ACCLAIM FOR
GLENN COOPER

"Cooper's name on a book's cover guarantees two things: an elaborate story with plenty of twists and turns and a swift pace that carries the reader through to the end." —*Booklist*

"Cooper's intelligent, heart-pounding homage to *Raiders of the Lost Ark* and *The Da Vinci Code* will appeal to fans of action, thriller and conspiracy genres." —*Booklist* on *The Debt*

"[Cooper] is no ordinary thriller writer, but one who asks big questions." —*Sunday Telegraph* (UK)

"The debut of a startling new talent. Here is a story both incandescent and explosive. A seamless blend of modern-day thriller and historical mystery with an ending that left me breathless." —James Rollins, *New York Times* bestselling author, on *Library of the Dead*

THE FOURTH PROPHECY

GLENN COOPER

GC

GRAND CENTRAL
PUBLISHING

NEW YORK   BOSTON

Copyright © 2022 by Lascaux Media LLC

Cover design by Ben Denzer. Cover photos: Saint Peter's basilica by salajean/Getty Images; aerial view of Rome © Alinari Archives, Florence/Bridgeman Images; eclipse © Ken Offit. Cover copyright © 2022 by Hachette Book Group, Inc.

Grand Central Publishing
Hachette Book Group
1290 Avenue of the Americas, New York, NY 10104
grandcentralpublishing.com
twitter.com/grandcentralpub

First Edition: May 2022

Grand Central Publishing is a division of Hachette Book Group, Inc. The Grand Central Publishing name and logo is a trademark of Hachette Book Group, Inc.

The publisher is not responsible for websites (or their content) that are not owned by the publisher.

The Hachette Speakers Bureau provides a wide range of authors for speaking events. To find out more, go to www.hachettespeakersbureau.com or call (866) 376-6591.

Library of Congress Cataloging-in-Publication Data
Names: Cooper, Glenn, 1953- author.
Title: The fourth prophecy / Glenn Cooper.
Description: First Edition. | New York : Grand Central Publishing, 2022. | Summary: "A beloved professor of theology and archaeology at Harvard, Cal Donovan has achieved renown - but he drops everything when he is called by his friend Pope Celestine to investigate the potential existence of a mysterious prophecy. And it soon becomes clear that another party is desperate and willing to kill for the same information. When the attacks begin and terror is brought to the very doorstep of the Vatican, Donovan finds himself in a race against time. From Lisbon and Rome, to London and Paris-he will push his limits in order to confront one of the greatest evils the world has ever known"-- Provided by publisher.
Identifiers: LCCN 2021053686 | ISBN 9781538721247 (trade paperback) | ISBN 9781538721254 (ebook)
Classification: LCC PS3603.O582627 F68 2022 | DDC 813/.6--dc23
LC record available at https://lccn.loc.gov/2021053686

ISBNs: 9781538721247 (trade pbk.), 9781538721254 (ebook)

Printed in the United States of America

LSC-C

Printing 1, 2022

THE FOURTH PROPHECY

1

It had rained hard the previous night, a blood rain whipped by wind, but the storm had passed, and the morning sky was luminous and nearly cloudless. A morning such as this seemed a magic trick conjured by a grand illusionist. The sirocco winds from North Africa had carried red Saharan sand clinging to raindrops, and when Romans awoke, they found their city steaming with humidity and dusted with rosy glitter. At Saint Peter's Square, the sun beat down at just the right angle, transforming the wet cobblestones from hardscape to light, a yellow light that danced with sparkles and flashes. Looking toward the Vatican obelisk from the Piazza Papa Pio XII, pilgrims and tourists appeared to be walking not on gray stones, but on the surface of a shimmering, mystical red sea.

A man made his way across the square at his usual plodding pace. Right foot forward, left knee raised high to clear the left foot from dragging. He was fine on a flat surface, but uneven cobbles threatened to catch his sole and pitch him forward. He loathed canes, for they marked one as disabled. His custom was to survey the ground and adjust his leg lift as required. He was well practiced; his foot drop was old. He had been five, playing near the gardener as the old man with sunbeaten skin pushed a lawn mower. The blade hit a rock and cracked, and a length of jagged steel kicked up from the turf and spun into the boy's leg just below the knee, breaking the fibula and nicking the peroneal nerve. In time, the bone healed; the nerve did not. When the boy returned from hospital, the gardener, whom he liked, had been fired. The boy protested, but blame had been assigned. His father showed him the rock. The boy recognized it by its color and shape, black and pyramidal. He had found it in a flower bed and had been using it to bash toy soldiers until it became lost in high grass. He wanted to tell his father that it was his fault, not the gardener's, but he worried that he too would be sent away.

The consequence of this small carelessness was permanent disability. First, he blamed the rock. When he was older and classmates made fun of his limp, he would stare at the statue of Jesus above the altar of his white-plastered church and blame a cruel God. It was only when he was an adult that he came to conclude that although God was indeed behind his accident, it had been a blessing, not a curse. A young man who could not play sports or dance with the girls had little to distract him from a life of study and spiritual devotion. His foot drop made him cast his gaze downward, but his mind had been freed to roam the heavens.

The exceptional beauty of the morning escaped him. In anticipation of the ordeal he was to inflict on himself, he had woken angry and brooding. He could have waited and avoided the opening-day crowd, or not gone at all, but in a fit of self-mortification, he hurled himself toward the spectacle as punishment for the great sin he was planning.

He arrived early to avoid the lines that would soon pack the square, but even so, there was a wait of thirty minutes to enter the basilica. On either side of the central portico, large placards announced the event, each with a photograph of the statue and two words: THE RETURN. When he was close enough to see a placard clearly, the photograph was confusing, but that was the intent, he supposed. The trickery infuriated him.

He reached the portico, where the brightness and heat of the morning gave way to the cool darkness of the atrium. Ahead, the line of visitors snaked to the right and disappeared from view. He slowly made his way forward on the mosaics. The floors of the basilica were often overlooked by tourists, who found loftier wonders to capture their attention.

He of downward gaze always noticed floors, and he knew the history of this one. Sixteenth-century stonemasons had used the finest Tuscan marbles and inlaid them with rose porphyry looted from ancient imperial temples and the Colosseum. Roman emperors had been drawn to the royal purple of porphyry and sent their minions to the single mine in Egypt on Mount Porphyrites, where the stone was known to exist. When the location of the mine was forgotten in the fourth century, the only way to obtain the ultrahard stone was to loot it. He had to take care, because the porphyry inlays were higher than the rest of the floor—unlike soft marble worn down by centuries of foot traffic, porphyry was indestructible. It would take a modern cutting laser an hour to penetrate a mere centimeter.

With each high step he took, the sole of his left shoe slapped down hard on these rarest of stones.

The queue moved slowly. Although it was the nearest chapel to the entrance, it took several more minutes to reach it. For hundreds of years, the chapel had been accessible, but that changed in 1972 when a deranged Hungarian named Laszlo Toth took a hammer to the sculpture while screaming, "I am Jesus Christ. I have risen from the dead." Since then, ballistic glass had greeted visitors.

When he arrived at the closest viewing point, he put his hands on the railing and peered through the thick glass at the cream-colored statue that filled the chapel. Since its creation in 1499, Michelangelo's Renaissance marble masterpiece, the *Pietà*, had inspired the highest emotions of faith through its elegant depiction of the body of Jesus Christ brought down from the cross and draped over the lap of a youthful Virgin Mary, who gazed upon him with maternal sadness. The *Pietà* was the only work Michelangelo ever signed, a petty reaction to a rumor that it was the work of his rival Solari. Until the catastrophe—that was how the limping man put it— the statue had left Rome only a single time since its creation, when it traveled by ship to New York City for display at the Vatican Pavilion at the 1964 World's Fair. This was precious cargo indeed, and its crate was waterproof, equipped with a marine beacon, and designed to float if the ship foundered.

For a moment, the statue evoked the same deep response it had done countless times. He caught himself and allowed anger to reclaim the space. A black plaque with white lettering was bolted to the wall. He knew what it said—he had read the text on the official Vatican website—but while he waited for the line to move him to the central viewing point, he read it again.

When Pope Celestine VI decided to create a 30-billion-euro fund to alleviate the suffering of the poor, the sick, and the victims of war, he directed the Vatican to sell selected treasures from its museums and churches. One of these treasures was Michelangelo's *Pietà*. At auction, the Louvre Museum acquired the magnificent statue with a bid of 1.5 billion euros, by far the highest amount ever paid for a work of art. As a condition of the sale, the Louvre agreed to undertake and fund the creation of a replica of the *Pietà* to once again grace its traditional chapel at Saint Peter's Basilica. For years, a team of Italian, French, and German engineers, scientists, and artists worked to produce a perfect full-sized replica.

This magnificent re-creation of the *Pietà* is the result. The original statue was scanned by lasers in Paris as the first step in producing a "digital twin." The data was then processed and fed into the largest 3D printer in the world, located in Hamburg. Over a period of months, the printer created the replica, layer by layer, utilizing special resins created for this project. The statue was then transported to Florence, where a group of art restoration experts polished it by machine and by hand, and added the finishing touches of color to perfectly match the tonalities of the original marble. The visitor to the chapel will see a scientific marvel virtually indistinguishable from Michelangelo's masterpiece. The *Pietà* has returned.

The line progressed until he reached the prime sight line. People on either side of him babbled and took photos, but he stared violently at the scientific marvel and thought, *No, it has not returned. This is a sleight of hand for the foolish and the gullible. It belongs in Disneyland, not the holiest of churches.* He had watched Pope Celestine on television at the papal viewing following its installation. He heard him extol the best of both worlds—amelioration of the suffering of the poor and the return of the *Pietà* in a form that would give even Michelangelo pause. He had hurled curses at his television. This pope was toppling the pillars of the Church. He was replacing centuries of orthodoxy with liberal garbage. He was replacing precious marble with cheap resin. He had traded the priceless cultural patrimony of the faith for pieces of silver. He gripped the wooden railing hard enough to blanch his knuckles. When the woman behind him told him the line was moving, he silently cursed the pope and gave this ersatz *Pietà* one final look.

He would never visit it again.

2

It was a small conference with sixty international participants who were mostly known to one another. The few
newcomers were younger academics, excited to have been invited into a circle of scholars whose work they had read but
whom they had never met in such close quarters.

The venue was the Lapa Palace Hotel in Lisbon, a
nineteenth-century palace with parklike gardens overlooking
the Tagus River. At the opening dinner the night before the
lectures, the host and clerical chair of the symposium, Cardinal Rodrigo Da Silva, had presented all the participants with
ecclesiastic-red T-shirts silkscreened with OFFICIAL MEMBER
OF THE THREE SECRETS CLUB.

It had been left to the academic chairman, Professor
Calvin Donovan of Harvard Divinity School, to deliver the
after-dinner remarks. He had knocked back a couple of vodka
martinis during the cocktail mingler and a couple of glasses
of wine over dinner, but he was a fast metabolizer, and rising
to the microphone, he displayed no signs of inebriation. Mere

seconds into his talk, he knew he had his audience, but then again in this arena, he never failed. He peered at his colleagues with lively eyes that crinkled at the corners when he laughed, and shifted his gaze to make strong contact with every table. When you'd done as many lectures and speeches as Cal had, you didn't sweat after-dinner remarks.

He winged this one, but it came out light and witty and erudite. Wrapping it up, he gave a warm toast to the bald, rotund Portuguese American cardinal.

"This symposium would not have occurred if not for the tireless efforts of Cardinal Da Silva," he said. "And more importantly, if not for him, the blessed event scheduled for less than two weeks from now, when a new saint will join the firmament, would not have come to fruition."

With that, Cal thrust his hand toward the ballroom ceiling, a gauzy mural of a blue sky with puffy clouds, a theatrical act that set the audience tittering. "So, please, ladies and gentlemen, lift your glasses to the finest bishop to ever serve Providence, Rhode Island, the finest cardinal to ever serve Boston, Massachusetts, the finest secretary of state to ever serve the Vatican...my dear friend, His Eminence Rodrigo Cardinal Da Silva."

As the cardinal got to his feet to bask in the applause, the professor, armed with a fresh martini, dispatched it with an energetic turn of his wrist.

Toward the rear of the ballroom, two women, who had only just met as tablemates, continued to talk over coffee. The younger one, Estel Coloma, a *profesora asociada* at the University of Barcelona, starstruck by her more senior colleagues, gushed over the Harvard prof. "He's amazing. How well do you know him?"

The older woman, Margaret Hawthorne, a British don who taught religious studies at Cambridge, looked over half frames, brushed back some errant strands of hair, and said, "I know him quite well."

"What's he like? Is he married?"

"Cal married? No. Never was, never will be."

"Really. How old would you say he is?"

"A few years younger than me."

"And how old are you?"

"Your age and double it." The waiter interrupted with an offer of more coffee. Hawthorne requested a glass of port instead and added, "And one for my colleague."

"Tell me more about him. Not his work—I've read his books. The other things."

"All right. For one, his name says a lot about him. He's a religious and cultural hybrid. His father was the famed biblical archaeologist Hiram Donovan, a staunch Boston Catholic. His mother was a vivacious New York socialite, a Jew. Apparently, at birth, they haggled and chose Abraham as his middle name as a nod to his mother's side. Amusingly, they found compromise and came up with an arch-Protestant first name, Calvin."

"How fantastic."

"Isn't it?"

"I've read about his friendship with Pope Celestine."

"Yes, they've been quite matey ever since Cal helped him sort out a mess over a young priest who blossomed with the stigmata of Christ. Cal had written a seminal book on stigmata years ago. The Vatican sent out the Bat-Signal, and he answered the call."

The young woman mumbled that she didn't know the book

and asked for its name. Hawthorne told her, and she began ordering it on her phone.

Near the head table, the cardinal was waxing lyrical on one of his favorite subjects. With his ample face, animated and mirthful, he would happily spout, to any and all, some variation of: *My vocation is the work of the Church; my avocation is food. I assure you, my only vice is overindulging.*

Cal wasn't standing particularly close, but Da Silva's bulging waist bumped against him whenever the cleric gesticulated. They effected a characteristic pose—Cal, far taller, would bow his head and lean, and the cardinal would counter by arching his neck as far back as its thick roll of posterior fat allowed.

"Please don't tell a soul, Cal," he said, "but I spent more time working on the menus than on my talk for tomorrow."

"The food was excellent, Rodrigo. I'm quite sure your talk will be as well."

"Did you like the carne de porco à alentejana? You know, being Portuguese, I felt a special obligation to treat our guests to the finest my homeland has to offer."

"It was superb. I don't think I ever had pork and clams in the same dish."

"Yes, completely local! The chef did himself proud. Do you like octopus?"

"I do."

"At the closing dinner tomorrow, we'll have polvo à lagareiro—octopus and potatoes, swimming in enough olive oil to float a boat. And pastéis de nata for dessert. Our famous custard tarts."

They first met when they appeared together on a panel on the history of Catholicism in Portugal. At the time, Da Silva ran the Diocese of Providence. Cal delivered a paper on the two Portuguese popes, and Da Silva spoke about the dissolution of the monasteries after the Portuguese Civil War. They easily fell into friendship and began to dine regularly on Cal's home turf in Massachusetts or Da Silva's in Rhode Island. When Da Silva was called to become a cardinal, Cal was a personal guest at his Vatican investiture. And years later, Cal again traveled to Rome for Da Silva's installation as cardinal secretary.

"Well, if you'll excuse me," Da Silva said, touching the sleeve of Cal's suit jacket, "I wasn't entirely joking about being unprepared. I need to retire to my room and do some editing."

Cal undertook the mission of schmoozing, gliding from table to table, gossiping with colleagues he had known for years. He arrived at Hawthorne and Coloma's table when they were on their second glass of port.

"Megs," he said, bending to give Hawthorne a peck on each cheek. "Having a good time?"

"What could be better than swanning around swanky hotels and gabbing about saints and secrets? You were your usual dazzling self tonight."

"Hardly dazzling. Twinkly at best."

"Have you met my new friend, Estel Coloma from Barcelona?"

He knew her particulars—he had personally invited all the attendees and had spotted her at the cocktail party but never made it over.

"I'm delighted to finally meet you," he said. "Your paper on Marian visions in the fifteenth century was excellent."

"Was it my ticket for admission?" she asked saucily.

"It was. Plus look at how ancient we are—Professor Hawthorne not included. We desperately needed fresh blood."

Coloma extended a hand and said, "I am very happy to be a blood donor."

His radar was a perfect instrument. It never failed to alert him to a woman's attraction, and it was pinging like crazy. Coloma's flush extended down her neck and disappeared under her blouse.

Hawthorne watched with a knowing bemusement and said, "We were just talking about your book on stigmata."

"You mean the one I signed a contract with my publisher to update and never have?"

"The very one."

Coloma looked at him rather slyly and said, "I have it on my tablet."

Cardinal Da Silva puffed his chest, climbed onto a box to get some height on the podium, and asked Cal to project the first slide. It was a split-screen image, a pair of photos of a young girl and an old woman. The photo of the girl was grainy and black-and-white. She had an oval face and a dark complexion. Her downturned mouth and wide eyes gave the impression that she hadn't enjoyed being photographed. She was dressed in peasant clothes, but Sunday ones, and her black hair was covered in a long veil of dark cloth. The old woman was a nun with the same downturned mouth, the same wide eyes, now under thick plastic glasses, and the same delicate nose, although her face was scrunched with age. Her Carmelite habit covered everything save the disk of her face and a bit of neck. She, too, appeared uncomfortable in front of a camera.

Da Silva said, "My friends, we are here today because of this girl, this woman, the Blessed Sister Lúcia, who, less than two weeks from today, will be canonized by Pope Celestine as Sancta Lúcia. Lúcia's journey has been a long one. It began on a fine spring day in 1917 in Fátima, in what was then a farming and sheep-raising community of peasants, and what is now home to one the most venerated shrines in Christianity, attracting millions of religious pilgrims and tourists every year. Has anyone in the audience not been to Fátima?"

There were a few apologetic hands.

"Well, you must go soon," Da Silva said warmly, "or you'll have to give your T-shirts back. As a Portuguese man and a member of the clergy, it is almost impossible to describe how gratified I am to speak to you this morning about Sister Lúcia and Fátima. I know that some of my comrades from the mainland look down their noses a little at us Azoreans—especially one like me, who emigrated in my youth to the fishing community of New Bedford, Massachusetts—but my every fiber is Portuguese, and my heart is in Fátima. Why is Fátima so important to me? Why is it so important to Christianity?

"It is because Fátima, along with Guadalupe and Lourdes, is one of the most significant Marian apparitions. When the Blessed Mother first appeared before the three peasant children on the thirteenth of May in 1917 and began to reveal her prophecies, she set in motion a chain of events that have rippled forward in time and that resonate today as strongly as they did over a century ago. For in these apparitions, the Blessed Mother gave the children a message to pass to the world, containing many central truths and devotions of the Catholic faith—the Trinity, the Eucharist, penance, the Rosary, and sacrifices for the conversion of sinners, all with special emphasis on the Immaculate Heart of Mary. It is that Immaculate Heart in which we of the faith find the refuge of maternal love and a sure path that leads to God.

"But of course, for over a century, the somewhat breathless focus of the secular world, the religious world, and even the academic world in which you, my friends, dwell, has been on the Three Secrets of Fátima that were divulged in slow motion over the course of the twentieth century. In the afternoon session, Professor Donatelli will speak about the First Secret, Professor Gray, the Second Secret, and Professor Donovan, the Third Secret. This morning, you will hear presentations on the cultural and religious contexts of Marian apparitions throughout history and presentations about the long life of Lúcia dos Santos and the tragically brief lives of the two other shepherd children, Jacinta and Francisco.

"But first, please bear with me a while longer as I tell you about the exhaustive process that led to Sister Lúcia's impending canonization. I never had a direct hand in the proceedings, but given my heritage and, in recent years, my duties as cardinal secretary, I have maintained an intense interest in those proceedings and perhaps I have nudged them along from time to time.

"The process was arduous and prolonged, because this was a woman who lived almost ninety-eight years and corresponded with all the popes from Pius the Twelfth to John Paul the Second, as well as many cardinals and bishops. Testimonies had to be obtained from sixty witnesses concerning her holiness and heroic virtues. All of her writings had to be collected and scrutinized, an immense undertaking, as she left us over ten thousand letters and a diary of two thousand pages. Thirty laypeople and theologians worked full-time for years on the *positio*, the official position document.

"And this was only the first, or diocesan, stage of Sister Lúcia's canonization phase. The matter was then passed on to the Vatican Congregation for the Causes of Saints, where documentary proof had to be obtained that a miracle had occurred through the intercession of the Venerable Sister Lúcia.

"Let me now show you the timeline of the process. Professor Donovan, could I have the next slide?"

Lunch was served on the lawn, and as Cal was placing a piece of fish on his plate, he detected a whiff of perfume. Estel Coloma had slid behind him in the buffet line.

"Looks delicious," she said.

"Doesn't it? Did you enjoy the session?"

"Very much. Mind if I join you?"

Cal's table filled quickly, and Coloma hardly got a word in while Cal and his buddies traded academic war stories. When one of them left to return to his room, the Portuguese historian Albano Baptista, from the University of Coimbra, took the empty chair and produced a book from his bag to show his colleagues. He was one of the few attendees who had actually met Sister Lúcia, and he proudly displayed a copy of one of her memoirs, inscribed and signed.

The book was passed from hand to hand until it wound

up with Cal, who read Lúcia's scrawled inscription and said, "You've got yourself a real treasure, Albano."

"Indeed I do. I have already bequeathed it to my university library, the beautiful Biblioteca Joanina. Have you been?"

"I haven't," Cal said, "but it's on my bucket list."

"You must come," Baptista said. "The city is blessed by Lúcia's spirit."

Deep into the afternoon, Cal took the podium for the conclusory talk. Coloma had bagged a front-row seat, and she smiled whenever their eyes met.

"Gaetano and Angela have done wonderful jobs covering the first two secrets of Fátima," he said. "So here's what we know about the Third Secret. According to the accounts of Sister Lúcia, the Virgin Mary first appeared to the children at noon on May thirteenth, 1917, telling them to return to the pasture the same day and time in the coming months. On June thirteenth, the children returned and were told by the apparition to come back the next month and, in the interim, to pray the Rosary and, interestingly, learn to read. We do know that Sister Lúcia took this encouragement to heart, as her voluminous writings attest.

"Then came July thirteenth, 1917—the main event, as it were—when Mary revealed to the children the Three Secrets. Gaetano has told you about the First Secret, an eschatological vision of hell, a warning of what fate would befall those who did not repent of their sins and follow the path of God. Angela has told you about the Second Secret, one that might be described as historical in nature, involving as it did predictions about the First and Second World Wars and the perils of an unconsecrated, godless Russia.

"Lastly, Mary revealed to them her infamous Third Secret, the subject of this talk. As you know, the children were instructed by the Virgin not to reveal the secrets, particularly the Third Secret. It was the bishop of Leiria who, in 1941, persuaded Sister Lúcia to give him a text of the first two secrets, and thus they were revealed to the world.

"In late 1943, the bishop instructed the gravely ill Lúcia, who was suffering from influenza, to set down the Third Secret in writing in case she died, and she did so in 1944. The bishop kept it in a sealed envelope at his residence, and it was not delivered to the Vatican until his death in 1957. And there it sat for forty-three years until, finally, it was publicly divulged on May thirteenth, 2000, a date chosen by the Vatican to match the first apparition.

"The path to its revelation was a curious one that has spawned a cottage industry of conspiracy theories about Vatican cover-ups and intrigues. As you are all, no doubt, aware, the Third Secret concerns a prophecy widely considered to be a foreshadowing of the assassination attempt on Pope John Paul the Second, but some of you may not know about the strange actions that were taken inside the Vatican from 1957 until the time of its disclosure."

With that, he projected a slide of an aerial view of the Vatican and said, "Buckle your seat belts, ladies and gentlemen, for an interesting ride."

When he was finished, Cal asked for the lights.

"Questions?"

Coloma's hand shot straight up. "Professor Donovan, you've addressed the theories about the existence of a Fourth Secret, a prophecy so alarming and diabolical that the Vatican has suppressed it all these years. What is your personal opinion?"

Laughter broke out when Cal responded with an exaggerated grimace. "I was afraid someone was going to ask me that. Look, I'll freely acknowledge that conspiracies do exist in this crazy world of ours. And because the Vatican is a constitutionally opaque organization, it's easy to impart all manner of conspiracy theories onto the Curia. But my opinion—and I come to it after having read all the stuff out there, some of it quite nutty—is that there were only three secrets. But let's ask the man who would know. Cardinal Da Silva, would you care to comment?"

The secretary of state rose, turned to the audience, and said, "The position of the Vatican has always been clear. Sister Lúcia never sent the Holy See a so-called Fourth Secret of Fátima or even a second part to the Third Secret, as some have claimed. When asked about this later in life, Blessed Lúcia consistently affirmed that she transmitted the entirety of the Third Secret in 1944. The matter is closed."

<hr>

The conference dinner had dragged on, it was late, and Cal was working on polishing off the bottle of Grey Goose the cardinal had sent to his suite. The sharp ring of the hotel phone didn't startle him. He was expecting the call.

"Do you mind if I come up now?" the woman asked.

"I'd mind if you didn't."

Before long, there was the lightest of raps on the door, a sort of faraway tattoo.

She led with her own half bottle of hotel vodka, sweating with condensation.

"I come bearing gifts," she said, moving inside.

"You know your customer, Megs."

She grabbed two cut-crystal glasses from the sidebar and settled onto the sofa, her shirt untucked over her skirt, her legs bare. He'd always liked the way she carried herself, with an effortless sort of highbrow, casual elegance.

"I wouldn't be here if you hadn't split with what's her name."

"Christ, word travels fast."

"You're not the only person I know at Harvard. Have a drink. I've missed you."

"Missed you too, Megs."

She got up to clink glasses with him. "So are you going to give it a rest, or are you going to flit?"

"Flit?"

"You know, jump straight into another relationship. You're a flitter."

"Am I?"

"What's the longest you've gone without a woman in your life?"

"It's not something I track."

"Perhaps you should."

"All right. I broke up with Jessica a couple of weeks ago, and here you are."

She snorted. "I don't count. You off tomorrow?"

"First thing. I'm up to my eyeballs in work back home."

"Planning on your usual two weeks in Rome in August?"

"Hopefully."

She slugged back her drink and slowly moved her arm until her hand was pointing toward the bedroom. "Well, the hour is late. What say we?"

They enjoyed each other, as they had done many times in many cities in years past. Her husband, a member of Parliament who sat on the opposition backbenches, had the decency not to ring her mobile until they were done. She breathed a "Bloody hell," unapologetically broke away from their embrace, and launched, as far as Cal could tell, into a heated discussion about some sort of unpaid household account.

Cal headed to the bathroom, naked. He didn't mind bedding another man's wife, but he drew the line at listening to their domestic chitchat. When he was done with his shower and was toweling his hair, she knocked and said, "Now it's your phone going off. It's your sister."

"I don't have a sister."

The caller ID read **Sister Elisabetta**. It was a strange time for her to call unless she thought he was stateside.

"Hello, Sister. How are you?" It was midnight, and he wondered where she was. Her office? Her room? Was she draped in her shapeless black habit or lounging in something secular? He had seen so many pictures of Sister Lúcia of late, a dowdy presence even in her youth, that the contrast in his mind's eye was jarring. Lúcia looked like most nuns did. Sister Elisabetta looked like a leading lady, perhaps the most beautiful woman he'd ever known.

"I'm fine, Professor Donovan. I hope I'm not interrupting."

He was watching Megs put herself back together. "No, I'm free. I'm in Lisbon, you know."

"Yes, the cardinal secretary's symposium. We spoke tonight."

"How can I help you?"

Her English was impeccable, her Italian accent strong. "The Holy Father wonders if you could possibly come to see him tomorrow."

"I was planning on heading home in the morning."

"I see." Down the line, he heard breathing. "It's an urgent matter. I hate to inconvenience you."

"Can you tell me what it's about?"

Another hesitation, then, "It concerns the secrets of Fátima."

Megs walked backward, gesturing for him to do the hooks on her bra. He recalled she always liked him doing the job, and he tucked his phone under his chin to oblige.

"I'll book the first flight out," he said.

"I've already taken the liberty," she answered. "I'll text you the details. Thank you, Professor. I'll let the Holy Father know."

Megs buttoned her blouse and said, "That sounded interesting."

"It was the Vatican. Celestine wants me there tomorrow."

"Can you say more?"

"I don't know more."

"What about your work?"

"I guess it'll have to wait."

3

At the entrance to the Domus Sanctae Marthae, uniformed Vatican gendarmes asked for Cal's identification and checked his name off a visitor list. It struck him as curious, because he had never gone through this kind of procedure before. After presenting himself to the receptionist, he found a chair and pulled out his phone to check his email.

Harvard was on its summer break, but departmental meetings at the Divinity School continued and he had two grad students who needed care and feeding on their theses. The Lisbon trip had come at an inopportune time, but there had never been any doubt he would deliver the goods for his friend the cardinal. Now, an ocean separated him from three books and two academic papers in various stages of tardiness and incompletion, multiple journal articles to referee, and one extremely busted-up relationship.

Jessica had been in the picture far longer than any of his previous partners, and Cal's friends had wondered whether she might be the one to get him down the aisle. On the face of it, they were a formidable match. She was a PhD geneticist, the CEO of a major biotech company, who at one time had been the youngest female to lead a publicly traded healthcare firm. Likewise, Cal had been one of the youngest faculty members at Harvard to be named to a full professorship.

Both were athletic. She had been a competitive golfer. He had taken up boxing in the army to blow off steam, and he continued to box at a Harvard club. Both were practicing Catholics, she born and bred, he a latecomer who had eventually made a choice among Judaism, Catholicism, or nothing. They were both wealthy in their own right, she from stock options, he from inheritance. And both could hold their liquor, or in her case, wine. Her penthouse in Boston had a legendary wine room, where she also kept a selection of rarefied vodkas to keep him happy.

They had divided their time between her condo and his house on a leafy Cambridge street populated by well-heeled professors. Looking back on the wreckage, they agreed that their relationship had worked best when travel schedules disjoined them for extended stretches. More recently, a confluence of obligations had kept both of them in Massachusetts, and that led to their downfall. For several months, there was seldom a night or weekend they weren't together, and as he saw it, domesticity crept in like a choking vine. The more comfortable Jessica felt with this new normal, the more agitated Cal became, and he found himself instigating petty arguments. Two weeks earlier, in the midst of a squabble about something inconsequential, she called out acidly from his bathroom as she removed her makeup, "Aren't we acting like the married couple."

That was the point. They were. And he hated it.

The innocent comment triggered a vodka-fueled eruption that, predictably enough, began with "It's not you. It's me..." before things went sideways fast. The argument ended an hour later with her angrily clearing out the closet and a few dresser drawers. In the morning, he sent a bouquet of flowers as a half-baked apology, but the gesture failed and he made no further attempts. Nothing she had said that night was untrue. He *was* a commitment-phobe. He *did* miss the exhilaration of brief, meaningless flings. It wasn't his fault that his narcissistic parents had screwed him over, but it was very much on him that he had never tried to tackle his issues with professional help, relying instead on eighty-proof dosing. On their last call before he flew to Portugal, she asked if he had ever loved her.

"I did, Jess. I did," he had said. "But I guess love isn't enough for me."

Scanning his new emails, he saw one from her with the subject line One more thing. He steeled himself for another reproach, but the message was: I think I left a thumb drive with some sensitive draft contracts in your living room. If you find it, whack it with a hammer.

He was constructing a witty, insouciant reply when Sister Elisabetta swept into the lobby with a gentle smile and an extended arm.

"Right on time, Professor," she said. "How was your flight?"

Her hand, warm and dry, disappeared for a moment into his, and the tops of his ears began to burn. Sister Elisabetta existed in a place in his mind normally walled off from conscious thought. Repression, the emperor of Freudian defenses, was in play, for how else could he deal with having feelings for a chaste woman? Since they first met, she had occasionally crept

24

into his thoughts, sometimes when he was working, sometimes when he was with another woman. These were brief incursions, easily brushed away. But in the wake of her phone call, his self-censorship had crumbled, and when he awoke in Lisbon that morning, she was as present as if she were lying beside him.

She was not yet forty, and she carried herself with the fluidity of the dancer she had been as a child. Her complexion was naturally flawless, her skin milky. She wore the black habit of her order, the Augustinian Sisters, Servants of Jesus and Mary. He had never seen her hair, as it was always veiled, but he imagined it to be black and unbearably silky.

"Were you able to speak with Cardinal Da Silva?" she asked.

"I left very early, so no. I assume he knows what this is about."

"He was informed. He was glad the Holy Father was asking for your help."

"I'm happy to assist in any way I can."

"It's greatly appreciated. He's waiting."

During the pontificate of Celestine VI, the nerve center of the Vatican had shifted a few hundred meters from the Renaissance Apostolic Palace to the modern and modest Domus Sanctae Marthae, the Vatican guesthouse. The pope had grown up humbly in Secondigliano, a working-class suburb of Naples. On his election, his humility led him to eschew the papal apartment in the palace for a two-room suite in the guesthouse. There he slept on a narrow bed, worked at a small desk in the adjoining study, ate communally in the cafeteria, and conducted morning Mass in the simple chapel. He used the palace to receive dignitaries and delegations, in a spacious library office, and following tradition, he appeared at the balcony of the papal apartment for his Sunday Angelus blessing, but he spent most of his time in the functional equivalent of a three-star hotel.

Elisabetta led Cal down one wing toward Celestine's suite, where Swiss Guards stood at attention. The adjacent guesthouse room served as her office. Her bedroom was two doors down.

Before her tenure, no woman had ever been chosen as first secretary to a pope, but Sister Elisabetta was unique in many respects. Although her mother had been religious, Elisabetta had never, even in passing, contemplated a life under religious orders. At university, she studied archaeology, the Roman catacombs specifically, and she had been on the verge of obtaining her PhD when she fell victim to a violent attack that almost took her life. During her long recovery, she had the kind of epiphany that some do when confronted by their mortality. In her case, she made the decision to abandon an academic life for a religious one.

She chose the Augustinian Sisters because of their educational mission, and following her vows, she taught at their primary school in the Trastevere area of Rome, the neighborhood of her youth. It was there that Cardinal Secretary Aspromonte, who would become Celestine VI, learned of her past. A crime had occurred at the Catacombs of Callixtus, and he needed someone with knowledge of the catacombs whom he could trust. Grateful for her faithful service, he paid homage to her surname, Celestino, when he was elected to the papacy, and also to Pope Celestine V, who, like him, had been famously reluctant to accept the job.

In time, the new pope tapped the young nun to be the first woman to lead the Pontifical Commission for Sacred

Archaeology, and in this role, she was among his advisors about which Vatican treasures to divest for his charitable foundation. Later, she made history again with her appointment as papal first secretary.

Midway down the corridor, Cal and Elisabetta passed an open door, where they saw a priest working at a desk. He rushed out and said, "I'm sorry to bother you, Sister, but do you know why the Holy Father had me cancel his morning meetings?" He was in his fifties, his clerical garb hanging loosely on his gaunt frame.

"Professor Donovan happened to be in Rome today," she said. "He wanted time to see him."

The lie took Cal by surprise. Something was going on. They were keeping the coterie tight.

"Professor, this is Monsignor Cauchi," she said. "He recently became the Holy Father's second secretary."

"I'm pleased to meet you," Cal said.

"And I, you. I've heard about the illustrious Professor Donovan," the Maltese priest said, bowing deferentially and then slipping back to his office.

The Swiss Guards parted, allowing her to knock.

Cal was sure that Celestine's jowly face had lost volume since his last visit. When they embraced, as they always did, Cal's arms seemed to reach farther around. Celestine was a large man, sturdy but given to fat, and undeniably there was less of him. One had only to read the papers to know he was beleaguered, but was there more? Was he ill?

As usual, the pope spoke to him in Italian. "It is so good to see you, Professor. It has been too long."

"I was planning on my usual visit later this summer, Holy Father, but the sooner, the better."

As he withdrew from the clinch, the pontiff's smile faded. He moved to his chair with an uncharacteristically shuffling gate, bent his knees, and let gravity take him the rest of the way down. He seemed to have leapfrogged years.

Celestine gestured for Cal to sit and asked Elisabetta to have the kitchen send in coffees. She made the call and took a small chair behind Cal, resting a leather notebook on her lap.

"Tell me how you have been," Celestine said, as a father might ask a son.

"I've been well. Busy as always. If funding comes through, I'll direct a dig in Israel next summer." The Divinity School occupied most of his time, but archaeology was a passion, so much so that Cal held a joint appointment at Harvard's Department of Anthropology.

"A biblical site?"

"A sixth-century Byzantine church in the Negev."

"Following in your father's footsteps. That is good." The pope paused to work his jaw a little. "I understand you have been with Da Silva in Lisbon. How was the conference?"

"It went well. There's tremendous interest in Sister Lúcia."

"As there should be. Da Silva tells me your lecture was on the Third Secret."

Cal nodded.

"Tell me, what is your opinion about the existence of a Fourth Secret?"

The question made his skin prickle. "I was asked that yesterday. I told the attendees I thought it was nonsense."

Celestine glanced at Elisabetta and then turned his watery

eyes—an old man's eyes—to Cal. "You are usually right. On this, my friend, you are wrong."

Cal moistened his lips with the tip of his tongue and pondered Da Silva's categorical denial.

"I know what you are thinking," Celestine said. "Da Silva told me about his statement to the contrary."

"Did he know he was in error?"

Celestine made an apologetic gesture with his large hands. "Put it this way—he knew what I knew, which was quite limited. But he was sworn to secrecy. You know the cardinal as well as anyone. He advocates for transparency at every turn. I would not say it was a lie, but it pained him to tell what might be called a half-truth. Last evening, we received new information. Out of necessity, I expanded the circle of knowledge to include Sister Elisabetta, the director general of the Vatican Gendarmerie, the commander of the Swiss Guards, and now you. Da Silva had appointments in Portugal today. He returns to the Vatican this evening. He urged me to consult you without delay."

"I'm at your disposal, Holy Father."

The pope showed his gratitude with a single deep nod. "Thank you. Thank you as always. I believe we should start by speaking about the past. You see, regarding Fátima, there are official versions and, shall we say, unofficial ones. Not only are you an expert in the official versions, but Da Silva informed me that you also are well versed in the conspiracy theories that have arisen over the years. Sister Elisabetta is new to the subject, so for her sake, let me review some salient details."

Cal heard her turn a notebook page and unscrew the top of her fountain pen.

Celestine spoke without notes, the relevant dates etched in his memory. "The Third Secret was revealed to the children on July thirteenth, 1917. Within three years, the brother and sister, Jacinta and Francisco Marto, were dead, leaving the legacy of the apparitions solely to Blessed Lúcia. In 1921, Lúcia went to school at the college of the Sisters of Saint Dorothy in Vilar. In 1925, she began her postulancy with the Sisters of Saint Dorothy in Pontevedra. In 1928, she took first vows in the order of Saint Dorothy, and made her perpetual vows in 1934. After this, she began committing her childhood experiences to writing, producing four volumes of memoirs between 1935 and 1941. In 1948, after receiving special papal permission to be relieved of her perpetual vows, she entered the Carmelite Convent of Santa Teresa in Coimbra, where she resided until her death.

"In the early 1940s, she made public the first two messages from Our Lady, which, until then, had been kept secret. The first concerned a vision of hell and how sinners might achieve salvation by praying to the Immaculate Heart. The second concerned a prophecy of the future world war that could be averted if Russia were consecrated to the Immaculate Heart. Well, we know what happened, don't we? Russia remained under godless communism, and the Second World War was terrible indeed.

"We now come to the Third Secret, which Our Lady ordered Blessed Lúcia not to reveal, and this is why its text is omitted in her memoirs. Toward the end of 1943, she fell seriously ill with influenza. It was thought she might die. The bishop of Leiria, fearful that the Third Secret might be lost forever, ordered her to write it down. She offered the bishop the opportunity to read the text, but he refused. It was sealed in an envelope kept by the bishop with the instructions that it should not be opened until 1960 or upon her death. When the bishop died in 1957, the envelope was sent to the Vatican. And now we come to the double-envelope problem." Celestine looked at Cal. "I assume you are aware of this."

Cal was well versed on the subject and had covered it in his lecture. "I am, Holy Father. When the envelope arrived at the Vatican, it was initially kept in a wooden box in the apartment of Pope Pius the Twelfth. It's said he didn't read it. For safekeeping, it was soon deposited in the Secret Archives of the Holy Office of the Congregation for the Doctrine of Faith.

"Pius died a year later, and Pope John the Twenty-Third was elected. The envelope was brought to him, but he, too, declined to open it, famously saying, 'We shall wait. I shall pray.' He prayed, he waited, and eventually he did read it but chose not to publish it. Someone must have translated the text for him from Portuguese to Italian, but we have no details. The envelope was returned to the Holy Office Archives.

"The so-called two-envelope problem arose during the papacy of Paul the Sixth." Cal heard a page rustling and turned for a moment to see Elisabetta furiously taking notes. "According to the official Vatican version," he continued, "Paul waited until 1965, almost three years after his election, to read the text himself. However, in 2006, Pope John's long-serving private secretary, Cardinal Loris Capovilla, who was then ninety and in retirement, made contrary statements to a journalist. He insisted that just six days after Paul's election, one of the new pontiff's representatives asked Capovilla where the envelope was hidden. Capovilla told him it was kept in a desk drawer in John's bedroom."

"It is called the Barbarigo desk," Celestine said, "a magnificent seventeenth-century piece that belonged to Saint Gregory Barbarigo, the bishop of Bergamo and Padua. It was given to Pope John as a gift. I should show it to you."

"I'd love to see it," Cal said.

"Please, go on," the pope said. "I am enjoying your version."

"All right. Capovilla seemed to have a very clear memory of the event. He said that one of Paul's men called him back an hour later to tell him the envelope had been found. He assumed that the new pope intended to read it, but he had no further information. Hence, the double-envelope problem was born. One envelope kept in Pope John's desk, a second kept in the Archives of the Holy Office. The conspiracy theorists seized on the discrepancy in the official record and said, 'Aha, there must be two texts, one that was revealed in 2000 and one that remains hidden. Was there a Fourth Secret too controversial to be made public? Was there a second part to the Third Secret?'"

Cal hoped for an answer, but instead, Celestine said in a quiet rush of words, "And now we come to Pope Saint John Paul the Second."

"And specifically to the terrible day," Cal added, "May thirteenth, 1981. John Paul had sent a message to the pilgrims gathered at Fátima to commemorate the anniversary of the first apparition, and at the very moment it was being read aloud, Mehmet Ali Agca shot him as he was touring Saint Peter's Square in his popemobile. He lost a great amount of blood and almost died."

Celestine interrupted. "John Paul always kept Fátima close to his heart, even before the assassination attempt. The Second Secret, with its anti-communist message, spoke to him in a profound way, because the defeat of communism was one of his bedrock principles. After the shooting, Fátima took on an even greater meaning for him, did it not?"

"Two months into his convalescence, John Paul asked for the envelope containing the Third Secret," Cal said. "He had never read it, but now he did. The prefect of the Holy Office presented him with not one, but two envelopes. Again, the official version is that the white envelope contained Sister Lúcia's original text in Portuguese and the orange envelope contained the Italian translation. The nonconspiracy types, myself included, take this to be the innocent explanation for Capovilla's recollections, namely that Pope John kept the Italian translation in the Barbarigo desk while the Portuguese original was kept in the archives."

Celestine nodded sagely and said, "Of course, John Paul immediately took the Third Secret to be a prophecy of his assassination attempt, and he went even further. He was convinced that the Virgin of Fátima had saved his life. Sister Elisabetta, there is a copy of the secret on my desk. Could you read the highlighted section?"

She found the document and read aloud: "*And we saw in an immense light that is God: something similar to how people appear in a mirror when they pass before it, a bishop dressed in white. We had the impression that it was the Holy Father. We saw other bishops, priests, men and women religious climbing a steep mountain, at the top of which was a large cross. Before reaching this point, the Holy Father passed through a big city half in ruins. He trembled with a halting step, afflicted with pain and sorrow, praying for the souls of the corpses he met on his way; having reached the top of the mountain, on his knees at the foot of the large cross he was killed by a group of soldiers who fired bullets and arrows at him, and in the same way there died one after another the other bishops, priests, men and women religious, and various lay people of different ranks and positions. Beneath the two arms of the cross there were two angels each with a crystal aspersorium in his hand, in which they gathered up the blood of the martyrs and with it sprinkled the souls that were making their way to God."*

Cal repeated what he had said in his lecture. "John Paul might have been convinced the Third Secret was about him, but when the text was eventually made public in 2000 to coincide with Jacinta and Francisco Marto's beatifications, not everyone agreed. Yes, he was shot. No, he didn't die. Leading some Fátimaists to believe that the prophecy referred to a different pope. The discrepancies didn't shake John Paul's absolute belief. As you know, he even had one of the bullets that was removed from his body inserted into the crown of Our Lady of Fátima's statue at the shrine."

Celestine was bobbing his head as Cal spoke, and now he said, "I admire John Paul's dedication to Fátima and his ironclad belief in the prophecy of the Third Secret. Blessed Lúcia was always steadfast in her accounts of what the Holy Lady told her. Bullets were indeed fired at John Paul on a holy day of Fátima, but he was not killed. Lúcia wrote down what the Virgin had told her many years after the fact—and she was but a young girl when the prophecy was revealed to her. Was her memory defective? Did John Paul err in his belief that the prophecy was about him? I think we may never know the answer to these questions. However, I have an answer to a different question, and that question is: Was there a Fourth Secret of Fátima? Yes, there was. It seems it involves me."

⁐⁐⁐

Cal forced himself to keep quiet. Everything that came to his mind, all the exclamations, if vocalized would only trivialize the moment.

"Indeed there were two envelopes," Celestine said. "The one kept in the archives at the Holy Office contained Lúcia's original text of the Third Secret written in Portuguese, along with an Italian translation made for Pope John. The second envelope, kept in the Barbarigo desk, contained a single page written by Lúcia, presumably at the same time she wrote her recollection of the Third Secret. Sister, could you get it for the professor? The orange envelope in the top drawer."

Cal took it from her. It was thin, nearly weightless, cleanly sliced by a letter knife.

"Do you read Portuguese?" Celestine asked him.

"Not perfectly, but yes." He pinched out the sheet of onion-skin, examined the messy scrawl, and translated as he read.

There is a Fourth Secret. The Holy Mother revealed it to me on 13 July 1917. She commanded me to never reveal it. I wrote a single copy to preserve my memory of the astonishing prophecy. Only I and Our Lady know its hiding place.

"Who knows about this?" Cal asked.

"Before yesterday, only myself and Da Silva. The envelope has been passed to successive popes, and like me, they informed their cardinal secretaries. Now, I am forced to tell others."

"Why now? What's happened?"

"This happened," Celestine said, reaching into his cassock for a folded paper. "This is a photocopy of a word-processed letter I received yesterday. It is anonymous, unsigned, with no return address or stamp. It simply appeared in my mail."

"It must have been hand-delivered from within the Vatican," Elisabetta said.

Celestine said, "The original is with the Gendarmerie, who have examined it for identifiable features. Here, read it."

It was brief, in Italian, a warning and a threat.

The Holy Father must resign and do so before the day Sister Lúcia is canonized. If not, he will suffer the most terrible of fates. If he wishes to know the reason he must find the Fourth Secret of Fátima. There is no other way.

"I have no intention of resigning," Celestine said wearily. "Nine days from now, on the thirteenth of July, the date of the third apparition, Lúcia will be canonized, and I will say her Mass."

"What would you have me do, Holy Father?" Cal asked.

"I would like you to use all of your skills to find the Fourth Secret, if it indeed exists. I know this is an imposition. You have many pressing responsibilities. But I do not believe the police can be helpful. I am already informed there were no finger-prints or DNA traces on the letter or envelope, other than the sister's and mine. There are no images from security cameras of the person who delivered the letter. I have sought your help in the past, Professor. I seek it again."

Things began to disappear. Cal's unfinished books and articles. His grad students. Jessica. Cambridge. All that remained was in this small room. An extraordinary nun and a pope in need.

"I'll do my best."

As Celestine haltingly pushed himself to his feet, Cal resisted the urge to lend a hand.

"Sister Elisabetta will assist you in any way she can," he said. "All doors the Church controls will open for you. Be well and be safe. I will pray for you." Celestine managed a wan smile. "By the way, you should take a moment to see our new *Pietà*. It is quite the marvel."

Cal and Elisabetta passed through the cordon of Swiss Guards.

"How did he seem to you?" she asked.

He followed her into her office. "Tired. Older. Is he ill?"

"The doctors say he needs rest. Physically, there's nothing specific. He's been under tremendous pressure since the sale of the art and antiquities. His critics have the loudest voices, like snarling dogs."

"I've read what they say."

"It weighs on him. His appetite is poor. He knows he did the right thing, and takes heart when he's informed about the positive effects of the charity work, but the constant criticism takes a toll."

"And now this," Cal said.

"And now this," she repeated.

"There's more security than usual."

"I've learned the term is 'hardened.' His security has been hardened. He insists on fulfilling his General Audience and Sunday Angelus blessings, but the police and Swiss Guards will be out in force."

"There's no way to persuade him to postpone the canonization?"

"You heard him."

"Then I'd better get to work."

"Where will you start?"

"My gut tells me the archives, but my head isn't telling me what to look for yet. I need a little time to think."

"I'll book your hotel. Your usual?"

"I'd rather stay here at the Domus if you have a room."

Her solemnity gave way to a smile. "Yes, I believe I can arrange that."

It was impulsive, but he let it out. "It would be good if I could bounce some ideas off of you. Are you available for supper?"

"Yes, of course. I can arrange that too."

As she spoke, that finely tuned radar of his was absolutely quiet.

4

Fátima, Portugal, 1917

She was a curious girl and unafraid. She could spend an hour watching a spider build a web, and she could hold spiders in her hand and let them crawl up her arm. She could gut a rabbit as well as her mother and aunts, but, unlike them, she studied the organs and wondered what each one did. When she chased after a runaway sheep, she could run like the wind, jumping fearlessly off high limestone outcroppings.

Lúcia de Jesus Rosa dos Santos had just turned ten.

It was the thirteenth day of May, but she was unaware of the date. There were no calendars in the dos Santos farmhouse. They followed the seasons. They followed the feast days and Christmas. All the other days of the week held a sameness, except Sundays, which were special. On Sunday mornings, the chores could wait. The sheep could wait. On Sundays, the family put on their best clothes and attended early Mass, as they had done that day.

War was raging across Europe, but their little corner of the world was still peaceful. Portugal, which had been neutral since 1914, was on the verge of declaring allegiance to the Allied forces, and prayers had been offered at Mass for the young men who would soon be swept into the conflict.

Now, with the sun overhead, the wisp of a girl, in a black shepherding dress, shawl, and boots, headed out the door toward the meadows.

Lúcia's father was in the garden, prying a nail from an old board. "Take them to the Cova da Iria today," he called out without looking up. "The lower meadow needs a rest."

"Yes, Papa."

Lúcia was seven when her parents put her in charge of their flock. The job had belonged to her sister, but when Carolina turned thirteen, she was apprenticed to a weaver to earn money for the family. Lúcia, the youngest of the seven children of António and Maria Rosa dos Santos, loved everything about being a shepherd. She cherished the woolly creatures and gave each one a name. She sang to them and gave them hugs. And to win them over and stop them from straying, she shared her lunch with them.

Each day, she was joined in her labors by her two young cousins—Jacinta, who was seven in 1917, and Francisco, who was nine. The cousins had begged their parents to let them care for their family flock so they could be with their best friend, and from dawn to dusk, the three children and their sheep were inseparable.

On this warm May Sunday, they met up at a point between their two houses and began to move the merged flock toward the Cova da Iria, a half-hour walk through the farmland where Lúcia's father cultivated maize, greens, and peas.

No one remembered why the grassy meadow was called the Cove of Irene, but its wild, natural beauty made it one of Lúcia's favorite spots. Leaving the cultivated fields, their path took them across a barren moorland, where Lúcia asked her cousins their opinion of the priest's sermon that morning. It was an unsurprising question, as they often discussed sermons and Bible readings.

"I thought it was lovely," Jacinta said. "Father's words about charity and kindness were beautiful."

"I liked it too," Francisco said.

Lúcia said, "When he read from Ephesians—'Be kind to one another, tenderhearted, forgiving one another, as God in Christ forgave you'—I felt my heart warm as the sun warms us now."

She squinted toward the midday sun and spontaneously broke into song, one of their favorite part-songs for boys and girls, "Congratulations with Illusions."

"You are the sun of the sphere,
Do not deny your rays!
These are the smiles of springtime,
Ah, change them not into sighs!
Congratulations to the maiden,
Fragrant as the dewy dawn,
Smiling, you anticipate
The caressing of another morn."

They were still singing when they entered the Cova da Iria, a wide pasture dotted with olive trees, oaks, pines, and holm-oak bushes.

"Go, my lovelies," Lúcia called to the sheep. "There is grass aplenty. Eat your fill."

Francisco declared that his stomach was rumbling and asked whether this was a good time for their lunch.

"Yes, perhaps there, on that sunny patch," Lúcia said.

They fell to their knees on the lush grass and unwrapped cloth bundles of bread and cheese, but before they took their first bites, Lúcia led them in a prayer of thanksgiving. Just as they were saying their amens, they were startled by two lightning flashes, followed not by thunderclaps but complete silence.

"Look there!" Jacinta said, standing and pointing toward a young holm-oak bush near the spot they had spread their lunch. It was a sapling, no more than a meter high, with glossy bright-green leaves.

Lúcia looked up and gasped.

Hovering just above the bush was a small cloud of mysterious vapor, and as she stared, a figure materialized, of a lady dressed in a white gown more dazzling than the sun. Her face was indescribably beautiful, and it glowed like a pale sunrise. Her expression was neither happy nor sad, but serious with an air of mild reproach. Her hands were clasped in prayer upon her breast. A rosary hung from her right hand. Her small feet seemed to be resting on the uppermost succulent shoots of the holm oak.

The children stood in awe within the arc of light that radiated from the lady.

And then, she spoke. "Do not be afraid. I will not harm you."

It was Lúcia who responded. "Where is Your Grace from?"

"I am from heaven."

"And what does Your Grace wish of me?"

"I have come to ask you to come here for six months in succession, on the thirteenth day of each month at the same hour. Later, I will tell you who I am and what I want."

"And will I go to heaven too?" Lúcia asked.

"Yes, you will."

"And Jacinta?"

"Also."

"And Francisco?"

The lady said, "Also, but he must say many Rosaries. Tell me, do you wish to offer yourselves to God to endure all the sufferings that he may be pleased to send you, as both an act of reparation for the sins with which he is offended and an act of supplication for the conversion of sinners?"

Lúcia nodded fervently. "Yes, we do."

"Well, then, you will have much to suffer, but the grace of God will be your comfort."

At that, the lady opened her hands, and an intense light spread from her palms, penetrating the children. As they would later say, it reached the core of their very souls.

The three shepherds fell to their knees and, unbeknownst to one another, inwardly repeated the same words: *O most Holy Trinity, I adore thee! My God! I love thee in the most Blessed Sacrament.*

And then the lady spoke one last time, saying, "Pray the Rosary every day to obtain peace for the world and the end of the war."

With that, she immediately rose toward the east until she disappeared in the distance.

Who knows how long they stood in stunned silence? In time,

Lúcia became aware of the flock bleating for bread and cheese, and Jacinta asking breathily, "Was that real or a dream?"

"It was real," Lúcia said. "It was Our Lady!"

"Why did she choose us?" Francisco asked.

"I do not know. But we must do as she said and pray the Rosary."

All of them carried rosary beads, the girls in their pockets, the boy on his belt. They knelt at the altar of the holm-oak bush, fingered the beads, and began to fervently pray.

Lúcia made Jacinta and Francisco promise not to tell anyone of their encounter. No one would believe them, she said, and they would be branded as foolish, even crazy. Jacinta was obedient, but Francisco could not contain himself and he blurted out the secret to his parents that very night. The response was as Lúcia had predicted. Their mother told her mother, and all the kids wound up in hot water, accused of being fantasists.

"Don't you dare tell anyone about this nonsense," Lúcia's mother hissed at her. She tried to make the girl confess to a lie, but Lúcia would not and could not do so.

Gossip was the lifeblood of their little community. When Jacinta and Francisco's sister told a friend, who told a parent, who told a neighbor, the entire village was soon buzzing.

Lúcia began paying attention to the days of the week, and the thirteenth day of June finally arrived. It happened to fall upon the important feast day of Saint Anthony of Padua, and Lúcia's parents hoped that the lure of the festival would draw the children away from the Cova da Iria. However, Lúcia was undeterred, and when they herded the sheep across the moorland to the meadow, they were accompanied by fifty curious villagers. At noon, the children stood before the holm-oak bush and began to pray the Rosary. The onlookers began to murmur and point, because a little cloud, this mysterious vapor, appeared over the bush. But they could not see what the children saw, the resplendent lady in white, her feet resting lightly atop the leaves.

"What does Your Grace wish of me?" Lúcia asked.

When the lady spoke this time, Lúcia and Jacinta could hear her, but Francisco could not. Lúcia had to hush him when he kept asking why he was deprived. As for the onlookers, they would later describe hearing only a small noise emanating from the little cloud, akin to the vibrations of a hummingbird's wings.

"I want you to come here on the thirteenth of next month, to pray the Rosary every day, and to learn to read. I shall later say what I want."

There was a sick man in the village, and Lúcia boldly asked for his healing.

"If he converts," the lady said, "he will be healed within the year."

Lúcia said, "I would like to ask you to take us to heaven."

"I shall take Jacinta and Francisco soon, but you will remain here for some time yet. Jesus wishes to use you in order to make me known and loved. He wishes to establish devotion to my Immaculate Heart in the world. I promise salvation to those who embrace it, and these souls will be beloved of God, like flowers arranged by me to adorn his throne."

"Will I stay here alone?" the girl asked.

"Does that make you suffer much? Do not be dismayed. I will never forsake you. My Immaculate Heart shall be your refuge and the road that shall lead you to God."

Upon saying these words, the lady opened her hands, and a bright light came from them, flooding the children. In later years, Lúcia would write that she felt as if she had been immersed in God. In the lady's right hand Lúcia saw a heart encircled and pierced by thorns, and she understood immediately it was the Immaculate Heart of Mary, insulted by the sins of humanity.

When the vision ceased, the lady rose from the bush and glided toward the east, surrounded by her radiated light until she disappeared. Some of the villagers who were close by noticed that the buds at the top of the holm oak bent in the same direction, as if they had been drawn by the lady's clothes as she departed. The gaggle of onlookers watched as the children cycled through their Rosary prayers. Some of the women joined in, and when the last of the prayers were said, everyone trekked back to the village and the feast that awaited them.

Not everyone who witnessed the shadow of the apparition was convinced of its miraculous nature, but some were, and word of the affair spread like wildfire throughout the region. Lúcia's father shrugged whenever someone asked his opinion, but her mother was vocal, and she was angry at Lúcia, because she was the oldest and the ringleader. "What will people think of us?" she would say. "I've heard whisperings at the market. Some are saying your father and I have raised a mischievous liar. I even heard someone use the word 'blasphemer.' You'll be the ruin of us."

But Lúcia was calm and serene and insisted that she and her cousins were telling the truth. The children attended to their shepherding, dutifully prayed the Rosary, and counted the days until July 13. When the day finally arrived, hundreds of people from Fátima and surrounding villages followed them to the Cova da Iria. While they walked across the moorlands, the children talked among themselves.

"When do you think Francisco and I will go to heaven?" Jacinta asked.

"Mother Mary said soon," Lúcia said.

"When is soon?" Francisco asked. He and his sister were not the least bit worried or anxious. The prospect of going to heaven thrilled them.

"Soon is soon."

They had timed their departure to arrive at noon. When they knelt at the holm-oak bush to pray the Rosary, many of the villagers did likewise. For the first time, Lúcia's parents joined the procession, and her father himself later reported that just when it seemed the children became aware of the apparition, the sunlight diminished, a cool breeze rolled off the mountain range, chilling the summer air, and a small grayish cloud hovered over the bush.

Everyone at the Cova da Iria heard Lúcia say, "What does Your Grace wish of me?"

The glowing apparition replied, "I want you to come here on the thirteenth of next month and to continue to pray the Rosary every day in honor of Our Lady of the Rosary in order to obtain peace for the world and the end of the war, for she alone can be of any avail."

The crowd of onlookers saw the three children suddenly lower their gazes and stare in awe at the ground. Years later, in her memoirs, Lúcia would give this account of the first prophecy revealed to them at that moment:

> Our Lady showed us a great sea of fire which seemed to be under the earth. Plunged in this fire were demons and souls in human form, like transparent burning embers, all blackened or burnished bronze, floating about in the conflagration, now raised into the air by the flames that issued from within themselves together with great clouds of smoke, now falling back on every side like sparks in a huge fire, without weight or equilibrium, and amid shrieks and groans of pain and despair, which horrified us and made us tremble with fear. The demons could be distinguished by their terrifying and repulsive likeness to frightful and unknown animals, all black and transparent. This vision lasted but an instant. How can we ever be grateful enough to our kind heavenly Mother, who had already prepared us by promising, in the first Apparition, to take us to heaven? Otherwise, I think we would have died of fear and terror.

The children then lifted their eyes toward the hovering apparition, who addressed them kindly and imparted the second prophecy. "You have seen hell, where the souls of poor sinners go. To save them, God wishes to establish in the world devotion to my Immaculate Heart. If what I say to you is done, many souls will be saved and there will be peace; the war is going to end. But if people do not cease offending God, a worse one will break out during the pontificate of Pius the Eleventh. When you see a night illumined by an unknown light, know that this is the great sign given you by God that he is about to punish the world for its crimes, by means of war, famine, and persecutions of the Church and of the Holy Father. To prevent this, I shall come to ask for the consecration of Russia to my Immaculate Heart, and the communion of reparation on the First Saturdays. If my requests are heeded, Russia will be converted, and there will be peace; if not, she will spread her errors throughout the world, causing wars and persecutions of the Church. The good will be martyred; the Holy Father will have much to suffer; various nations will be annihilated. Finally, my Immaculate Heart will triumph. The Holy Father will consecrate Russia to me, and she shall be converted, and a period of peace will be granted to the world."

Lúcia concentrated hard on Mother Mary's utterances, trying to burn each word into her memory so when the day came that she could read and write, she could commit the prophecy to paper. When the lady finished, she announced there was a third prophecy. As with the first prophecy, it was shown to them in a vision that played out as they stared upon the ground. Lúcia watched aghast as a pope reached the top of a mountain, knelt at the foot of a large cross, and was killed by soldiers, who shot him through with bullets and arrows. Her eyes filled with tears at the thought of the cruel fate that would befall the Holy Father.

When she was done, the lady looked down with pity on the children's wet cheeks and said, "There is a fourth prophecy. It is the most important of all. It is for you and only for you. It is a message from God about an Italian pope and the fate that awaits all God's children."

And with that, she told them the fourth prophecy.

When the Virgin had finished her deliverance, Lúcia tried to speak, but words stuck in her throat.

"These are secrets you must carry within your hearts," the lady said. "You are the ones God has chosen. Keeping your silence will be a great grace."

Lúcia looked to the people in the murmuring crowd, who were in rapt suspense, then back to the lady. "I would like to ask you to perform a miracle so everyone will believe that Your Grace appears to us," the girl said.

"Continue to come here every month. In October, I will perform a miracle that everyone shall see so as to believe."

As the apparition sailed away to the east, the children prayed. Many of the onlookers began to pray too, as a congregation follows the lead of its priest.

On the way back to the village, the people hurled questions at them. What had they heard? What had they seen?

Lúcia answered. They could say nothing.

"Why not?" an enraged woman shouted into Lúcia's face.

Jacinta flew to her cousin's defense. "Leave Lúcia alone. The lady made us promise we would keep her secrets." But the questions kept flying, and the children ran ahead to escape.

Francisco pumped his little legs to keep up and asked, "Can I speak about the Holy Father and the soldiers who killed him?"

"No! Never!" Lúcia said. "Don't you see? That's part of the secret."

"What about the amazing last prophecy?" he asked.

"No! Especially not that!"

"All right. Then I'll say nothing."

In the days that followed, Lúcia's parents grew increasingly distraught as word reached them of threats the provincial mayor was making. He, like many, thought the children were making up stories for attention, and he fumed that the monthly events at Fátima were becoming politically disruptive. If the children didn't recant, there would be consequences.

On the morning of August 13, the mayor acted. As twenty thousand people streamed into the village, the police arrested the children on their way to the Cova da Iria, bundled them onto a donkey, and hauled them away.

At the provincial capital of Ourém, the mayor subjected the children to withering rounds of questions. He shouted, he threatened, and he cajoled. "Admit you are liars!" he said. "Do you take us for fools? Why would the Virgin Mary appear to silly little peasant children? What do you think you will get from this? Prove you are telling the truth!"

To each question, Lúcia patiently answered on behalf of her cousins. "We are telling the truth. We do not know why Our Lady appears to us. We seek nothing, only her blessings. The lady told us she would offer proof in October."

The mayor tried every tactic. He questioned the children separately. He said he would fine their parents. He threatened to lock them up in jail for the night.

It turned out that Lúcia's mother was in cahoots with the mayor. He shuttled back and forth between the interrogation room and the room down the hall, where Maria dos Santos was waiting. They collaborated on lines of questioning, trying to persuade the children to end the affair and admit to their falsehoods.

Nothing worked. The children held firm.

Meanwhile, the crowd of twenty thousand had assembled at the Cova da Iria, encircling the holm-oak bush, waiting for a sign. At noon, there was a sudden cooling of the air. The sun dimmed enough for the stars to come out, and the skies opened up with a rain resembling iridescent petals.

At the end of a long and frustrating day, the mayor made good on his threat and threw the children into a cell with common criminals. But the criminals knew about the apparitions and treated the youngsters sweetly, giving them food and the cleanest mattress and begging them to ask the Virgin for blessings.

In the morning, the mayor changed course and announced he had come to believe them. He told them he would let them go free if they revealed the secrets.

Lúcia shook her head emphatically and said they were under strict orders not to do so. The best she could do to placate him was to offer to ask the apparition for permission to tell him. The mayor finally relented and let them go.

A month went by, and when the children returned to the Cova da Iria on the thirteenth day of September, thirty thousand people accompanied them. At noon, the atmosphere changed as it had done before. The air cooled, the sun dimmed, and, this time, everyone could see a glowing orb of light that moved slowly through the sky from east to west until it hovered over the holm oak. But only the children could see the lady.

The apparition said, "Continue to pray the Rosary to obtain the end of the war. In October, Our Lord will also come, as well as Our Lady of Sorrows and Our Lady of Mount Carmel, and Saint Joseph with the Child Jesus, to bless the world. God is pleased with your sacrifices."

Lúcia told the lady that there were many requests. Requests for cures for sick people. Requests for blessings. Requests for proof of the lady's existence. The mayor's request that the secrets be divulged to him.

The lady replied, "Yes, I will cure some; others not. Some I will bless; others not. In October, I will perform a miracle for all to believe. Keep the secrets locked in your hearts. Jacinta and Francisco will not have to hold them long, for they shall enter heaven soon. You, Lúcia, will carry the burden and the grace for a long while."

And rising into the sky, she disappeared as she had done before.

The day arrived that brought the sixth and final Fátima apparition. It was October 13, 1917. The crowds were truly massive. Some seventy thousand pilgrims had arrived from far and wide, hoping for the proof that the little seers had promised. Again, the lady appeared to the children bathed in light against a sky turned dark and cloudy. A gentle iridescent rain began to fall.

"What does Your Grace wish of me?" Lúcia asked.

"I wish to tell you that I want a chapel built here in my honor. I am the Lady of the Rosary. Continue to pray the Rosary every day. The war is going to end, and the soldiers will soon return to their homes."

"I have many things to ask of you. Will you cure some sick people? Will you convert some sinners?"

"Some yes, others no. They must amend their lives and ask forgiveness for their sins." The lady became sadder and added, "Let them offend Our Lord no more for he is already much offended."

Lúcia said, "You told us you would offer proof of your existence to the world on this day. Will this be done?"

Opening her hands, the lady threw light from them overhead, and as she rose and disappeared into the expanse of the firmament, her own radiance was cast onto the sun.

Lúcia cried out, "Look at the sun!"

The great throng of spectators at the Cova da Iria and many throughout the region witnessed the miracle of the sun that would be chronicled in all the newspapers. That was the day Fátima earned its place in history.

As Lúcia pointed and shouted, the clouds parted, revealing the sun, a shining silver disk burning with an intensity no one had seen before. And although it was amazingly bright, it was not blinding.

Then the immense disk began to dance.

The sun spun rapidly like a gigantic circle of fire and then stopped for a few moments before spinning wildly again. Its rim became scarlet, and red flames were strewn across the sky. The light from the flames reflected on the meadow, the trees, the bushes, and the upturned faces.

The globe of fire seemed to tremble and shake, and then plunge in a zigzag toward the terrified crowd before zigzagging back to its original place. Then, in an instant, the sun was normal again. The miracle had ended.

In less than three years, Jacinta and Francisco would succumb to influenza. Lúcia would live for the better part of ninety years more, and every day of her pious life she thought about her little cousins, about the lovely meadow at the Cova da Iria, about the glowing, graceful face of Mary, mother of God, and about the great and terrible secrets that had been entrusted to her, especially the fourth and last one, the one that always made her tremble so.

5

Elisabetta ate her caprese salad with precision, cutting the slices of mozzarella and tomatoes into little squares and neatly delivering them to her small mouth. Cal had ordered pasta dripping with a thick ragù, and he felt a little self-conscious, shoveling messy forkfuls.

The sunlight was streaming through the windows of the ancient Tonnarello restaurant in the Trastevere neighborhood of Rome, and Elisabetta adjusted her veil to shield her eyes. It was early in the evening, the restaurant was uncrowded, and the other patrons surely must have noticed how the owner and his waiters lavished their attention on the nun, treating her as they would a family member or a celebrity.

When Elisabetta was growing up, her father regularly took the children to Tonnarello. After she became a teaching nun, it was a short walk from the Teresa Spinelli School and her residence hall on the Piazza Mastai. In recent years, as the pope's private secretary, she left the confines of the Vatican infrequently, but when she did, the restaurant was a favorite destination.

The owner stopped to ask if they were enjoying their meal.

"Marvelous, as always," she said.

"Good, good. How is your father, if I might ask?"

"He's well."

"Did he solve his problem?"

"He's still working on it. It keeps him going."

"Well, give him my regards. And how is the Holy Father?"

"He's well too."

"Can I give you a dish to take to him?"

"Of course."

"What would he like?"

"Perhaps what Professor Donovan is having. There's nutmeg in the dish, isn't there? The Holy Father likes nutmeg."

The owner bowed in pleasure. "An excellent choice."

Cal was bemused by the exchange. "How did you know they used nutmeg? Have you had this before?"

"I've not had that dish, but I have a rather acute sense of smell. It's a blessing around pleasant smells and a curse with unpleasant ones."

"What did he mean about your father—did he solve his problem?"

"My father is a retired mathematics professor. His great obsession has been trying to find a proof for the Goldbach conjecture, one of the great unsolved theorems."

"I'm afraid I don't know it."

"It states that every even integer greater than two is the sum of two prime numbers. It seems elementary on the face of it, but it's bedeviled the likes of my father ever since the eighteenth century. I live in fear I'll awake one morning to read that someone else has solved it. It's his raison d'être."

"Did the acorn fall far from the tree?" Cal asked.

"Do you mean, am I good at math?" she asked with a grin. "I'm not bad, actually. I taught it at my school."

"An archaeologist, a mathematician—is there anything you can't do?"

She didn't seem to enjoy the flattery—her jaw tensed, and her smile was artificial. He regretted the flirtatious comment. Why had he asked her to dinner? What had he hoped to achieve? He quickly changed the subject.

"How is your brother?"

"He's always busy, and with this threat, he's even busier. He keeps a calm exterior, but I know how much pressure he's under. He's completely dedicated to the Holy Father, as am I. I can only attempt to protect his agenda. Emilio protects his life."

Emilio was Colonel Emilio Celestino, the inspector general of the Vatican Gendarmerie Corps. Cal knew him professionally as the pope's personal bodyguard, and he admired the officer's intensity and intellect.

"He's lucky to have both of you at his service."

"It's our honor."

"Will you give Emilio my regards?"

"I will. He knows you're here. He asked me to pass along an offer of any assistance you require."

The waiter returned to pour more wine, and they fell into a brief silence. She had hardly touched her drink, and the waiter politely added a few drops to her glass and filled Cal's.

Cal knew he needed to bend the discussion to Fátima, but he wanted to take the opportunity to know Elisabetta better.

He said tentatively, "There's something I've always wanted to ask you."

"You want to know why I became a nun."

He sat back. "You're a mind reader."

"Not a good one. It's an obvious question."

"If it's too personal, I understand."

"It's very personal, but I'm happy to tell you. I was finishing my doctorate at the University of Rome when my boyfriend and I were stabbed one evening while out on a walk. He died. I survived. I endured a long and difficult convalescence in a rehabilitation hospital, where I was attended by a wonderful group of nursing sisters who were always so kind and relentlessly positive in their outlook. For my entire life to that point, I had always done everything for the exclusive benefit of myself. Yet here were these women who were happy and satisfied doing for others. Their devotion to their patients and to God was pure simplicity and joy. The scales fell from my eyes—I know it sounds melodramatic, but it's true. I reexamined my life. I began to pray more. What began as a germ of an idea grew into a passionate new calling. And here I am."

"You never looked back?"

"Oh, I look back sometimes, and forward sometimes, but mostly I stay in the present. The present can be a very good place to dwell." Before he could say more, she said, "And how did you come to your calling, Professor?"

"I wish you'd call me Cal."

"All right."

He surprised himself by opening up then, and it was only

later that he guiltily realized it had been something of a tactic to draw her in. "I grew up despising my father. He was distant and cruel. He did a lot of damage to my mother with his brazen affairs. But he was a, quote, unquote, great man, a giant in his field of biblical archaeology, an esteemed Harvard professor, the author of definitive books, and he expected me to follow in his footsteps. I rebelled, as kids do. I was wild in a lot of unpleasant ways. Instead of going to college, I enlisted in the army, and that really sent him into orbit."

She cut a tomato and said, "I'm sure it did."

"In the army, I kept on rebelling, which wasn't a huge surprise, and I got booted out for punching my sergeant. My father fixed it. He couldn't have the family name stained by a dishonorable discharge. He used his political clout to have my discharge classification changed to honorable. Then he made sure I got into Harvard. I didn't have anything else going for me, so I went. A year later, when I was a freshman, he died on a dig in Iraq. It shocked me, but I wasn't sad."

"My goodness. I'm sure you don't mean that. He was your father."

"Let's just say, you didn't know him. The irony, of course, is that he got his way from the grave. I got hooked by a course on the religious history of Europe, and twenty-five years later, my career is a mirror image of his. One of my offices, the one I keep at the Peabody Museum, used to belong to him. There's a plaque with his name on it."

"I find that comforting. Have you reconciled with him?"

"He's dead."

"You know what I mean."

"I suppose I have, in my own way."

"He was a Catholic, was he not?"

"Boston Catholic, through and through."

"And you? I read a newspaper article where you spoke about having a Jewish mother."

He liked that she had been curious enough to dredge up that old interview. "I study and I teach the history of European Christianity. For a thousand years, until the great schism between the Church of the West and the Church of the East, this was a Roman Catholic story. Even after the Reformation, the Roman Catholic Church was the dominant force in European political and cultural history. I suppose it was inevitable I'd fully immerse myself and become a practicing Catholic."

"Your father would have been proud, I think."

"Maybe, but my mother was not best pleased."

The restaurant door opened, and street sounds carried in. A voice boomed, "There they are!"

Cal recognized it and turned to see Cardinal Da Silva bounding toward them, and the restaurant owner hurrying with another chair for the table.

Cal rose to embrace him. "I didn't know you were coming, Rodrigo."

"It's rude of me to come unannounced," he said. "I looked for you at the Domus, and then I looked for you, Sister. Monsignor Cauchi was good enough to check your calendar. I love Tonnarello, and I am very hungry. Excellent company, excellent food, so I came. I do hope I'm not interrupting."

Elisabetta assured him that he was most welcome, and he donned his glasses and began studying the menu as carefully as if it were a religious tract. He told the hovering waiter, "Cacio e pepe, followed by filetto di salmone alla Ghiotta. Actually, bring them together, because my friends are ahead of me." He turned to Cal. "What wine are you drinking?"

One glance convinced Cal that Elisabetta was relieved that the twosome had become a threesome. Her face softened and became even lovelier, and her shoulders relaxed. Maybe he was relieved too. The dinner invitation had been rash and impulsive. Celestine had called for his help, and what had he done? Used the opportunity to pursue a woman who happened to be unobtainable. Megs was right about him. He was hopelessly flitting.

"Have you seen the Holy Father?" Elisabetta asked Da Silva.

The cardinal leaned forward and spoke in a hush. "Yes, yes, we talked. He showed me the letter. It's a great worry. He's had so many threats lately, but this one is highly specific. How is it possible that someone knows the Fourth Secret when the Vatican is in the dark?"

Elisabetta said, "I can't understand the motivation of the letter writer. Is it to harm the Holy Father or save him?"

"It is a mystery," Da Silva said. "It seems the best way to solve it is by placing ourselves in Cal's capable hands."

Cal frowned. "Look, I'll do what I can, but for everyone's sake, I hope you have good backup plans."

"My brother's team and their counterparts in the Swiss Guards are formulating enhanced security protocols for the canonization Mass," Elisabetta said. "Beyond that, we can only pray."

"Have you thought about how you'll approach this, Cal?" the cardinal asked.

"Elisabetta and I were just about to discuss that," he said, catching a flicker of a smile rippling her face. "I think I'll start here in the Vatican at the Lúcia archive at the Congregation for the Causes of Saints. It's a long shot, but maybe the researchers overlooked something in her papers that should have triggered a review by your people in the secretariat. I mean, nobody was specifically looking for clues about a hidden secret, were they? The next place I'll go is the Pope Pius the Twelfth section at the Vatican Archives."

"Why there?" Elisabetta asked.

"Modern archives aren't in my wheelhouse, but I understand his papers were recently opened to academics studying the Vatican's diplomacy with Nazi Germany during the Second World War. Pius was pope in 1957 when the bishop of Leiria died and Lúcia's envelope with the Third Secret was sent to the Vatican. We don't believe that Pius unsealed the envelope, but we now know, or at least *I* now know, that it held the message about a fourth prophecy. But maybe the historical record is incorrect. Maybe the envelope was opened and read when it was received, and if so, maybe some internal Holy See communications survived."

Da Silva looked pained. "I'm so very sorry that I couldn't share this information with you, Cal. I was truly torn."

"It wasn't something I was entitled to know, Rodrigo."

"Any other places?" Elisabetta asked.

"The Pope John the Twenty-Third, Pope Paul the Sixth, and Pope John Paul the Second papers, for the same reason. Any one of them could have made further inquiries to Lúcia about the Fourth Secret, directly or indirectly."

Da Silva shook his head miserably. "Do you have any idea how many hundreds of thousands or perhaps millions of documents you'd have to review?"

Cal nodded and took a large gulp of wine. "Classic needle-in-a-haystack problem. Got to try, right?"

The cardinal cheered at the arrival of his heaping plates. "When will you begin?" he asked, twirling cheesy spaghetti onto his fork.

"In the morning, if that's possible."

"I'll make the arrangements when we return to the Vatican," Elisabetta said.

"What will you do tonight, Cal?" Da Silva asked.

"It's a nice evening. I'll wait for the food to settle, then I'll probably go for a run."

"My goodness, that's virtuous of you," Da Silva said.

Elisabetta returned to her salad, and Cal was almost sure he detected a hint of a smirk. *She is a mind reader,* he thought. She knew it wouldn't be virtue driving him to pound the pavement. It would be frustration.

The man with a limp greeted each visitor with a solemn hand-shake and a choice of beverage. As per their practice, they arrived in a staggered fashion to avoid arousing the suspicion of neighbors. Sometimes they met during the day, sometimes in the evening. He lived modestly, in an inexpensive part of the city. His only luxury was the elevator service in his building, which allowed him to rent a fourth-floor apartment with a view over a park.

Assembling this fraternity had been a painstaking and deli-cate process undertaken only after he convinced himself of the need for assistance. His personality was not that of the lone wolf. He had always relied on the affirmation of others for important decisions. Beyond the psychological support, he realized early on that there were operational necessities that exceeded his capabilities.

He had chosen his confederates one by one. They suggested themselves by a stray comment or perhaps an eye roll at an opportune moment. Once a person became a target, he performed his grooming exceedingly slowly. Over weeks and months, he probed attitudes and then pulled back. He provoked strong reactions and then pulled back. Only when he was certain the fellow was going to be more than simpatico, but also bold, did he explicitly ask how far he would be willing to go. The day his first recruit shook his hand and said, *I will join you. I will go to the end with you,* a dam broke and he sobbed. This was going to be possible. The pope would die. The prophecy would be fulfilled. He was God's instrument, lame in body but strong in mind.

Each new man brought into the fold represented a heightened risk, so he shared the vetting and aimed for consensus. In time, two became three, three became four, and four became five. Five men, a cabal, united in righteous certainty. They used first names only. The man with a limp was known to his friends as Hugo, and by now, he considered these men to be his friends. He knew everything there was to know about the other four, and he assumed they might have done their own sleuthing to discover the identity of their comrades, but he never asked. The facade of anonymity provided something akin to Dutch courage.

"It won't be long now," Martin said, placing his glass of beer on a coaster.

Angelo, whose usual drink was orange soda, asked their host, "How are you feeling?"

"I was feeling good," Hugo said, "but now I'm a little worried."

"About what?"

"Cal Donovan, a professor from Harvard, was seen at the Vatican today. Do you know who he is?"

Two of them didn't, and Hugo educated them.

"Why does he worry you?" Leone asked.

"He was at the cardinal secretary's Fátima conference in Portugal the day before. So I ask myself, is his visit related to Fátima?"

"I understand he often comes to the Vatican," Martin said.

"He does," Hugo said, "including times when the pope needs something of him. Maybe it's nothing, but maybe it's something. We are so close. In nine days, everything changes! We can't take chances. I want to know if Celestine has suspicions. I want to know why Donovan is here. We should have him followed."

Christopher was the newest member of the group. "Who can do this?" he asked, sipping tea.

Hugo pointed toward the orange-soda drinker. "What about your cousin, Angelo? You spoke of his skills, but we never needed him. Do you think he would be available?"

"I can check. As far as I know, he doesn't care about ideology. He would need to be paid."

Christopher asked about this cousin.

"He is sometimes hired to find people and deal with them," Angelo said.

"What do you mean, 'deal with them'?"

"You can imagine."

"Has he killed?"

A shrug. "Other relatives say yes. I'm not sure. He seems capable of violence. It's unbelievable we share blood."

"Is he Mafia?"

"No. But the Mafia hires him to do jobs."

Leone asked, "Is there money to pay him? I'm sure he doesn't come cheap."

Hugo limped to the table for more red wine. "I can put my hands on money. By the time I'm discovered, it will be too late."

"Thank you for seeing me at short notice," Cal said in Italian, reaching across the desk to shake Monsignor Bonifácio Jordão's hand.

"The Holy Father's secretary asked me to provide assistance," the priest said. "I am happy to do so."

It was a poorly lit ground-level office with a single window facing one of the small courtyards of the Congregation for the Causes of Saints, an oddly shaped triangular building just off Saint Peter's Square. Built in the Fascistic style by Mussolini's favorite architects, the building and its twin across the Via della Conciliazione symbolized the Lateran Pacts that Mussolini forged with the Holy See. It was now home to the uniquely Vatican institution that oversaw the process whereby mortal beings became saints.

Cal sized up the priest, a prototypical Vatican functionary working in the bowels of a congregation. Everything about him seemed bland and uninteresting, as if the Curia had ground his personality to dust. The only color in his pale face came from reddish bumps on his chin and neck, the razor burn from his morning shave.

"I need access to Sister Lúcia's papers," Cal said.

"I was told. May I ask why?"

"It's a special project for Pope Celestine."

"Ah."

"Is the archive in one place?"

"Indeed, yes. The papers are in boxes in a storage room down the hall. After the canonization, they will be deposited in the Archive of the Congregation for the Causes of Saints."

"Is there an index?"

"There is. I personally edited it."

"You're Portuguese."

A nod. "That is why I was chosen to lead the project. I performed some of the translations of her letters and diaries."

"How long have you been working on her case?"

The priest went quiet, furrowed his brow, and looked to the window as if the answer were in the courtyard. "Formally, ever since Pope Benedict initiated her beatification process in 2008."

"It must be gratifying to reach the end of the road."

"It is, although I confess to be a little sad at the conclusion to this chapter of my life. You spoke at the conference in Lisbon, I believe."

Cal asked how he knew.

"The Secretariat of State circulated a notice about the conference. I would have liked to attend."

"It was recorded," Cal said, aware of the man's disappointment. "Cardinal Da Silva announced that the transcripts will be published as a monograph."

"I will enjoy reading it. I did receive an invitation to be an honored guest at Blessed Lúcia's Mass." The priest's tone bordered on pathos. "I will have my assistant open the storage room for you. Perhaps if you tell me the nature of your inquiry, I could point you to the correct box or boxes."

Cal answered obliquely. "Her correspondence, mainly. I believe she wrote many letters."

"She did indeed. Well, I hope you find what you are looking for."

A young Irish priest, a Father Flynn, took Cal to a locked room that was stacked, floor to ceiling along one wall, with uniformly sized cardboard boxes, each bearing a number. A thick index binder lay on the table. The priest walked him through the binder, explaining that the boxes were broadly organized chronologically, although, for ease of reference, some papers had been grouped by theme, for example, Comments and Recollections Concerning Her Cousins. There was a separate index of named individuals, with corresponding box and folder numbers.

"Do you read Portuguese?" the priest asked.

"I'm not an expert, but yes."

"Her use of language is fairly basic, so that's for the good. The problem you'll have is with her handwriting. I'm in room 121B if you need help. It's near the lavatory."

"You speak Portuguese?"

"I learned it for this assignment. Now that we're done, the knowledge will likely fade. I suppose I could request an assignment to a parish in Portugal or Brazil, but to be honest, I'm better with documents than people."

Cal took a sip from the bottle of water the priest had left him and began leafing through the binder. He had a feeling it was going to be a long day.

After getting the lay of the land, he searched for *Pope Pius XII* in the index. There were two entries, the first a letter sent to the pontiff by Lúcia in April 1939, shortly after his pontificate began, and his reply in May.

He found her letter in box 18:

Holy Father, I write to Your Holiness that, according to a heavenly revelation, the good God promises to end the persecution in Russia. I beg of Your Holiness to make and order that all the bishops of the Catholic World together make a solemn and public act of reparation and consecration of Russia to the most Holy Hearts of Jesus and Mary and approve and recommend the practice of reparatory devotion, which consists in receiving Holy Communion, reciting the Rosary, making fifteen minutes of meditation on the mysteries of the Rosary, all this on the first Saturday of five consecutive months.

Yours in Christ,
Sr Lúcia, Convent of St. Dorothy, Pontevedra

He found the brief, solicitous reply of the pope in the same folder, praising her piety and devotion and promising that he would take the matter under advisement.

Cal knew the history of her request and the political

difficulties it created for Pius with respect to the sensitivities of the Russian Orthodox Church. It took Pius three years to issue a papal bull that did as she asked, formally consecrating Russia to the Immaculate Heart of Mary. However, Lúcia was unsatisfied, because it was a unilateral declaration of the Vatican, not a unified agreement by all the bishops of the world. Lúcia had to wait for Pope John Paul II, the dedicated Fátimaist and anticommunist that he was, to fully satisfy her request in 1984 with a papal bull that was endorsed by all corners of the Church.

Cal shifted his search to the number two man in Pius's Holy See, the secretary of state, Cardinal Luigi Maglione, but the index didn't include him. He had better luck within the papacies of John XXIII, Paul VI, and John Paul II. Each pontiff and their respective cardinal secretaries had corresponded with the nun. For the next hour, Cal pulled down boxes and read their letters but found no allusion to a Fourth Secret.

He turned to the bishop of Leiria, the Portuguese cleric who persuaded Lúcia to commit the secrets to writing. José Alves Correia da Silva (no relation, his friend the cardinal had assured him) was referenced in numerous documents, mainly letter exchanges from the 1930s until his death in 1957. Cal decided to review them chronologically and began shifting boxes again.

The first mention of the secrets of Fátima was in a 1941 letter from the bishop encouraging Lúcia to continue with her memoirs. She had written four volumes to this point, and although she had spoken of and written about the existence of the secrets of the Virgin since the fateful days of 1917, she had never expounded on them.

He wrote: *Perhaps this is the appropriate time to tell the world about Our Lady's prophecies.*

Cal found her reply in her chicken-scrawled penmanship: *If you command me to do so, I will comply. However only the first two secrets should be revealed, as God has not authorized me to go beyond this.*

The bishop wrote back: *I will come to Tuy in a fortnight. Please commit the secrets to writing. We must let the Vatican see them before your new memoir is published.*

The next mention of the secrets was in a letter from the bishop dated late in 1943. He wrote that he had received a telegram from her Mother Superior informing him that Lúcia had contracted influenza: *The time has come, my dear Sister, to reveal all else revealed to you by Our Lady, lest we lose you to the bosom of Our Lord. You will see me very soon.*

The historical record was clear as to subsequent events: The bishop was successful in persuading her to write down the Third Secret. She acquiesced in January 1944. Her sealed envelope was given to the bishop, who chose not to read it, keeping it among his personal effects until his death in 1957, at which time his secretary delivered it to the Vatican.

Cal spent the next few hours reading the other exchanges between the bishop and the nun, but he found no further discussions of the secrets of Fátima and nothing to indicate whether the bishop was aware of a separate note concerning a Fourth Secret. He was back scouring the index when the young Irish priest poked in and asked how he was getting on.

"You were right about her handwriting," Cal said.

"Yeah, brutal, no?"

"It looks like she wrote letters to people I assume are

relatives," Cal said. "There's a Glória de Jesus Rosa dos Santos, a Carolina de Jesus Rosa dos Santos, a Manuel Rosa dos Santos."

"Brothers and sisters. Plenty of correspondence. Nothing terribly interesting or important, if you want my opinion. Mostly family doings, exchanges of blessings, and the like."

"I think I'll grab a bite," Cal said. "Want to join me?"

"Would love to, but I've got a meeting with Monsignor Jordão to go over the final texts of the canonization encyclicals. I can point you to a good café."

"Thanks, but I know my way around the neighborhood."

When Cal returned from lunch, he spent the rest of the afternoon reading exchanges between Lúcia and her sisters. Father Flynn hadn't been wrong. The tide of banalities numbed Cal's mind. The correspondence between Lúcia and her brother was even worse. Manuel's letters were rather basic. The most interesting tidbits concerned the birth and death of farm animals. Cal's eyes were drooping when, late in the afternoon, he came upon this in a letter Lúcia wrote to Manuel in April 1944.

Brother, with a war on you would think the Vatican would have more to do than question your humble sister. I wrote to the Bishop and said, have them send me their questions in a letter. He should not travel to Galicia again, but it seems Cardinal M insists, and so the Bishop is coming.

Cal snapped to attention, took a photo of the paragraph, and immediately called Elisabetta.

"Can you get your hands on a list of cardinals at the Vatican in 1944 whose surnames start with 'M'?"

"Do you need it now?"

"I do."

"I'll ring you back."

She called several minutes later. "There was only one. Cardinal Maglione."

He pumped his fist and said, "The secretary of state. I'll need to get into the Pius the Twelfth archives first thing in the morning."

"You found something. I can hear it in your voice."

"Nothing to talk about yet, but I think history might need a rewrite. I've got a feeling the Vatican knew about the Third and Fourth Secrets in 1944, thirteen years earlier than everyone thinks."

6

By order of the pope, the Vatican Apostolic Archives had recently undergone a name change. Its old Latin name, dating back centuries, was Archivum Secretum, the Secret Archives, a label meant to convey that it was the pope's private collection. However, the word *secret* had long emitted a sinister whiff that encouraged conspiratorial thinking, and the Vatican believed a more anodyne designation would better reflect the institution's service to the Church and the larger world of culture.

The archives were maintained by a professional staff overseen by layers of Curial officials. There were strict rules regulating how academic researchers could access archival documents, rules that applied to everyone except Cal Donovan, whose golden library card gave him free rein.

The origin story of the golden library card was legendary. It was told to every new member of the archives staff, and it was gossip fodder among Cal's envious colleagues. In gratitude for helping him with the delicate case of the young priest with the stigmata of Christ, Pope Celestine granted Cal an academic's dream—unlimited and unfettered browsing rights to the Vatican Archives and Apostolic Library.

Whenever he presented himself to the reception desk, a Vatican archivist would give a knowing smile and let him pass through the private entrance into the restricted areas. And then he would be on his own, free to wander from floor to floor, to stop at any cabinet or shelf and peruse any document or folio, with the exception of some modern documents that remained under quarantine.

All others had to make a written request to use the archives or the adjacent Apostolic Library. Some fifteen hundred researchers a year qualified for admittance. They had to make specific queries for books or documents, and to do so, they relied on imperfect catalogues and indices, and accepted the possibility that a document had been accidentally or purposefully misplaced at some point in the past. Their requested documents were delivered to the reading rooms, then returned to the stacks upon completion of their work.

The first time Cal used his golden library card, he took a long and languid walk through twelve centuries of history. He started at the top floor, the frescoed Tower of the Winds, built in the sixteenth century as a solar observatory by Pope Gregory XIII. Then he inhaled the mustiness of the second level, the so-called Diplomatic Floor, commissioned in the seventeenth century by Pope Alexander VII as a central depository of the complete diplomatic correspondence of Holy See legates, nuncios, and other agents. All the written communication between the Vatican and the states of the ancien régime were still stored in the same wooden cabinets that Alexander had constructed, an archive spanning the fifteenth century to the Napoleonic era.

His next stop was the thirteen kilometers of documents housed in the long gallery built in the early twentieth century to the west of the Cortile del Belvedere, dubbed by insiders as the Gallery of Metal Shelves. The documents stored there included the archival material of the Curial offices, various Vatican commissions, and papers from the papal household. Nearby was another archive, the so-called Soffittoni, built after the Second World War above the gallery of geographical maps in the Vatican Museums, containing the documentary history of the Congregation for Bishops and other Vatican congregations.

Finally, he descended to the basement to explore the newest archival space, known to insiders as the Bunker. There, under the Cortile della Pigna, were forty-three kilometers of shelving dedicated by John Paul II in 1980, a fireproof two-story reinforced-concrete structure that was temperature- and humidity-controlled. The Bunker housed a huge array of documents ancient and modern, ranging from the archives of the most important families of the Vatican city-state to various institutions of the Roman Curia and its councils, to the Congregation of the Rites, to the near-modern archives of the Secretariat of State. To Cal's delight, he was even allowed into the most secure storerooms adjacent to the Bunker, which contained the archives' greatest treasures, such as the letter from English noblemen to Pope Clement VII concerning the "Great Matter" of Henry VIII's divorce, the Edict of Worms with the signature of Emperor Charles V, and the bull excommunicating Martin Luther.

Now, after a small breakfast in the guesthouse cafeteria, Cal checked in at the reception desk at the archives and asked for Maurizio Orlando. Orlando was the assistant archivist, the number two official on the professional staff, and over the years he and Cal had forged a pleasant friendship. He emerged from his back office in his signature sweater vest, emanating aftershave vapors.

"Cal, it's so good to see you. Everything is prepared. I've had people working on your request all night."

"I'm sorry for the short notice, Maurizio."

"Actually, the staff was quite energized by the challenge. As you know, the rhythms of the archives are slow and, some would say, gentle. We rarely receive urgent assignments. So, when Sister Elisabetta said, 'Jump,' my reply was, 'How high would you like me to jump?' Come, let's go to the Bunker."

The Pius XII pontificate ended in 1958, and under the seventy-year rule, its papers would not have been released until 2028. However, controversy over Pius's relations with Nazi Germany during World War II and the alleged failure of the Vatican to use its moral authority to protect Jews during the Holocaust had scholars clamoring for access to the archive while some Holocaust survivors were still alive. The Vatican heeded the call and lifted the embargo early.

On the stairs to the basement, Orlando told Cal, "The Pius archive consists of approximately two million documents that take up precisely three hundred twenty-three meters of linear space in the Bunker. The documents cover an extensive area of activity—the actions of the Holy See during the war, concordats that were negotiated, the humanitarian work of the Church, reports on religious and political issues, and documents concerning the Vatican city-state. The material spanning 1939 to 1948 was fully catalogued before the quarantine was lifted.

"Of course, the war years were of the most interest to academics, and that's where we put our manpower. Work is advancing for 1948 to 1958, but it is far from complete," Orlando told Cal. "Fortunately, your request centered on 1944. My people relied on the digital catalogue to generate lists of documents that might be of significance for your work."

They walked along fluorescent-lit corridors, past football-field lengths of metal bookcases with shelves stacked floor to ceiling with countless red-and-gray storage boxes. The Bunker brought to mind Borges's Library of Babel, an infinite library containing all possible books, and Cal sniffed appreciatively at the mustiness of old cardboard and paper.

"This is where the Pius archive starts," Orlando said, brushing a hand along a cage. "You can't even see the end of it from here."

In a far corner of the Bunker was a room set up with a large table and multiple computer workstations. Cal noticed a trash bin filled with plastic coffee cups, water bottles, and a crushed pizza box, the detritus of junior archivists burning the midnight oil.

"Here, let me show you what they found," Orlando said. The two sat at the table sharing a line listing of potentially interesting documents with their catalogue accession numbers. "Although all the pontificate documents from 1944 have been digitized, many are handwritten and can't be easily subjected to word or phrase searches. If you see a document that might be important to your queries, you'll have to review it on this workstation by typing in the accession number, or, should you wish to see the actual document, you can go into the stacks."

Cal scanned the memo. The archivists had adhered to his search parameters. Although there were no documents with the search terms *Fátima* or *Lúcia dos Santos* in their descriptors, there were hundreds of notes and letters between Pope Pius and Cardinal Maglione, dozens between Maglione and the bishop of Leiria, and a few between Maglione and other Portuguese prelates.

"Let's say letters were written from the Vatican to the bishop of Leiria," Cal asked. "Would they have found their way into the archive?"

Orlando replied, "Well, this is always a problem we face in reconstructing the historical record. We often must rely on only one side of a communication stream. I would say that in the postwar period, there was little to no inclination for a provincial diocese in Portugal to send documents to the Vatican for archival storage. It's possible that the Diocese of Leiria has their own archives with correspondence from this period, but, remember, this was during the war, and they may have been cautious and destroyed documents in case neutrality crumbled and Portugal was invaded by Germany. In your favor, a good portion of the official Vatican correspondence from this period was typewritten, and it was common practice to retain an unsigned carbon copy for the files. These we have."

"Thank you, Maurizio. I'll be sure to let the Holy Father know how helpful you've been."

"Good, good. I'll leave you to your work then. The mobile signal down here is weak. If you need me, use the phone on the table."

Cal generally preferred to work with original documents. There was an intangible vitality in holding a paper, parchment, or papyrus in one's hand, as its writer and its readers had done, but time was short, and he made do with digital images. Lúcia's letter to her brother about an upcoming visit from the bishop of Leiria at the insistence of Cardinal M was dated April 18, 1944, so he centered on the surrounding months and began searching the letters between Cardinal Maglione and Bishop da Silva.

Cal had read up on Cardinal Maglione the night before. He was the consummate Vatican insider, a man with an academic training and advanced degrees in philosophy and theology, who spent only a brief period doing pastoral work in Naples before his transfer to the Holy See as an operative in the Secretariat of State. What followed were diplomatic postings to Switzerland and France and his elevation to archbishop, then cardinal.

As a cardinal elector, he participated in the 1939 conclave that chose his former schoolmate Eugenio Pacelli to become Pius XII. Pius promptly appointed his friend secretary of state and was so reliant on his counsel that until Maglione's death in August 1944, Vatican wags liked to joke that whenever the pope goes outside without a *maglione* (Italian for *sweater*), he catches cold.

Cal reviewed carbon copies of letters that Maglione sent to Leiria in January and February of 1944. They were diplomatic in nature, expressing concerns that, for the sake of the nation, the Church must do nothing to upset the fragile balance of Portuguese neutrality. He repeatedly noted that it was the bishop's responsibility to make sure that the priests in his diocese, regardless of their personal opinions about

Nazi Germany, do nothing to incite discord or undermine the positions of Portugal's Salazar government. Although the ancient Anglo-Portuguese alliance remained intact, the British had not sought Portugal's assistance and the country remained one of the Europe's last escape routes for refugees and Allied fighters.

Then Cal found an intriguing carbon of a brief letter from Maglione to da Silva dated late February, with a crucial sentence: *I am in receipt of your letter regarding the nun in Pontevedra. The Holy Father has taken an interest and wishes to know more.*

That sparked a feverish search for the da Silva letter to which Maglione was referring, but it appeared it hadn't survived.

His interest at a boil, Cal began working through a voluminous swath of correspondence from March 1944. It wasn't until he looked up accession number 1239-3339-44, *Letter from B. da Silva to C. Maglione,* that he got a jolt of discovery. It came from the short note dated March 20 that was handwritten in Portuguese on diocese letterhead.

Eminence, I did as you wished although I admit my reluctance as I did not think it my place to know what was written. Please find within my transcriptions. I will retain the originals.

da Silva

Please find within? Transcriptions of what? Lúcia's letters? Where were they, these transcriptions? The digitized letter was a single page in length. Could it be that the original was longer, that the transcriptions existed but hadn't been scanned? The possibility sent Cal flying from the workroom, heading down the corridor through the stacks. His leather soles skidded on the poured concrete as he jogged through the Bunker, peering through the cages at the accession numbers on the end racks. When he found the right row and opened the cage door, he groaned. The file box he wanted was on a top shelf. It took time to locate a stepladder and a while longer to riffle through the box and locate the original letter, but there were no "transcriptions" attached, or elsewhere among other documents in the box.

He endured a disappointing walk back to his workstation, where he plotted his next move and made the decision to start looking for the letter or letters in which Maglione expressed an insistence that da Silva visit Lúcia to put questions to her. Unfortunately, there was a gap in their correspondence. The next communiqué between the two men was from May of that year, a carbon of a letter from Maglione inquiring about a church fire in Porto.

His mobile rang, a call from Elisabetta's office. When he answered, the signal dropped, so he used the room phone to call her back. She asked how his inquiries were going.

"Nothing definitive yet. A few green shoots."

"Green is good. It's the color of life."

"I've hit a dead end on correspondence between Maglione and the bishop of Leiria. There's a large number of letters between Pius and Maglione, and that's where I'm going next. It looks like most of it's going to be about official secretariat and Holy See business, but hopefully there'll be something useful."

"Thank you, Professor. I'll let the Holy Father know."

"I thought it was going to be *Cal*."

"Thank you, Cal," she said with similar formality.

The letters and memos between the pope and his cardinal secretary might have been interesting to historians of the period, but for Cal, they were a blizzard of unhelpful documents. He broke for lunch at a restaurant he liked on the Via Aurelia and checked in with Maurizio Orlando on his return.

"How goes the war?" the archivist asked.

Cal chuckled. "It feels like one. It's a challenge. If these papers weren't digitized, it would be hopeless."

"We archivists have one foot in the analog world, the other in the digital world. Maybe one day, you'll be able to tell me what you're looking for."

"Over a very good bottle of wine," Cal said.

An hour into his afternoon session, he came upon the index descriptor *Memo from Maglione to P XII, 27 March 1944: Travel to Neutral Countries*. He punched in the accession number and saw the handwritten document.

Holy Father, I can confirm the difficulties I would face undertaking a journey to neutral Spain. All civilian air travel has been suspended. It might be possible to arrange a military flight in cooperation with Bastianini at the foreign ministry. However, there is the risk of Allied planes, and it is debatable as to whether the Spanish government would allow us to land. Travel by rail through France is unacceptably hazardous and disrupted. Regretfully, we must ask da Silva to make the visit in my place.

Maglione

Cal took a screenshot with his phone, muttered, "Another green shoot," and pressed on.

He could count on one hand the times in his professional life where discovering a document made him feel as if his heart would explode. The note that set him off was dated March 30, 1944, and written in a flowing hand on Vatican stationery embossed with *Stato Della Citta Vaticano*.

Maglione, Regarding your missive on travel to Spain, I agree that risk to life and limb is unacceptable. Send da Silva. We must ascertain whether the scenario applies to me, as I fear it does. Pressure must be brought to bear for her to divulge additional clarifying recollections. Furthermore, she must reveal the nature of the undisclosed scenario. We must know if it involves the Vatican and the Third Reich. Convey to the bishop the urgency.

Pius pp. XII

Cal waited for his heart to slow and thought, *My God, Pope Pius thought the Third Secret was about him!*

7

Tuy, Spain, 1944

Sister Lúcia had celebrated her thirty-seventh birthday a month earlier. After supper in the refectory, she was presented with a candle stuck into a muffin. When she tried to share the treat with the other sisters and novices, her Mother Superior insisted that it had been baked for her. Sister Lúcia, as always, was stubborn. There is a war on, she said. People are hungry. Sugar is scarce. I will not consume an entire treat on my own. So the muffin was diced, and everyone had a morsel.

She was eighteen when she joined the Sisters of Saint Dorothy as a postulant, a sprig of a woman who still looked like a child. The convent was in Tuy, in the Spanish province of Pontevedra, just across the northern Portuguese border. To hide Lúcia's notoriety as the little seer of Fátima, the Mother Superior assigned her an assumed name, Sister Maria das Dores, Mary of the Sorrows, but by the time she took her perpetual vows nine years later, everyone in the religious community knew who she was, and she was ordained as Sister Lúcia.

She was a headstrong woman with a fluid tongue, and a

confidence that came from a childhood spent in the limelight. When she no longer had to hide her identity, she talked freely about some, though not all, of her childhood visions and the lessons she had learned from the Holy Virgin. Every day, she prayed the Rosary, prayed to the Immaculate Heart of Mary, prayed for the consecration of Russia, and prayed for the souls of Jacinta and Francisco. She was a shining inspiration to her fellow sisters, and they all tried to emulate her piety and purity.

The trauma of nearly losing her a year earlier was still percolating within the community. Influenza had swept the nunnery during November and December of 1943, and two elderly sisters had died. At first, Lúcia's illness had not seemed too bad. After a few days of confinement, the fevers and aches had subsided, and she was able to return to the chapel and perform light kitchen work. Then, on Christmas Eve, the sickness returned with a vengeance. She began to cough. She developed a fever. She stopped eating and teetered on the edge. Her Mother Superior, fearing the worst, sent a telegram to Lúcia's patron, the bishop of Leiria, Bishop da Silva.

Da Silva crossed the frontier into Spain and arrived in Tuy on a blustery January day. Upon entering Lúcia's cell, he saw a number of sisters praying the Rosary at her sickbed. He quietly bowed out and waited in the hall for them to conclude. When he entered again and approached, he was greatly alarmed. The normally robust middle-aged nun was gaunt, her skin whiter than the bedsheets. He had never seen her without a habit, and although she wore a stocking cap for warmth, he was surprised her hair was prematurely gray. Propped on two pillows, she tracked his movements and blinked in surprise.

"Eminence? Is that you?"

"Yes, dear Lúcia, it is I."

"You have come all the way from Leiria?"

"I have indeed."

After a brief fit of coughing, she said, "But why?"

"Don't you remember the letter I sent? The one where I asked you to write down the last of Our Lady's secrets?"

"Perhaps. I have been forgetful. I have not been able to take in fresh air. My lungs have been weak."

"Yes, I've been told about your condition. That is why it is so important to have a complete record of what occurred in Fátima in July of 1917."

"Such a long time ago," she said.

"Yes, a long time ago. Were you able to write down your recollections?"

She looked toward her nightstand and then to her desk. "I cannot recall. I feel I have been in a fog these past weeks."

Her cell was typical for her order, sparse and bare. There was no rug, no electric fire. There were a few pieces of cheap furniture, a lamp, a small wardrobe, and lace curtains on the two narrow street-facing windows. The windows were shut, and the airless room was heavy with the odors of infirmity. Someone had placed a sack of potpourri on her desk, likely done to sweeten the atmosphere for the bishop's sake.

"May I check your drawer? Your desk?"

"Of course, Eminence," she said weakly.

Da Silva was a doughy man with a kindly face, who seemed to be in a perpetual state of fatigue. He bent to explore the drawer of her nightstand and then sat at her small desk to examine its contents.

"I cannot see it, Sister."

"Then perhaps I did not write anything."

He took a sheet of onionskin paper from the desk drawer and tested a fountain pen. "I need to find something for you to write on."

"I have books there," she said, pointing to a small bookcase.

"The covers are too rough for this thin paper," he said.

"There is a shirt box in the wardrobe, where I keep my old letters. Give me the lid."

He retrieved the box and peeked in. Lying atop stacks of opened envelopes were two sealed ones with nothing written on them.

He waved them in the air. "What are these, Sister?"

"Bring them closer," she said, and when they were under her nose, she said, "Oh, yes! These are for you. I must have asked someone to put them into the box."

"These are your recollections of the secrets?"

She nodded weakly. "I remember now. There was a day last week when I felt strong enough to sit at my desk for a spell."

"Why are there two envelopes?"

"It is because there were two further secrets revealed on that day. Would you like to read what I wrote?"

"No, Sister. They are not for my humble eyes. They are for posterity. Do you know who Cardinal Maglione is?"

"No, Eminence."

"He is the Vatican cardinal secretary. Only the pope is more important."

"Oh."

"He is aware of your illness, and he instructed me to secure the full accounting of the Fátima apparitions."

"Well, now you have what I have written. Could you ask one of the sisters to assist me with a bedpan?"

⁌————⁍

What a difference three months made.

When the bishop returned to the convent in April, the weather was milder, and Sister Lúcia had regained much of her strength and vitality. She received him in the library. The convent of the Sisters of Saint Dorothy was on a busy road in town, the Rua Martinez Padim, and a din of street noise made it into the library. Along with her strength, she had regained her feistiness, and she immediately lit into the cleric.

"Eminence, you surely have more important things to attend to than this poor nun. There is a war. There is suffering. Why make a long journey to see me again? You were here such a short time ago. Surely you have heard of my recovery."

Da Silva was weary from his journey, and he sat heavily on a library chair. "Everyone is grateful for your recovery, dear Lúcia. Our prayers were answered. Did the Virgin not tell you that you would have a long life?"

"Longer than my beloved cousins. What are the questions this cardinal wishes to ask?

"Cardinal Maglione."

"Yes, him."

"I must tell you, Sister, that the cardinal had me provide him with a copy of what you wrote concerning the Third and Fourth Secrets."

"You read them?"

"Reluctantly. He gave me an order, and I complied. I made transcriptions."

"Then you know everything you might know. I should not have agreed to write what I did. Our Lady told me not to reveal the Third Secret. You caught me in a weakened state."

The bishop pulled absently at a thread on the sleeve of his cassock. "Yes, I can appreciate that. Might I ask some questions about it?"

Her dark eyes flashed through her thick lenses. "You are here, are you not? You are my bishop, are you not?"

He deflected her anger with a fraternal smile. "The Holy Father in the prophecy, the one felled by arrows and bullets, how would you describe him?"

"What do you mean, Eminence? He was the Holy Father. He was dressed in white, as Holy Fathers are."

"Was he thin? Was he fat?"

"I cannot say."

"Was he tall or short?"

"I cannot say."

"Did he speak? If so, what was his language?"

"I heard nothing. I remember the sadness I felt. I was sad the Holy Father was suffering so."

"The soldiers who killed him. What were their uniforms like?"

"I cannot say."

"You know the swastika, do you not?"

"Of course. I live in a convent, not under the ground."

"Did the soldiers wear swastikas?"

"Eminence," she said with exasperation, "why all these questions? What is the purpose? I gave you my best recollection, even though the Holy Mother told me to keep the secret. I have done penance. I will continue to do penance."

"The questions, dear Lúcia, do not come from me. They do not even come from Cardinal Maglione. They come directly from the Holy Father, Pope Pius. I must tell you, he is concerned that the prophecy is about him. He is concerned that he will be the one who is set upon by soldiers, perhaps soldiers of the Third Reich."

"I have told you what I know, Eminence. I can say nothing else."

"But, my dear Sister, there *is* more you can say. You also wrote of another prophecy, a Fourth Secret, that you would not disclose. The pope demands to know if this last prophecy confirms or refutes his assassination. He demands to know if Axis soldiers will attack the Vatican."

Her veil was tight around her face, and when she moved her jaw, the veil moved with it. "I will say nothing more about it. Our Lady was clear. God decreed that only we children were allowed to know. Jacinta and Francisco have already taken the secret to heaven. When it is my time, I will take it to heaven."

"But this comes from the pope!"

"Who is a higher authority, Eminence, God or the pope? Now it is time for chapel, and I must go."

The bishop went to the Mother Superior's office and closed the door. The dour, elderly Spaniard asked whether his visit was satisfactory. It was far from satisfactory, he replied. He was on a mission from the Vatican and demanded she help him.

"Sister Lúcia has hidden a letter. I must see it."

92

"Have you asked her for it?"

"She refuses."

"You are her bishop. Demand it."

"It seems she answers to a higher authority," he said wearily.

"Do you want me to make the demand?" the nun asked.

"It will do no good. She is willful."

"She sees herself as special. Perhaps she is. What can I do?"

"Search her room, if you will. It is a letter we are after, probably no more than a page or two. She writes on onionskin. It might be loose or in an envelope. Look everywhere."

"You want me to invade her privacy?"

"I do."

"Now?"

"While she is at chapel."

"This does not sit well."

"If it were not important, I would not insist."

Da Silva waited in the office, standing at the windows, sipping a glass of mineral water, watching dark sedans drive past the drab convent.

The nun was gone for half an hour on the clock. When she returned, he knew instantly from her puckered expression that she had found nothing.

"You looked everywhere?"

"Everywhere."

"Among her box of letters?"

"Inside each envelope."

"Under the mattress?"

"Everywhere, Eminence."

"The Vatican will want details. Give me an inventory of her possessions."

She sat at her desk and wrote a list for him. "What else do you want of me?" she asked.

"Might she have hidden something elsewhere in the convent?"

"If it was something important, it would be reckless of her to do so, don't you think? Someone could come upon it."

He grunted his agreement. "Might she have passed it to someone outside Saint Dorothy? A visitor? Via the post?"

"You are the only visitor she has had in months. She is an avid letter writer, so that is possible, I suppose. Eminence, we are always pleased to receive you, but I do have a convent to run."

The bishop took the stairs to his waiting car and driver. Before climbing in, he glanced at the second-floor windows of Lúcia's cell. Through the lace curtains, he saw her looking down, and he sincerely hoped that the Mother Superior had made every effort to cover the traces of her intrusion.

8

I t was easy to lose track of time in a windowless room with
no wall clock. Cal worked methodically into the afternoon,
reviewing every piece of correspondence between Cardinal
Maglione and the pope.

The war was raging across Europe, and April was a deadly
month. Pius seemed reliant on his cardinal secretary to keep
him informed, and Cal found a steady flow of memos updating
the pontiff, often several per day.

On April 1, the Waffen-SS massacred eighty-six men in
Ascq, France. On April 4, Bucharest was bombed for the first
time. On April 7, Hitler suspended all laws in Berlin and made
Goebbels the sole administrator of the city. On April 10, the
RAF dropped almost four thousand tons of bombs in a single
raid on Germany, France, and Belgium. On April 15, the
Soviets liberated Tarnopol. On April 20, the RAF commem-
orated Hitler's birthday by dropping an even greater tonnage
of bombs on Germany. On April 25, Adolf Eichmann and

the Nazis offered to exchange a million Hungarian Jews for a large supply of trucks and food, a deal that, Maglione noted, would be seen as blackmail and would never be accepted by the Allies.

Moving into the May correspondence, Cal clicked on a file blandly labeled MEMO FROM MAGLIONE TO P XII, 2 MAY 1944, INVENTORY.

Holy Father, The inventory at Pontevedra was as follows: one box of letters——thoroughly examined, one pair shoes, one habit, two vests, ladies undergarments, one umbrella, blank writing paper and pens, photos of the Shrine of Fátima, photos of Jacinta and Francisco Marto, one broken rosary, a small wooden statue of the Virgin, books——the Portuguese prayer book O Livro Das Minhas Orações, a Spanish Bible, a Portuguese Bible, the 19th-century Portuguese missal Visitas ao Santissimo Sacramento e a Maria Santissima, Ágreda's Mystical City of God in Portuguese. Nothing else was found. Maglione

Cal hadn't realized he had been holding his breath, and now, he sat back in his chair repaying his oxygen debt. The bishop of Leiria had fulfilled his assignment. He had gone to Lúcia's convent. Presumably, he had questioned her. He had searched her room, looking, no doubt, for the Fourth Secret. She must have remained tight-lipped and resolute if he had to resort to rummaging through her things. *Nothing else was found.* The green shoots were turning brown.

He had plowed on through May and into June and July when he heard a rustling behind him.

"I got lost," Elisabetta said. "I rarely come down here. The endless corridors remind me of the catacombs."

Cal pushed his chair from the table and disguised his pleasure by yawning and stretching his arms. "It can be disorienting."

"I wasn't sure of this room's extension. I tried calling your mobile, but it didn't go through."

"Cell phones and basements," he said.

"I needed the exercise. Any progress?"

He showed her the March 20 and March 27 exchanges between Maglione and Pius and Maglione's May 2 inventory memo.

"I have to agree with you," she said. "In 1944, the Vatican knew as much as we know today. Pope Pius probably envisioned a direct attack by the Nazis or perhaps a betrayal by Mussolini. He had Lúcia's room searched! The desperation!"

"There's absolutely nothing to suggest they found the Fourth Secret," Cal said. "I've almost come to the end of the correspondence between Maglione and Pius. Maglione died in late August 1944, and Pius didn't name a new secretary of state. He personally assumed control of the secretariat until the end of his pontificate."

"I'm sure they never found it," she said. "Future popes would have known. Future cardinal secretaries would have known. No, I fear Sister Lúcia took the secret to her grave."

"Can you put me in touch with someone at Saint Dorothy convent in Tuy?" Cal asked. "I need to ask if they have any of Lúcia's belongings on display or in storage. Maybe Bishop da Silva missed something."

"I'll find you a contact."

"Thanks. I don't want to waste a day on an unnecessary trip.

We've only got a week. If I need to go, I can catch an early flight tomorrow."

"That's fine. Let me know, and I'll make the arrangements. I passed along your greetings to my brother, and he'd like to see you. Tonight is our monthly supper at my father's. Would you like to come?"

Time was of the essence, but Cal didn't know what his next move would be. Spending the evening with Elisabetta sounded good to him.

"I'd be delighted."

When Cal returned to the guesthouse, there was a note under his door with the phone number for the convent, the Orden Católica Religiosas Santa Dorotea en Tuy, and a message that the Mother Superior would be expecting his call. Elisabetta had added her father's address.

He sat on his bed and punched in the number. The Mother Superior, Sister Curbelo, answered, and Cal introduced himself in Spanish.

"I speak English, if that is easier, Professor Donovan."

"It is," he said. "Thank you for taking my call."

"We are honored to help the Holy Father in his inquiries about Blessed Lúcia. Her special day is almost upon us."

"That it is. My understanding is that she remained in Tuy until 1948."

"Yes, she desired to become a Carmelite, for obvious reasons. Their order, as you are probably aware, is under the special protection of the Blessed Virgin Mary. In March of 1948, she returned to her native Portugal and entered the Carmelite Convent of Santa Teresa in Coimbra."

"While in Tuy, did she have the same room her entire stay?"

"It is likely that when she came as a novice in 1925 she would have been housed in the novitiate dormitory. After she entered into orders, she would have been assigned her own room. That room was hers until she left us."

"Did she leave anything behind? Books, letters, personal possessions?"

"None that I am aware of. We would have treasured anything belonging to her."

"You're sure."

"Quite sure."

"What about the room itself? We're interested in anything she might have hidden—maybe under a loose floorboard, maybe in a vent."

"Oh my goodness." The nun laughed. "I can assure you that nothing is hidden in that room."

"How can you be certain?"

"When I came to Saint Dorothy in the 1980s, we experienced an increasing number of Fátima pilgrims wishing to visit her cell. The diocese decided to convert the room into a small chapel where pilgrims might pray. An altar was installed. Pews were added. The ventilation had to be improved, and to do this, the ceiling had to be dropped. The room was taken apart before it was put back together. Nothing of the Blessed Sister's was found. I was there."

"Ladies and gentlemen, we're just over Bangor, Maine, and the captain has turned off the seat-belt sign. You are now free to move about the cabin."

The atmosphere in the business-class cabin was as bubbly as the flowing champagne. This was the high season, and vacationers outnumbered business travelers.

The atmosphere in row four was particularly giddy. Laughter spilled from the three middle seats, occupied by friends who were on something of a lark. Jessica Nelson had been down in the dumps, and her two best friends had presented the vacation as a fait accompli.

"You're both sweethearts, but I can't possibly go," she told them. "I've got a meeting with the FDA."

Carrie Weinstein, a cardiothoracic surgeon at Boston Medical Center said, "It's not for three weeks."

"How'd you know that?"

"Eleanor told us," Margo Thorn said. Margo was the main anchor for the CBS affiliate in Boston.

"You called my assistant?"

"Operation Cancel Cal demanded it," Carrie said.

"Look," Margo said, "one week in the sun at a fabulous resort, spa treatments, a warm sea, good wine, cute waiters— it'll do you a world of good, honey."

"You can't say no," Margo said.

"Oh yeah? No."

Carrie pulled out her trump card. "We bought everything with nonrefundable reservations to make sure you'd play along."

The three of them combined had the wherewithal to buy their own island, but walking away from nonrefundable bookings wasn't a concept.

"I hate you," Jessica had said, "but I love you."

Now, at cruising altitude with ten hours until touchdown, they clinked glasses.

"To Operation Cancel Cal," Margo said, snapping a group selfie for Facebook.

"Who?" Jessica said.

Carrie laughed. "It's working."

A single square kilometer on the western bank of the Tiber had been Elisabetta's childhood universe. The flat on Via Luigi Masi, her school, and her church were all within a few city blocks. As a girl, she had needed nothing more than her neighborhood could provide, and whenever she returned to it as a woman, she felt swaddled by its familiarity. Arriving at her father's door, she braced herself, as she always did, for a backhanded comment—although no longer delivered out of bitterness, she supposed, but out of habit. Her father had been horrified by her decision to leave academia for nunhood, but that was long ago, and at least he was proud she had broken through the Vatican's glass ceiling as much as any woman could have done.

"How's your boss?" Carlo asked, planting a small kiss on her cheek.

"The Holy Father is well."

"I saw him on TV the other day. He looked like shit."

"Hardly the way I would describe him," she said, putting her bag of groceries down. "Am I the first?"

"They're on the way. So who's the mystery guest?"

"It's Professor Donovan from America. You met him once at the ceremony at the Vatican where Emilio was made inspector general, remember?"

"I'm old, not senile. Of course I remember. I recall I didn't hate him."

"High praise," she said.

"Why did you invite him?"

"He's in Rome helping the Holy Father with a project. Emilio wanted to see him. The professor was on his own tonight, so I thought it might be nice."

"He's at Harvard, no? A professor of religion?"

"He is, Papa."

"I would have preferred a mathematics professor."

"I'm sure you would have. Now go smoke your pipe, and I'll start on supper. And comb your hair."

Carlo Celestino was spright and robust—a good eighty, most would say. He had the square shoulders, squat legs, and ruddy complexion of a farmer, and that had always made him the odd man out among his spindly colleagues in the Department of Theoretical Mathematics at La Sapienza. How a brilliant mathematician had sprung from a family of Abruzzo dairymen was always fodder for family jokes. *Maybe Albert Einstein delivered milk to Grandma one day*, Micaela, the youngest daughter, liked to say.

Elisabetta followed her father into the sitting room to see if it needed tidying, her nose twitching at the bouquet of Cavendish tobacco. Growing up, she had never liked it, especially when someone at school sniffed her woolen sweater and teased her. Now she didn't mind it at all—it was the smell of her father and the smell of a pleasant childhood.

The flat occupied the top floor of an apartment block along a narrow, sloping street. There were three bedrooms, one Micaela and she had shared until she left for university, one for Emilio, and her parents' room. The children's bedrooms were essentially museums now. The door to her father's bedroom was always closed, and she had no idea the state it was in. "Do you let the cleaning woman in, Papa?" she always asked. He said he did, but she and her sister weren't so sure. The sitting room, cluttered as always with books and papers, was presentable enough, and she went to the kitchen to unpack her groceries.

Her paternal grandmother had been a master of lamb dishes, and Elisabetta had bought a shoulder joint to make a family recipe, a roast with a rich anchovy sauce. Micaela arrived as the roasting pan went into the oven, gave her sister pecks, and followed the trail of pipe tobacco to her father, where they did their usual routine.

"So, Papa, how's Goldbach?"

"Goldbach is fine. He says hello."

Micaela started working on the side dishes. She was a fiery sort, whose red hair dye matched her personality.

"It's hotter than hell," she told Elisabetta. "Why don't you change into civilian clothes?"

"Did you forget we have a guest coming?"

"So this guy can't see you have arms and a neck?"

"It wouldn't be appropriate."

"Collapsing in a hot kitchen from heatstroke is more appropriate?"

"I'll be fine, Elisabetta said, then changed the subject. "I'm sorry Arturo and the girls aren't coming."

"They've got the sniffles, and I don't want Papa catching anything. Besides, Arturo's beside himself with joy that he's off service until day after tomorrow, and Roma's on TV tonight. He put on his jersey to watch the game. He's like a child."

They had met at the Gemelli University Hospital, where Micaela was a gastroenterologist and Arturo was an emergency department physician, and they had managed through busy schedules and mutual temper tantrums to make a go of family life.

Emilio was next to arrive. He peeled off his suit jacket, removed his tie, and discreetly hung his Glock shoulder holster under his jacket at the door. The aroma of roasting lamb drew him into the kitchen, where he kissed his sisters and rolled up the sleeves of his dress shirt.

He was the oldest child, in his midforties, a handsome, athletic fellow, whose job required him to be impeccably groomed. As inspector general of the Carabinieri and Celestine's personal bodyguard, he was always at the pope's side, and his rugged face was constantly in the papers. Growing up, his mother treated the overactive boy like a princeling and approved of almost everything he did, but his father couldn't understand where the urge to become a policeman had come from. The only thing he disapproved of more forcefully was his daughter's tilt to the cloth.

Even as Emilio moved to the Vatican Gendarmerie from Rome's Polizia Municipale and climbed the ranks of the corps to the top of the pyramid, his father showed a lack of interest in his career. He viewed the institution of the Vatican with general distaste and lamented the fact that two-thirds of his offspring wound up working there. He generally approved of

Micaela's career, although, for him, the practice of medicine was very much on the soft side of science.

"How's Papa?" Emilio asked.

Micaela said, "He's got a pencil in his hand, so he's good."

"Donovan's not here yet?" he asked.

"I told him half past," Elisabetta said, opening the oven door to check the roast.

"You're not going to talk shop at the table, are you?" Micaela asked. "I can't picture anything more unpleasant."

"Yeah, just like you and Arturo rattling on about some disgusting case you saw," Emilio said.

"We don't do that. Well, not often."

"Don't worry," Elisabetta said. "We'll save the shoptalk for later."

Cal was punctual to a fault and showed up with a bottle of wine. Emilio answered the buzzer, warmly shook his hand, and brought him down the hall to the kitchen to meet Micaela.

"Thanks so much for inviting me into your home," Cal told them. "Something smells terrific."

"The nun's a good cook," Emilio said.

Elisabetta dismissed him with a wave. "The nun says, get the professor—sorry—get Cal a drink, and have him say hello to Papa."

When Emilio led him away, Micaela whispered, "Why didn't you tell me that this guy is gorgeous?"

"Why would I?"

"You know he fancies you, don't you?"

"What on earth are you talking about?"

"You didn't see the way he looked when he saw you?"

"You're nothing but a troublemaker. Put the pasta on."

Cal hit all the high notes in the dining room. Although Elisabetta had dismissed her lamb as *cucina casalinga*, housewives' cooking, he praised it to the rafters. He had done his homework between showering and dressing for dinner, and although he wasn't much at math, he had crammed enough on the history of the Goldbach conjecture to engage Carlo in an animated discussion. Having won over the patriarch, he captured the rest of them by praising their mother's book, *Elizabeth and Pius V: The Excommunication of a Queen*, which he had downloaded and started to read.

"Flavia was a marvelous writer, it's true," Carlo said. "She was taken from us at such an early age. The children hardly remember her."

"Nonsense," Emilio said. "I remember her well."

"Me also," Elisabetta said.

"Me not at all," Micaela said.

"That was her first and only book," Carlo said. "Imagine what she would have produced if she had lived."

Cal set his sights on Micaela and asked about her job, and once her start button was pushed, there was no turning her off. She rattled on about her work in the clinic, Arturo's demanding emergency department schedule, hospital politics, and the Italian health system at large.

Elisabetta finally intervened and said, "Why don't you show Cal pictures of the girls?"

"They're gorgeous," Cal said, handing back her phone.

"Do you have a family?" Micaela asked.

Elisabetta gave her a sharp look. Micaela had asked her the same question in the kitchen, and the only reason for asking it again was to be an agent provocateur.

"Never married," he said.

"A confirmed bachelor, like me," Emilio said.

After supper, Carlo invited Cal to the sitting room for cognac. The three siblings did a quick cleanup while Cal was subjected to an in-depth discussion of the Goldbach conjecture that sailed over his head. The washing-up done, Micaela said her goodbyes and Elisabetta suggested that the rest of them leave Carlo to his pipe and notepad and take a walk.

Before they left, Cal asked for the restroom and was pointed down the hall. On the way, he peeked through the open door into the bedroom the sisters had shared. It was clearly unaltered from the day the last one had left for university. He could tell which half belonged to which. A Bon Jovi poster hung over Micaela's bed, and over Elisabetta's, a beautiful stag with giant antlers, cave art from Lascaux. Micaela's bookshelves were stuffed with pop and fashion magazines, Elisabetta's with history and philosophy books and classic novels. He retreated before he was caught and wondered where he could find pictures of Elisabetta as a child, as a teenager, as a young woman in university, and then caught himself. *Stop*, he thought. *Just stop.*

It was a warm, humid evening, and the air was carried the tang of sautéed onions from a restaurant on the corner of the steep street. Elisabetta said, "Come, I'll show you my church. It's just up the hill."

As they walked, Cal gave Emilio the rundown on the day's fragmentary discoveries.

"The Holy Father has been briefed on this?"

"I gave him an update this afternoon," Elisabetta said.

Emilio asked if he thought Lúcia might have mailed the secret to someone—a family member, a friend.

"It's possible," Cal said, "but I doubt it. It's pretty clear she felt she had a sacred oath to keep the last prophecy a secret. It's hard to believe she'd stick a stamp on it and send it into the world."

"Where do you go from here?"

"The Mother Superior in Tuy was very credible, so I don't think there's any point in going to Spain. It's more likely Lúcia took the text with her, hidden somewhere, when she left for Portugal in 1948. I'm going to Coimbra first thing tomorrow."

They stopped at the entrance to the Basilica di Santa Maria in Trastevere, its portico awash in yellow light. There were some tourists in the square and a young couple sitting on the low wall surrounding the fountain, holding hands.

"I support your trip to Portugal," Elisabetta said, "but I'm a bit concerned about stopping the archive searches at the Pius the Twelfth era. There could have been communications about the Fourth Secret in subsequent pontificates."

"I don't disagree," Cal said. "I'd like your permission to give Maurizio Orlando just enough information for his people to search through the John the Twenty-Third, Paul the Sixth, and John Paul the Second years while I'm away."

"We can't reveal too much," Emilio said.

"I thought I could simply ask them to flag any documents that mention Lúcia, Fátima, and the secrets of Fátima. That way we cover all the possibilities. When I get back, I'll go through what they found."

Emilio and Elisabetta agreed, and they stepped inside the nearly empty basilica. They took in the lighted dome and apse, which were festooned with golden frescoes and intricate mosaics.

"It's one of Rome's earliest churches," she said. "The first sanctuary dates to the third century. Do you know it?"

"I've meant to come but never have."

"Look," she said, pointing toward the biblical scenes set against a sea of golden tiles. "The dome was made by Cavallini in the thirteenth century, and the stories he depicted in mosaic were so intricate that, after all these years, I'm still discovering images I never noticed before. My favorite is a little mocking-bird mosaic. It's terribly difficult to find."

"I've never found it," Emilio said.

His sister chided him. "That's because you're always looking down at your phone."

Cal craned his neck and squinted.

"It's okay. Don't strain your neck," Elisabetta said with a laugh. "I'll show you."

It was childish, really, but he had never wanted to succeed at a challenge more than at this moment. He pressed for more time and kept probing the dome.

"There!" he said, pointing triumphantly. "Seven o'clock. I think that's it, next to those bunches of grapes."

"My goodness," she exclaimed. "That's remarkable. You have a very keen eye."

In the scheme of things, it was a minor accomplishment, but it seemed to have an outsized meaning for him, and he basked in her praise.

Emilio said, "This is a good sign. If you can find the bird, maybe you can find the Fourth Secret. Come, I'll give both of you a ride back to the Vatican."

As Cal was wheeling his roller bag through passport control at Fiumicino Airport, headed toward Terminal 1 for a flight to Coimbra, Alitalia Flight 615 from Boston was deplaning at Terminal 3.

The harsh sunlight streaming through the windows of the transit hall forced Jessica to fumble for her sunglasses.

"I drank too much," she groaned.

"We all did," Carrie said.

"Operation Cancel Cal requires a commitment to inebriation," Margo said. "We were just doing our job."

"I don't know where we're supposed to go," Jessica said blearily. "This is your deal. You lead the way."

Carrie took charge and asked an Alitalia rep, "Where's the flight to Messina?"

"Through customs and follow the transfer signs to Terminal Two. It's Gate B12."

"Ladies," Margo said, "we're only about three hours away from prosecco on the beach."

Cal bought a newspaper and took a seat at his departure gate. Nearby, a man slowly paced the hall, a phone to his ear. Nothing about him stood out. In his line of work, that was an advantage. He was neither young nor old. He was of medium height, medium build, his hair not long, not short. His nose was a little flattened and crooked, from fights as a youngster, but his features wouldn't catch anyone's eye. There were times in the past when the police had asked witnesses to describe the man they had seen, and the usual response was that he was just a guy—nothing special about him.

Inside Hugo's flat, a phone rang. It was across the room, and to answer it, he had to move as quickly as his foot drop allowed. The caller was professional and cautious to a fault. On the job, he used only prepaid phones. He had given one to his new employer.

"Yes?"

"It's Nino."

They had met a single time in a park, where Hugo gave him an envelope with cash and enough information about Cal Donovan to get him started.

"I'm at the airport. He's here. We're boarding in a few minutes. I'll call you from Portugal."

"Remember, I want to know everything he does and everyone he sees."

"Don't worry. I told you, I'm good at what I do."

9

Elisabetta had arranged everything. At the Coimbra Airport, a car was waiting to take Cal to the university district of the city, where a suite had been booked at a boutique hotel, the Sapientia.

At check-in, the manager was called from the back.

"Professor Donovan," he said, "we've been expecting you. Pope Celestine's private secretary personally made your reservation. It's an honor for us. We have our best one-bedroom apartment for you. Come, I'll show you everything."

Cal's credit card was waved off.

"It's all been taken care of by the Vatican. Food, drinks, everything."

The taxi hired at the airport to follow Cal's Mercedes left the unremarkable Nino at the hotel. He loitered in the lobby until Cal got into the elevator, and only then did he approach the registration desk.

"Do you have a reservation, sir?"

"No."

"What kind of room did you want?"

"A simple room. I want to pay with cash."

Cal's suite was large and stylish, and the manager was an ambassador for his city.

"Have you been to Coimbra before?"

"First time."

"It's very old and very beautiful. Six of our kings were born here, you know. Our university is the oldest in Portugal. Our incredible twelfth-century cathedral is the most important example of Romanesque architecture in the whole country. And were you aware that Sister Lúcia from Fátima, the one who will be made a saint soon, lived most of her life in our Convent of Santa Teresa?"

"Actually, I did know that," Cal said.

His appointment with the Mother Superior of the convent wasn't until the late afternoon. He unpacked his bag, ordered room service, and made a call to Albano Baptista from the Department of History at the university, who had extended an invitation at the Lisbon conference. Aside from being a charming fellow, the professor had actually met Sister Lúcia, and Cal was keen to pick his brain.

"Cal!" Baptista exclaimed. "I can't believe you're in Coimbra. Why didn't you tell me you were coming?"

"It was last-minute, Albano."

"You felt compelled to satisfy your bucket list."

"Exactly. I don't expect you to drop any appointments, but I've got a couple of free hours after lunch, if you're available."

"Yes, of course. Come to the university. I'll give you a tour."

Professor Baptista had a courtly presence, with an air of deliberate formality. He wore tan suits with bright silk ties and carefully folded pocket squares. Because he was either naturally swarthy or a sun worshipper, his skin tone always contrasted beautifully with his white hair.

"It is so lovely to see you here," he said, grabbing Cal's hand and pumping it several times.

"I really hope I'm not interfering with your work, Albano."

"Nonsense. Come, let's not stay in my dark office. It's a sunny day. Let's walk."

The hilltop university commanded magnificent views over the Mondego River. Its central courtyard was a broad plaza surrounded by grand colonnaded buildings with red-tiled roofs and a high bell tower. Baptista gave Cal a running commentary—it's the eighth-oldest university in the world; it has over twenty thousand students; it's a UNESCO World Heritage site—before he asked the obvious question, "So tell me. Why the sudden urge to come here?"

Cal dissembled, but as little as possible. "I came in search of Lúcia. The conference inspired me. I was thinking I could write something about her."

"A book? A paper?" Baptista asked.

"Not sure yet. Maybe it'll only wind up as a lecture. I'm not in Portugal often, and I thought I'd take the opportunity to visit her convent, have a little look around."

Baptista chuckled. "It's quite the magnet. A lot of tour packages to Fátima include a coach trip to Santa Teresa. To keep the tourists from rattling the quiet world of the Carmelites, they built a separate museum, complete with a replica of her cell. Do you want me to take you there?"

"No, no. I'll go on my own."

"Well, then, let us visit our famous Biblioteca Joanina."

They walked across the courtyard, through throngs of students, to the Baroque library adorned with the national coat of arms over its entrance. Every list of the most beautiful libraries of the world included Joanina. Inside were three great rooms, divided by elaborately carved arches. The walls were covered in two-story bookcases of exotic wood, some gilded, some brightly painted. The ceilings were also lavishly decorated. Cal breathed a low "Wow," and told his host it felt like being inside a golden jeweled box.

"A gold box with a quarter million volumes," Baptista said.

Something on high caught Cal's eye. "Was that a bat?"

"Yes, indeed. We have bats, and we adore them. Unlike other old libraries, our books have no insect damage. At night, the colony of bats consumes the insects. You might say they work for food. Before the library closes, all the credenzas are covered with sheets of leather, and that is how we clean the guano."

Outside, in the harsh sunlight, Cal put his shades back on and said, "Albano, you were saying at the conference that you knew Lúcia."

"I had the honor of interviewing her at the convent on one occasion. As you may know, Carmelites are a closed order and the sisters are under strict lockdown. Permission to visit is controlled by the Vatican. The bishop of Leiria-Fátima was kind enough to help me secure an appointment, and I accompanied him to the convent."

"What was she like?"

"Well, let me say that this was over a decade before her death. She was already an old woman, and I was a much younger man. She was sharp in more ways than one. Sharp mentally and sharp in temperament. You see, I was merely a young professor, not a man of the cloth, and she was impatient with me. The occasion was the seventy-fifth anniversary of the Fátima apparitions. I was on the lowest rungs of the academic ladder here at the university and was paid rather poorly. The municipal authorities of Coimbra thought it would be good to have a pamphlet commemorating our famous resident, and they offered to pay me for the work, with the stipulation that they wanted an interview and a photo."

"What kind of questions did you ask her?"

"A broad array. Her childhood, the visions, her life as a nun, her reaction to John Paul's assassination attempt. She was rather short with me and irritable—maybe I caught her on a bad day. The only time she smiled was when I asked her what her favorite thing was as a child. She told me she loved to dance! Imagine that coming from this woman of great piety. I don't think I broke any new ground with my interview—but I did get paid, and I went on, as you know, to write that book of mine on the place of Fátima in Portuguese religious traditions."

"Where did you conduct the interview?"

"Where? Why, in her room. She sat in her little chair, bundled against the cold."

"Do you recall if she had many possessions?"

Baptista closed his eyes, as if to riffle through the banks of his memory, and said, "I really can't recall. I'm sure she had some books and photos. Some pictures on the wall. Definitely a picture of the pope."

"Did you talk about the secrets?"

"Yes, for sure. Keep in mind, this was 1992, and the Third Secret had not yet been revealed. The very last question I asked was, Were there more secrets than the two she had written about? I remember because she basically kicked me out at that point without answering. She said it was time for her nap."

Their first order of business was finding a common language. The Mother Superior of Santa Teresa was an elderly Portuguese nun, Sister Beatriz, who spoke no English, and Cal's Portuguese was inadequate for the task. Fortunately, she had lived in Florence for a few years, and they managed in Italian. Sister Beatriz was small and round, all hips, with a bulbous nose and thick lips. She made it clear enough that if not for the intercession of the Vatican, he would not have been welcome.

"We are a cloistered order, Professor Donovan."

"I'm well aware," he said solicitously, "and I appreciate the time you're giving me."

She sat stiff and immobile behind her desk. Her office was spare, adorned with only three objects: a crucifix, a photo of Pope Celestine, and a photo of Sister Lúcia. "What can I possibly tell you about the Blessed Sister that is not already known?"

"I understand you knew her well."

"Not as her Mother Superior. As a fellow sister."

"How many years were you together before she passed?"

"I came here in 1995, so ten years."

"What was she like?"

"She was a woman of immense piety. That is one of the reasons she wished to come into this order. She desired a more contemplative life of prayer and silence. Many sought her attention, but here we have strict rules of seclusion, and in her case, the Vatican decreed that no one, not even a priest, could visit with her without obtaining the permission of the Holy See."

"Did she speak freely about her apparitions?"

"Quite freely. And not just her Fátima apparitions. She continued to have divine visitations throughout her most holy life, not only from Our Lady but also from Jesus."

Cal pressed on. "Specifically, did she ever speak about any Fátima revelations that did not make it into the official record?"

The nun grew irritated. "How can you even ask such a question? The Blessed Sister forcefully denied the existence of more Fátima secrets."

"Yes, she did," Cal said evenly. "Can you tell me who Sister Lúcia was allowed to correspond with?"

"There were not so many. She was allowed to receive and reply to letters from her siblings—she outlived them all. She corresponded with bishops and cardinals and even popes. She received a great number of letters from all over the world from the faithful and the curious. She was shielded from these distractions, and most of the letters were sent to the Vatican for—well, I don't know what was done with them."

"What about visitors?"

"There were prelates, of course. They did not come often, mind you, but they did come. I believe the Vatican permitted people like you on rare occasions."

"People like me?"

"Historians." She made the word sound distasteful.

"I talked with one of them today," Cal said. "Professor Baptista from the university here. He told me about a visit he made in 1992."

"It was before my time."

"Do you know who the others were?"

"We have a visitors' book. You signed it today. The older ones are in storage."

"Could I see them?"

"I was told to cooperate with your requests, so yes."

"I'd like to see her room."

"It is no longer her room. It remains in use. Sister Ana lives there now."

"I'd still like to see it."

"May I know why?"

"The Holy Father asked me to make an investigation on some matters prior to the canonization. I need to see her living quarters and any of her belongings that remain at Santa Teresa."

"Then you do not want the old cell of the Blessed Sister. The physical remnants of her life at Santa Teresa are in the museum."

The nun scraped her chair backward, and Cal followed her out the door. The eighteenth-century convent occupied a large tract of land near the center of Coimbra. Although it was surrounded by a bustling city, there was a sense of calm isolation within its high perimeter walls. Passing by the unoccupied chapel, they went outside and traversed a cloistered garden to a small, modern building with a plaque on the door, MEMORIAL

DA IRMÃ LÚCIA. The museum had closed for the day, and Sister Beatriz used the intercom to ask for the museum director. The woman who came to greet them was a secular employee in a stylish dress and heels. The Mother Superior briefed her in Portuguese, and the woman engaged Cal in English with a delighted, throaty voice. "Ah, you are from Harvard? My nephew is a graduate student at Harvard in chemistry."

"It's an excellent department."

"How can I help you, Professor?"

He said he hoped to see Lúcia's personal belongings.

"Which items in particular?"

"All of them."

"All of them! Very well. Some are in display cases; others, in the replica of her room. This way, please."

Cal had hoped that Sister Beatriz would have left them, but she followed along for the visit, his minder.

"We are open for six hours per weekday, three hours on Saturdays and Sundays," the director said. "The fee for admittance goes toward the upkeep of Santa Teresa." She pointed at the large photos along the hall, chronicling Lúcia's life: the first one, a 1917 photo of her with Jacinta and Francisco, the last, Lúcia lying in her coffin, her rosary beads wrapped around her fingers.

At the first glass display case, the director said, "Here are some of the goods she fashioned with her own hand. The sisters sold them to help keep the convent afloat. These are rosaries she made. Here is some lovely embroidery. She was quite good, wouldn't you say?"

"Very nice," Cal mumbled.

At the next case, she said, "Here is one of her personal

rosaries. See how worn the beads are? And here is her scarf. This rope is the one she wore around her waist. These are a pair of her actual sandals. Look how small her feet were."

"I'd like to see them, if I could."

"You mean outside the case?"

"Yes."

That triggered an urgent conversation in Portuguese, during which the Mother Superior shook her head and fixed Cal with a deathly stare.

"Not possible," Sister Beatriz said in Italian.

"I'm afraid I'm going to need to examine her possessions closely."

She repeated, "Not possible."

Cal offered an apologetic smile as he phoned Sister Elisabetta.

"I'm in Coimbra at Santa Teresa," he said. "I'm going to need your help."

He handed his phone to the nun, who explained the unreasonable request of this American professor, and in the back-and-forth, she was unyielding. Sister Beatriz abruptly stopped talking and told Cal, "She put me on hold!" A minute passed, and the elderly nun suddenly looked as if a current had passed through her body. She pressed the phone hard against her ear and listened, with amazement filling her eyes. "Yes, Holy Father. Certainly, Holy Father. God bless you, Holy Father."

Cal kept himself from smiling.

"That was the Holy Father."

"So I gathered," Cal said.

Sister Beatriz told the museum director in Portuguese, "The

professor is free to inspect any of the Blessed Sister's personal items."

The case was duly unlocked, and Lúcia's slippers were in Cal's hands. They were simple and woolen, with crocheted straps and cork soles. He gently probed the soles, but there were no hiding places.

"Are there any other items of clothing on display or in storage?" he asked.

"Only a pair of shoes, in her room upstairs," the director said. "She was buried in her habit."

"Can I see the room?" he said.

The replica of the cell in which she had lived for over half a century was on the second floor. At its threshold, the director commented that it was the most popular display. "It is a perfect copy of her room. Every detail was reproduced."

He stepped inside and took in the austere white-walled chamber, not much larger nor better-appointed than most prison cells. The Carmelite bed was a simple affair made from two benches and a few planks, topped with a thin mattress, rough linen, and a scratchy brown blanket.

Next to the bed was a small one-drawered chest with a removable top that Lúcia used as a writing board while reclining in bed. Her Olivetti typewriter sat on a little desk. Next to it were the few books she owned, stacked in three small piles.

There was a large cross of dark wood affixed to the wall. It was as tall as a man and draped with a rosary. Over the bed was a framed photograph of Jacinta and Francisco, which Cal imagined Lúcia had gazed at during the first minutes of the morning and the last of the night.

Across from the desk was a painting of the Holy Virgin, given to her by Pope John Paul II, her red Immaculate Heart beating outside her chest. Lúcia's cane was propped by the door. Her shoes were on the resin floor by the bed.

"All the items in the room are her actual possessions?" Cal asked.

"They are," the director assured him.

"I'm going to have to look at everything."

The Mother Superior and the director watched in dismay as he executed his papal search warrant. He inspected her cane and her shoes. He unmade the bed and searched the mattress and frame. He looked for hiding places in the chest and desk. He turned the typewriter upside down. He took the photos and the painting off the wall and checked the backings. He even took the crucifix down and inspected it for a hollowed-out space. Finding nothing, he turned to the stacks of books, snapped a photo of each one, then riffled the pages. There was a complete set of her memoirs in Portuguese. A worn Portuguese Bible. A Bible in Spanish. An authorized biography of Pope John Paul II, inscribed and signed by the pontiff. An illustrated children's book about Fátima. A Portuguese book of prayers.

"These are all the books she had?" Cal asked.

The director angrily said, "Yes."

Cal was deflated, but at the same time, he was profoundly guilty about violating the sanctity of the exhibit. "I'm sorry I had to do this. I really am."

He moved to put the bed together, but the director told him not to bother. "I'll have everything put back to normal," she said.

It was then that he noticed a ventilation grate in the wall near the door. "Did Lúcia's actual room have a grate?"

"It did," he was told. "This room is a perfect copy."

He switched to Italian and told Sister Beatriz, "I'm going to need to see that room."

The old nun seethed and muttered as he followed her across the sunlit courtyard into the dim halls of the convent. They walked along the tiled, empty corridors with only the sound of their footsteps, the light ones of the small nun and his own heavier clods. The dormitory doors were unnumbered, each marked by identical embedded crucifixes. The Mother Superior stopped at one and knocked.

The door opened almost immediately, as if they had been expected, although he knew Sister Beatriz had not given notice. Sister Ana was a middle-aged Black woman with full cheeks and an expression of wonderment, courtesy of thyroidal eyes. The Mother Superior explained the reason for the visit and introduced her. Their best common language was English, and Cal apologized for the intrusion and asked how she knew it.

"I learned English in school," she said shyly.

They chatted at the doorway. "And where was that?" he asked.

"In my country, in Angola."

"How long have you been at Santa Teresa?"

"I came here one year after Sister Beatriz, I believe."

"How is that possible? You seem so young."

She flashed her teeth. "I am not as young as you might think. I was twenty years old when I arrived."

"So you knew Sister Lúcia for a decade."

"We were very close, yes. She was like a mother to me. I loved her very much." She spoke in a precise cadence, each word crisply separated from the next.

"And now you have her room."

The woman's voice lifted. "It is such a blessing. She requested that I receive it when she passed, and Sister Beatriz granted her wish."

"Do you think I could come in?"

Sister Ana asked her superior if it was permitted, and she received a curt nod in response.

The museum had done well in its reproduction of Lúcia's cell. The layouts were identical. Cal surveyed the plastered walls and ceiling and the resin floor and could see no possible hiding place. That left only the ventilation grate, secured to the wall by four screws.

"I'll need a screwdriver," he told Sister Beatriz.

She abruptly turned her back and went clopping down the hall without a word.

"I hope she's coming back," Cal said.

"I am sure she is summoning our maintenance man. What are you looking for? Perhaps I can help."

"Did Sister Lúcia ever tell you that she hid something? A document or a letter?"

"Never."

"Did she ever talk to you about the secrets of Fátima?"

"Yes! On many, many occasions. She was such a holy woman. It is no wonder that Our Lady entrusted her with the revelations."

"Did she talk about the existence of another revelation?"

"Beyond the Third Secret?"

"Yes."

"No, nothing like that. I was taught there were only three secrets, and she never contradicted that."

He heard footsteps and said, "I think they're coming." Then

he had a thought. "Did Sister Lúcia ever give you anything of hers? A gift? A memento?"

"Why, yes, she did. She gave me one of her books shortly before she passed. It was her missal book, *Visitas ao Santissimo Sacramento e a Maria Santissima*. She told me that when I prayed from this book, I would feel her spirit and the spirit of Our Lady."

He recognized the title from Cardinal Maglione's inventory of Lúcia's meager possessions. "May I see it?"

Just then, Sister Beatriz returned with the maintenance man, who crouched and began unscrewing the grate.

"I no longer have the book," Sister Ana said.

"What happened to it?"

"My sister was very ill with cancer. I sent it to her with the hope that it might bring about a healing. Unfortunately, the Lord took her."

"How long ago was that?"

"Eight years."

"Do you know what happened to the book?"

"I suppose her husband has it."

"Where does he live?"

"In Paris."

The grate was removed, and Cal used his phone as a flashlight to explore the duct. The only thing he saw was dust.

"All right," he said, picking himself off the floor. "Nothing."

"Are we finished, Professor Donovan?" Sister Beatriz asked icily.

"Almost." He turned back to Sister Ana. "Do you have your brother-in-law's phone number and address?"

She retrieved it from a worn address book.

"I hope you find what you are looking for," she said. "I will pray for you."

Cal's last stop was the closet where old visitors' books were stored. Because few people were allowed at the cloistered house, there were only four of them spanning the relevant decades. He was given an office and began flipping through them.

It seemed that, throughout her seclusion at the convent, Lúcia did not receive many guests. In the early years, José da Silva, the bishop of Leiria, came to see her once or twice annually, and after his death, his successors continued the practice. Cal found Albano Baptista's signature from June 1992, confirming his account.

In March 1998, she was visited on the same day by Cardinals Antony Padiyara of India and Ricardo Vidal of the Philippines. The names rang a bell, and a quick phone search led Cal to an article in the Catholic Portuguese magazine *Christus* that he had read before. The cardinals had interviewed Lúcia near to her ninety-first birthday, two years before the Third Secret was divulged, and had asked her whether she thought the pope would reveal it. She responded that he could do so if he wished, but she didn't recommend it. If he went ahead, she said, she urged him to be very prudent.

The interview touched on communism, atheism, and materialism before she was asked to conclude with a message she might wish to pass to the world. She responded with an exhortation that demonstrated her reverence for Pope John Paul II.

"He who is not with the pope is not with God; and he who wants to be with God has to be with the pope."

In November 2001, a Monsignor Charles Graves visited. Again, the name seemed familiar, although Cal couldn't quite place it. He was about to do a search when Sister Beatriz returned, insisting it really was time for him to go. Evening prayers were about to begin in the chapel, and the convent would be locked for the night.

He quickly turned through the last few pages of the fourth book. Lúcia had no more visitors during the final four years of her life, but that small revelation didn't strike Cal as particularly sad. She hadn't died alone. She died surrounded by her family, her Carmelite sisters.

The hotel bar was made of railway ties, a rustic touch in an otherwise chic, modernist room. Cal took a stool, and, before ordering, he tried to reach Sister Ana's brother-in-law in Paris. No one picked up, and there was no prompt to leave a message. Next, he called Elisabetta to brief her on the day but only got as far as her voicemail. He turned his attention to the woman tending bar, a raven-haired beauty with olive skin and a saucy attitude, who proved to be Cal's favorite kind of bartender— quick-witted and funny. He didn't require a brilliant mixologist. His standard request was vodka martini, twist, extremely cold, and don't even think about vermouth.

"What brings you to Coimbra?" she asked in English, plonking the cold glass onto a bar mat.

"I heard you make the best martinis in Portugal." He took a sip. "I heard right."

"Well, the way you like it, it's not so complicated."

"Don't sell yourself short," he said. "Perfect temperature, hardly diluted in the shaker, great little lemon twist."

"You're a real connoisseur. It's like serving James Bond."

"Thanks, Moneypenny."

Another customer, who had been taking a light meal in the adjacent café, sauntered over to the far end of the bar, waving a banknote. She slid off to take his order.

"Beer," Nino said, glancing Cal's way.

Cal picked up where he had left off at the convent and Googled *Monsignor Charles Graves*. The first item that appeared refreshed his memory. He had written a book Cal knew, *From Little Seer of Fátima to Venerable Sage of Coimbra: The Remarkable Life of Sister Lúcia dos Santos*. He had a copy back in Cambridge and had briefly consulted it when he put his Lisbon talk together. His impression was that it was a minor book that added little to the Fátima canon, and, as such, he hadn't given it much attention. Now he wished he had. It didn't seem to be available online.

He had created a tab in the Notes app on his phone labeled 4th Secret, and it was time to update it. So far it included:

- Pius XII knew it existed in 1944!
- Pius had her room in Tuy searched
- Talked to Mother Superior at Tuy—dry hole, no need to go there
- She spent rest of life at Santa Teresa. Need to go to Coimbra. Could she have hidden it there, overlooked since death?

Now he added to it.

- Coimbra—nothing found among her personal effects at museum

- Searched her actual room—nothing
- Sister Ana—L gave her a prayer book (Visitas ao Santissimo Sacramento e a Maria Santissima) as a gift before she died. Ana gave it to her sick sister in Paris. Sister dead. Hidden inside the book?
- Sister's husband—Ramiro Loureno, 156 Rue des Poissonniers, Paris—can't reach by phone, need to visit
- Charles Graves, English priest—visited L in 2001—doubt importance

He looked up when the bartender said, "You must be a magician."

"Why is that?"

"You made that drink disappear. Another?"

"Why not? Who knows when I'll be back in Coimbra again."

"For the best martini in Portugal," she said. "Leaving us soon?"

"Afraid so."

"For home?"

"Not yet. Paris in the morning."

"I like it there," she said, "but we make better cocktails, I think."

He put away another one before bidding her a fond adieu and heading for his room. He had gone through his usual checklist with this purveyor of vodka. Pretty? Check. Sexy? Check. Available? Check. Anonymity of a hotel? Check. But he didn't try to close the deal, and as he pushed the button for his floor, he wondered why, before answering his own question.

He couldn't purge Elisabetta—a nun, for God's sake—from his thoughts. Trysting with this other woman would feel oddly sacrilegious. Such was his state of mind.

Nino polished off his beer and beckoned the bartender.

"Another?" she said.

"I'm good. I've got a question for you."

"Oh, yes? What?"

"How would you like to make a thousand euros?"

Cal was reaching for another vodka from the minibar when Elisabetta returned his call from her mobile.

"I'm sorry I missed you earlier," she said.

He heard footsteps on gravel and the gurgling of a fountain.

"It sounds like you're outside," he said.

"I'm having a walk in the Vatican Gardens. It's my only exercise, I'm afraid. Did you find anything?"

"No, but I need to go to Paris in the morning."

"Why Paris?"

He gave her a blow-by-blow of the day.

"Have you called Sister Ana's brother-in-law to ask him about the book?"

"I've tried. No one picks up. I'm going to have to go in person."

"What if her prayer book is just a prayer book?"

"Then we've lost another day. Like I've been saying, I really hope you and Emilio are working hard on plan B."

"I can assure you that Sister Lúcia's Mass will be the most secure event in Vatican history. Every man in the Gendarmerie and Swiss Guards will be on active duty, and there will be a high level of coordination with the Rome police authorities. I'm just off to another meeting tonight with Emilio and Commander Studer. We have less than a week to go."

"I'm well aware."

"I'll arrange your travel bookings and text you the details."

"There's one more thing. Can you see if someone can lay their hands on a book by an English priest named Charles Graves? It's called *From Little Seer of Fátima to Venerable Sage of Coimbra: The Remarkable Life of Sister Lúcia dos Santos*. If it's in the Vatican Library, could you express-mail it to my Paris hotel?"

"What's its significance?"

"Probably nothing. I just want to be thorough."

"I'll send someone to look for it. Have a good night, Professor. Goodness, I've done it again—have a good night, Cal."

They had taken to meeting at Eric Studer's private accommodations. The commander of the Pontifical Swiss Guards' apartment on the top floor of the nineteenth-century Swiss Guard barracks was in a discreet corner of the Vatican, tucked away from the tourists. Emilio and Elisabetta climbed three flights of stairs and were greeted at the door by Studer's housekeeper, an Ursuline nun, who took them to a reception room.

Before his appointment, Studer had been deputy chief of the Swiss Armed Forces, and he had brought his military bearing with him to the Vatican. Given the hour and the heat, Emilio had lost his necktie and jacket, but Studer appeared ramrod-straight, in a black suit, dark tie, and polished shoes. He immediately got down to business and acted, as was his practice, as if he were in charge of their group, not an equal participant.

"Have we given sufficient attention to the reception that follows the Mass?"

"What do you mean?" Emilio asked.

"Whose responsibility is it to do background screening of the attendees?"

"My intelligence officers are handling it," Emilio said. "They should be finished unless there have been last-minute invitations."

Elisabetta had the roster with her. "The final count is one hundred twenty," she said. "None have been added since last month."

"And who are they?" Studer asked.

"Two-thirds are prelates, mostly cardinals, bishops, and Curial officials from the Congregation for the Causes of Saints. The remainder are foreign dignitaries—from Portugal, especially—and lay representatives of worldwide Fátima organizations, such as the World Apostolate of Fátima."

"Beyond background screenings," Emilio said, "there will be a two-stage physical screening on the day. As you know, Eric, everyone in the crowd who enters Saint Peter's Square for the Mass will pass through magnetometers. And the invitees to the reception will be wanded again when they enter the Apostolic Palace."

"Even the cardinals and bishops?" Studer asked.

"Yes, even them."

"And what of Donovan and his wild-goose chase?" Studer asked.

Elisabetta visibly bristled at Studer's mocking tone. "The professor is in Portugal, where he visited Lúcia's convent," she said. "Unfortunately, he didn't find anything. He'll travel to Paris tomorrow to look for one of Lúcia's books that passed to a family member of a fellow Carmelite sister. The Fourth Secret could possibly be hidden within it."

"Such a waste of effort," Studer said. "I would not have authorized it."

"Then perhaps you should have a word with the Holy Father," Elisabetta said with a treacly smile, "because Professor Donovan's mission was his idea."

⁌⸺⸻⸻⸺⸻⸺⸻⸺⸺⸻⸺⸺⸺⸺⸺⸺⸺⸺⸺⸺⸺⸺⸺⸺⸺⸺⸺⸺⸺⸺⸺⸺⸺⸺⸺⸺⸺⸺⸺⸺⸺⸻

Cal was in bed drifting off when his buzzer rang. Without getting up, he shouted toward the living room, "Who is it?"

The muffled reply was, "Room service."

"I didn't order anything," he bellowed.

"No, no, I think you did."

He swore, got to his feet in his boxers, and used the peephole.

"Oh Christ," he said, opening up.

The raven-haired bartender had a tray, and on it were two of her perfect martinis. The top buttons of her starchy white shirt were unbuttoned, and her black skirt was tight around her hips.

"I just got off work," she said. "I hope I didn't wake you."

He was tired and drunk, and his defenses crumbled against the frontal attack. As he stepped aside to let her in, a few things came to mind, but Elisabetta wasn't one of them.

Later, in the small hours, the bartender crawled from her side of the bed and did as her paymaster had instructed. Cal's iPhone was charging on the night table. She unplugged it, woke the screen, and held it up to his sleeping face. When it was unlocked, she crept into the bathroom and used her own phone to take photos of his recent phone calls, emails, notes, and texts, including info on his flight to Paris and his hotel booking. Then she put the phone back on its charger, got dressed, and left the room, sporting a smile that said it all—this had been a red-letter night.

10

Nino took the first flight to Paris and arrived in the heart of the city while Cal was still at the departure lounge in Coimbra. Wearing dark glasses and a hoodie, Nino entered the high-rise and rode the elevator to the ninth floor. His French was rudimentary, and when the tall Black man answered the bell, he said, "Excuse me, do you speak Italian or English? I have a message from your sister-in-law in Coimbra."

Ramiro Loureno was still in his robe. He answered in English, "My sister-in-law? The nun?"

"Yes, Sister Ana. May I come in?"

Loureno let him in, and Nino, hoodie down and glasses off, took stock of the flat. Kitchen there, living room there, bedroom there.

"How do you know Ana?" Loureno asked.

"I did some renovations at her convent," Nino said. "I'm a builder. We got to talking. I told her my next job was in Paris, and she asked if I'd visit you."

Loureno was heavyset with droopy eyes. In his youth in the

slums of Luanda, he'd been something of a brawler, but he was in his late sixties now, his large hands arthritic.

"She asked you to visit me," he said, narrowing his eyes. "Why?"

"She gave you a book. She would like the book back."

"She didn't give me a book."

"She told me she did."

"She gave it to my wife."

"Is she here?"

The kettle whistled, and Loureno backed into the kitchen. Nino followed, step for step.

"Who are you?" Loureno growled.

"I told you who I was. Why are you being unfriendly?"

Loureno seemed to reach for the knob on the stove but, instead, pulled a kitchen knife from a rack and brandished it. "Carmelite nuns don't talk to builders, and if Ana did, she would have told you her sister was dead. What do you want?"

Nino was laser-focused on the knife. "Relax, friend. I only want the book."

"Get out, or I'll call the cops."

The Italian, though smaller, was younger and more agile. He had a claw hammer in the pouch of his hooded sweatshirt that he had bought an hour earlier from a hardware store. Hammers were his weapon of choice. Guns were loud, bullets could be traced, but hammers were just hammers. He used his new one to deliver a lightning-fast blow to Loureno's head. The large man bled and staggered and fell to the floor. It was then that Nino realized his adversary had been quicker than he had thought. His arm was slashed, and it was bleeding. He swore and swung his boot hard into Loureno's head.

When Loureno came to, he was zip-tied to a chair, a sock stuffed in his mouth. He was in his living room, but he seemed not to fully recognize it—perhaps from the blows to his head, perhaps because nothing was where it was supposed to be. The furniture had been overturned and slit open, the shelves and drawers emptied, and a chessboard and pieces were scattered on the rug.

Nino was standing over him, brandishing his hammer.

"I'm going to take the sock out. If you shout, I'll bury the claw inside your brain. Understand?"

Loureno grunted, and Nino removed the sock.

"Where's the book?"

"I don't have it."

"But you did have it."

"Not me, my wife."

"What happened to it?"

"I gave all her stuff to a charity shop when she died. It was years ago."

"I don't believe you."

"It's true."

Nino picked up a photo from the floor of a young Black woman. "Who's this? Your daughter?"

Loureno fixed him with hate-filled eyes and didn't answer.

"Because I can find her easily, and I could hurt her if you're lying to me. Just tell me the truth, and I'll leave her alone."

"I swear, it's the truth."

Nino sighed heavily and rubbed at his arm. The gash needed stitches, but he'd have to make do with the face-cloth and electrical tape he'd wrapped around it. He stuffed the sock back in Loureno's mouth and said, "Okay, friend,

I believe you. I think I'm done here. You shouldn't have stabbed me."

A new country, a new language. Cal signaled the waiter and asked for another coffee in French.

The waiter raised his eyebrows, for this was the third cup the American had ordered in a span of half an hour. Cal had fought the midday traffic from the airport and had arrived at the small hotel on Rue de Bruxelles bleary from the excesses of his night in Coimbra. He staggered into the lobby and, suspecting a mistake, checked Elisabetta's emailed itinerary, but this was, unaccountably, the correct hotel.

Cal usually made his own travel arrangements, drawing on his preferred hotels and airlines, but given the crush of time, he had left the mechanics in Elisabetta's hands. He was sure she had no idea that someone in the Vatican travel office, given the instructions to find a good hotel near the eighteenth arrondissement, had placed him at a converted brothel. The décor was over-the-top Belle Epoque, a dazzling sea of opulent red velvet with damask wall coverings, crystal chandeliers, and gold-leafed Moorish arches.

The brochure at the desk confirmed that the site had indeed been a turn-of-the-twentieth-century pleasure palace near the Moulin Rouge, recently restored to its former bawdy glory. He would never tell Elisabetta that his Paris hotel had been a whorehouse, but he was confronted with a painfully ironic re-minder that, once again, he had succumbed to the temptations of the flesh. Flitting, he thought, was putting it mildly.

He was taking his coffee in the hotel library bar that looked, he imagined, exactly like what a library in a brothel would look like—dark millwork, red settees, never-read books arranged by the color of their bindings, set on brightly lit shelves. He had hoped the third cup of coffee would finally clear his cobwebs, but it was not to be. He tried Sister Ana's brother-in-law one more time, and again the number rang through.

"Can you have the front desk get me a taxi?" he asked the waiter. He could have walked, but he was dragging.

"Where are you going?"

He checked his notes. "It's 156 Rue des Poissonniers."

The waiter gave him some side-eye, suggesting it wasn't a neighborhood that guests of the hotel typically frequented.

The eighteenth arrondissement, the Château Rouge district, was sometimes called Little Africa, for its heavy population of sub-Saharan and North African immigrants. While gentrification had been pushing immigrants farther into the peripheries and outer-ring suburbs, the ethnic specialty stores of Château Rouge drew them back, and the streets were bustling with shoppers.

The taxi driver was Senegalese and chatty, and he talked over the Afropop music blaring from his radio. "You're American, no?"

"I am."

"Where you from?"

"Boston."

"I've got a cousin in New York. One day—hey, what's going on up there?"

Police cars with flashing lights had Rue des Poissonniers

completely blocked off. The driver hit his brakes and looked to back up.

"How far are we?" Cal asked.

"Just up there."

Cal got out, joining a stream of curiosity seekers on the sidewalk. He walked one block, past high-rise apartments overlooking the metro tracks, and continued until he got to another high-rise block, 156–160 Rue des Poissonniers, a fourteen-story modernist complex that also abutted the tracks. There was a heavy police presence in the courtyard, and techs in forensic overalls at the entrance, coming and going.

"What's going on?" he asked a gawker.

"Don't know. Nothing good."

There was no barricade, only a loose cordon of policemen around the courtyard, but when Cal tried to get to the building, a policeman asked him where he was going.

"I'm seeing someone at number 156."

The cop shook his head. "No, you're not."

"Why?"

"It's a crime scene. No one's going in until it's cleared."

Cal tried to project a friendly urgency. "Look, it's important. I've come all the way from America to see a guy. Isn't there anything you can do to help me out?"

"Not until it's cleared."

Cal's charm wasn't working on the hard-boiled cop. France being France, the odds were that he was Catholic, so he played the Vatican card. "Can you let me speak to someone in charge? I'm here on a personal mission for Pope Celestine."

The cop looked him up and down and said, "Are you bullshitting me?"

"No, I swear."

"Come with me, but if you're bullshitting me, I'll charge you with interfering with police business."

He was led to a middle-aged guy in a muted-plaid sports coat, black slacks, and a dark-blue necktie, who was smoking a cigarette near the entrance to 156. He appeared either bored or tired, or perhaps some combination.

"Lieutenant, this guy says he's on a personal mission for Pope Celestine to see someone in the building."

The detective hardly looked at Cal before saying, "I'm too busy for this kind of crap."

Cal quickly interjected, "Lieutenant, my name is Professor Calvin Donovan. I was sent here by the pope to interview a man who lives here. If you like, I can connect you to someone in his pontifical office, even Celestine himself if it's necessary."

"What are you, an American?" the detective said, flicking his cigarette stub.

"I am. I'm a professor of religion at Harvard University."

The detective shook his head in a show of annoyance. "Religion. Wonderful. And who is it you're supposed to see?"

"His name is Ramiro Loureno."

The detective's face instantly changed. "You know Ramiro Loureno?" he asked aggressively.

Cal caught his breath and looked toward the entrance with an awful foreboding. "We've never met. I know his sister-in-law."

"What's her name?"

He realized he only knew her first name. "She's a nun at the Convent of Saint Teresa in Portugal. Her name is Sister Ana."

"This Ana is Ramiro's wife's sister, you say? What's her name?"

"Isabel Loureno."

"Do you know where she is?"

"I was told she died of cancer."

"When did you last speak with Ramiro Loureno?"

"I've been calling since yesterday. I never got through. Did something happen to him?"

The detective ignored the question. "What did you want to see him about?"

He knew his answer wasn't going to work wonders, but he gave it anyway. "It's a long story."

"Fine. You can tell me your long story at the station."

"He's dead, isn't he?"

The detective smirked at him. "It must be true what I hear. You Harvard types are real geniuses."

As Cal followed the detective to his car, a nondescript man on the other side of the police cordon placed a call.

"Donovan showed up," Nino said. "He's being taken away by the police." He listened for a few moments and then cut in, "I don't know what you want me to say. I already told you, the book wasn't there."

The voice on the other end got louder, and he put some air between the phone and his ear.

"I know I said there wouldn't be violence. That was the plan. Sometimes things don't go to plan. The guy stabbed me. It was self-defense. If you want me to keep following Donovan, I've got to go."

143

The sea was impossibly blue, and as warm as a blanket. The three Americans were stretched out on towel-draped chaises on a strip of white beach, naturally drying themselves in the midday sun. Small boats bobbed in a mooring field beyond the marked swimming area, and behind them, the Villa Sant'Andrea resort sprawled along the shore under craggy cliffs.

"Is it almost time to switch over?" Margo said.

"From what to what?" Jessica asked, holding her hand over her eyes to shield the glare.

"Nonalcoholic to alcoholic drinks."

"God, yes," Jessica said. "Down here or up on the veranda?"

Carrie stretched and yawned. "We could do both."

Margo praised the decision and waved her arms until a waiter noticed. "Rosé, ladies?" she asked.

"Silly question," Jessica said.

A bottle of icy rosato arrived, and appropriate toasts were made.

"To Sicily!"

"To X chromosomes!"

"To not checking email for a whole hour!"

Jessica fessed up. "I sneaked a peek five minutes ago."

"Traitor," Carrie snarled.

"I still have a company to run, love. My board doesn't even know I'm out of the country."

"And how does that make you feel?" Carrie asked, effecting the tone of a psychiatrist.

"It actually makes me feel...pretty terrific. You guys are the dictionary definition of 'best friends forever.'"

"It's working," Margo said.

"You sure?" Carrie asked. "I think we need to do a test.

Okay, Jess, tell me the name of the asshole this trip is meant to cancel."

Jessica pouted. "Jeez, I'm not sure. Is it Hal? Val?"

"Yeah, it's working," Margo said. "What are we doing after lunch?"

Carrie said that she'd talked to the concierge about getting a guide to take them to the ruins of the Teatro Antico di Taormina.

"But that would involve putting real clothes on," Margo moaned.

"Let's go tomorrow," Jessica said.

"So decisive," Margo said.

"It's almost as if she's a CEO of a big-shit company," Carrie marveled. "Tomorrow it is."

The police station for the eighteenth arrondissement was on Rue Marcadet on the ground floor of an apartment block. Detective Andre Canuel escorted Cal through an open-plan office into a stale-smelling interrogation room. It was uncomfortably warm, and, like the detective, Cal removed his jacket.

"The air-conditioning sucks in here," Canuel said. "You want a police coffee? I'm having one."

"Sure."

The detective came back with a couple of plastic cups and stirrers. "Okay, let's hear your long story."

"How did he die?" Cal asked.

"I see you're turning the tables on me. Okay, I don't mind.

Someone wanted to see if he could bleed. He could. It's your turn. Tell me this story of yours."

"The Vatican is looking for a document. It could be inside a book given to Isabel Loureno by her sister, Ana, about eight years ago. I was sent to retrieve it."

"What kind of document?"

"I'm not at liberty to say."

Canuel lit a cigarette. Smoke curled up the wall and fogged a yellowed No Smoking sign. "You're not at liberty. Okay, I'll try not to get angry. Is this document valuable?"

"The information is valuable to the Holy See, but I wouldn't say it has monetary value."

"How valuable is a man's life, would you say? Because maybe Ramiro Loureno lost his life for this document of yours."

"Why do you think there's a connection?"

"Oh, I don't know," the detective said, waxing sarcastic. "A man with no police record is murdered and a Harvard professor sent by the Vatican to look for a mysterious document shows up a few hours later? Where were you this morning between nine and ten?"

"On a flight from Portugal to Paris."

Canuel developed a hard edge. "Give me the flight number and let me see the stamp on your passport."

Cal obliged. Canuel grunted and then lit a new cigarette on his dying one.

"What's the title of this book you're looking for?"

"*Visitas ao Santissimo Sacramento e a Maria Santissima*. It's a Portuguese prayer book."

"Write it down for me."

"Do you know if the book was in his apartment?"

"You want me to tell you details about an active police investigation? Are you serious? Tell me something, Professor, how do I even know if your story about being on a mission for the Vatican is true? Why should I believe you?"

"Would you believe another policeman?"

"It depends who he is."

Cal pulled out his phone, perilously close to losing his temper. "How about the inspector general of the Vatican Carabinieri?"

"I don't speak Italian."

"He speaks English. Do you?"

"Actually, my English is better than your French."

Cal wondered why the hell they weren't speaking English.

He reached Emilio Celestino, quickly explained the situation, and then put the phone on speaker. Canuel appeared skeptical that he was actually speaking to the head of the Vatican Carabinieri, so Emilio humored him by switching the call to FaceTime and showing him the view of Saint Peter's Square from his office window. That hurdle cleared, Emilio refused to divulge the nature of the document they were seeking but stressed that it was a matter of grave importance for the security of the Holy See.

"May we have your assistance, Detective? Alternatively, I can go directly to the prefect of police, Maurice Voison, who I know quite well, and discuss your reluctance to offer assistance to a sister agency."

Canuel kept his chain of cigarettes going, puckered his mouth, and caved. "What do you want to know?"

"What happened to Ramiro Loureno?" Cal asked.

The detective took a particularly deep drag. "What happened

to him was not pleasant. From what we can tell from the crime scene, one, perhaps more than one person, went to his ninth-floor flat this morning. There was no sign of forced entry, so he likely opened the door. A neighbor below him heard something like a thud on her ceiling at half past nine. The flat itself was a shambles. They tossed it completely. Nothing was where it should be. There was blood everywhere. A chef's knife, one from a matching set in the kitchen, had blood on it. He was on a chair, bound with plastic ties, with a sock in his mouth. He'd been beaten on the head, and his throat had been cut. A friend of his came by at ten for their morning game of chess and found him."

"Did anyone see someone suspicious?" Emilio asked. "Do you have any leads?"

"We're in the early stages of forensic analysis. Most of the cameras in and around the building are disabled, which is a chronic problem in the area. Drug dealers, you see. We interviewed his chess friend and some neighbors. He was a nice guy, they say, very quiet fellow. No one had problems with him. He was retired. A bus driver. He lived alone. He had no arrests, no contact with the police. Usually, I would say this type of crime relates to drug dealing, but there's no indication that this is the case here. There's a daughter, Chloé, who's been notified and is coming from Noisy-le-Grand. That's all we have so far."

"The prayer book," Cal said. "Was it there?"

"I didn't see a single book in the flat," Canuel said. "I don't think he was a bibliophile."

Emilio asked, "Could you or one of your men return to the flat and make a specific search for this book?"

"Yes, we can do that. And now, let me ask you gentlemen

a question. If, and I stress if, this has anything to do with the Vatican, this book you talk about, this document you won't talk about, doesn't it suggest that someone else knows about this book and this document and is also looking for them?"

Emilio simply said, "It would suggest that."

"So who else knows?"

"Only an extremely small group of people surrounding the Holy Father," Emilio said.

"One of them could be an accessory to murder," the detective said.

"I very much doubt that," Emilio said.

"Whatever you say. But, listen, cooperation is a two-way street. You keep me informed about your investigation into leaks from your extremely small group of people surrounding the pope, which I'm sure you'll be conducting, and I'll keep you informed about my investigation."

On his way out, Cal saw a young Black woman in the lobby sobbing into a tissue.

"That will be his daughter," Canuel told him. "I'll call you later, after we've had another look for your book." Cal held back and watched the detective greet the woman, extend his condolences, and take her to the back.

The day had turned dull. There was a café across the street with a view of the police station, and Cal crossed for a coffee. After a few minutes of sipping the strong brew, he realized that the shock of the murder had left him clearheaded, although it wasn't a hangover remedy he'd recommend.

When he called Elisabetta, she said, "I've heard. Emilio told me what happened. He thinks it's because of Lúcia. Do you?"

"If not, it's an amazing coincidence. Who else beside you and me knew about the book?"

"I informed Emilio, Cardinal Da Silva, and the Holy Father. Emilio briefed Commander Studer. That's as far as it went."

"What do you know about Studer?"

"He has impeccable credentials. The Holy Father has complete confidence in him."

"And Emilio? What does he think?"

She hesitated for a moment and said, "I would say that there are always certain natural, and, some might even say, healthy tensions between the Gendarmerie and the Swiss Guards, but he admires Studer's ethics and dedication."

"That sounds awfully diplomatic."

She ignored his comment and said, "What about the Carmelites? Sister Ana and Sister Beatriz knew of your interest in the book."

The thought of cloistered nuns rushing to a telephone amused him. "I can't really see them as leakers, can you?"

"Perhaps not. Did you receive the Graves book? I had it sent by courier service."

"I haven't been back to the hotel yet. I'll let you know."

"Will you please be careful, Cal?"

The question pleased him. It was a small bright spot in a bleak day.

Cal was keeping watch, and when Chloé Loureno left the police station, he rushed across the street to introduce himself. "I'm very sorry for your loss."

The young woman's eyes were red, and she seemed profoundly confused by his approach. "How do you know about my loss?"

"I was trying to see your father today. I arrived too late."

"You knew my father?"

"I'm afraid I didn't. I was with your aunt yesterday, and she told me about him."

"My aunt? My auntie's a nun."

"I was with Sister Ana yesterday in Portugal. I came to Paris today to see your father."

"I'm sorry, I don't understand. I don't understand anything," she said in bewilderment.

"I know," he said as soothingly as he could. "What happened is incredibly tragic. I can't imagine how you feel."

"Thank you, but why are you here?"

"Your aunt gave a book to your mother eight years ago. It belonged to a very special person."

"Yes, Sister Lúcia."

"You know about the book?"

"Before she passed, my mother gave it to me."

Given the circumstances, he was shamed by his elation, and he masked it as best he could. "It's a terrible time to ask, but could I see it?" he said. "It's extremely important."

"Why?"

"The Vatican sent me on a mission. I answer to Pope Celestine. Sister Lúcia might have hidden something inside the book, something the Holy Father needs."

"I'm sorry, what did you say your name was?"

"Cal Donovan." He gave her a Harvard calling card from his wallet.

"It says you're a professor of religion."

"I am."

"I must"—she broke down but managed to finish—"go to the morgue to identify my father. If you need to see the book, you can come to my apartment later this afternoon."

Noisy-le-Grand was a multicultural city with a large African population about fifteen kilometers from the center of Paris, the kind of suburb that was a magnet for immigrants originally from Château Rouge in search of greener pastures. Cal took the RER line and walked the short distance to Chloé Loureno's address, a run-down building of a couple of flats above an optician. She had been sitting in the dark, and when she invited him in, she turned on the lights and parted the curtains. Her dress from earlier in the day was gone, replaced by jeans and a T-shirt that made her look much younger. He had initially thought she was about thirty, but he revised his guess downward.

"I'm so sorry to intrude," he said.

"It's okay. I can give you something to drink."

"I'm fine, thanks."

The apartment was small and tidy and decorated in bright colors. There were a few books in a silver bookcase that looked like textbooks. A red stethoscope was coiled on one of the shelves.

"Is that yours?"

"Yes. I'm studying to be a nurse. My mother was a nurse. She wanted me to be a nurse too."

"Were you born in France?"

"Angola. We came when I was a baby." She clearly had something on her mind, and she abruptly pivoted. "You saw my aunt yesterday? Is that what you said? I'm sorry, but everything that has happened today is fuzzy."

"That's completely understandable. I was in Coimbra with her yesterday. Have you been?"

"Never. Her life is very isolated. When my mother became ill, my aunt needed special permission to communicate with her, and then only by letter. I was a small child when I last saw her. I wanted to ask your opinion. Do you think she would want to know about my father?"

"I'm sure she would. She would want to pray for him."

"I thought so too. I don't know how to get a letter to her. Could you help me with that?"

"Of course."

"Let me get the book for you."

It was a small leather volume of crinkly pages with extensive foxing. It smelled of mold. He opened it to find its title and date: *Visitas ao Santissimo Sacramento e a Maria Santissima, 1851, Lisboa.* On the front endpaper was a juvenile-looking signature—*Lúcia dos Santos*—the *i* dotted with a tiny cross. Evidence, he supposed, that Lúcia had received it as a girl.

This was the missal book documented to be in Lúcia's possession in Spain in 1944. This was the book she had bequeathed to Sister Ana. This was the book Ana had given her ailing sister, Isabel. He stopped himself from exploring it right away, because Chloé's large, pleading eyes demanded his attention.

"The policeman said that my father's killer tore up his

apartment like he was looking for something. Is this why my father was murdered?" she asked. "This little book?"

"I don't know. That's for the police to say. It wouldn't be the book itself. It would be something hidden inside it."

"What could be so important for a good man to die?"

"Nothing," he said quietly. "Nothing is that important."

"You look for it. I will write my auntie a letter."

He thought about it. If Lúcia had simply inserted a folded paper into the pages of the missal, Sister Ana or Isabel Loureno would have found it long ago. There were only three ways she could have effectively concealed her message: by secreting a piece of paper into the binding, by writing in the margins, or by marking words or letters in some form of code. The binding was tight and well glued. Cal probed the endpapers for a subtle bulge and used a fingernail to see if the edges had been lifted. He bowed the book until he heard the binding start to crack and peered down the headband into the void of the spine.

He began his page-by-page inspection as Chloé began composing at her kitchen table. They finished at roughly the same time. She produced a letter. He found nothing. No marginalia, no markings.

"Did you find what you were looking for?" she said, giving him the letter.

"No. Here's your book."

"You take it. I don't want it anymore. It will only remind me that I'm an orphan."

On the way back to Paris, he called Elisabetta and relayed the disappointing news. She took it calmly and asked, "Where do we go from here?"

"I don't know. We may have hit a dead end. I'll look at the Graves book, but, let's face it, it probably won't be helpful."

"I'll inform the Holy Father. We're running out of time, Cal."

Hugo's four coconspirators dutifully answered his calls and assembled at his apartment. None knew the reason for the summons, but from his tone, they understood there was an urgency. No one was more uneasy than Angelo. He was the one who had brought a viper into their tent, his cousin Nino, the wild one, the outcast, the family leper. It was a mistake to involve him, he had told himself whenever he awoke from a fitful sleep, but a decision had been made, a collective one. Nino had been summoned, he had been paid, he had been activated.

They sat in the warm living room, the curtains drawn, the windows open. An ambulance wailed in the distance. Hugo sighed heavily and limped to his usual chair.

"Something happened today, something unpleasant. A man was killed."

The others exchanged panicky glances.

"Who? Donovan?" Christopher asked.

"Not Donovan. His name was Ramiro Loureno. He lived in Paris."

Angelo stood up and nearly shouted. "You say a man was killed. Are you saying my cousin killed him?"

As Hugo nodded, Angelo collapsed back onto his chair, tugging at his hair and sobbing, "My God, no, no."

"Nino told me it was unavoidable. There was some sort of struggle."

"What does this man have to do with us?" Christopher asked.

"Donovan was looking for a book that belonged to Sister Lúcia. This book might have been in this man's possession. Nino got there first."

"What book? What is Donovan looking for?"

Hugo calmly said, "We now know what Donovan is doing. He's looking for the Fourth Secret."

Everyone went quiet. Even Angelo stopped sobbing and raised his head.

"I think you should tell us how you know this," Christopher said.

Nino had texted him the 4th Secret note from Cal's phone. Each man passed a printout of it to the next.

"How did you get this?" Angelo asked.

"Your cousin is resourceful."

Leone said in a torrent of words, "But how does the Vatican know there was a Fourth Secret? How do they know there's a copy? How do they know to look for it now? They must know what we're planning."

"I have no idea how they know of its existence," Hugo said. "And I don't know how they discovered that a hidden copy exists. All we can be sure of is that the pope asked Donovan to find it. If he succeeds, everything will be ruined. I sincerely doubt they know about us and our intentions. If they did, the plans for the canonization would have been altered. We would have been arrested."

"What about the book?" Martin asked, putting down his beer. "Did he find it?"

"It wasn't there. Donovan went to another address, where Loureno's daughter lives. Nino followed him. We don't know if Donovan found anything there. We will try to find out."

Angelo blanched and gripped the arms of his chair. "This is my cross to bear. Nino is my cousin. I brought him in. Because of me, a man has died. Because of what we did, a man has died. Call him back and stop this before someone else is harmed."

"My friends, please," Hugo said. "In five days, the prophecy will be fulfilled, and all will be cleansed. What will follow will vastly outweigh the moral offense of what happened today in Paris. The only one who can stop us is Donovan. If he finds the Fourth Secret, everything collapses."

Christopher looked stricken. "You're not suggesting we have Donovan killed, are you?"

"No, I'm not suggesting that," Hugo said. "Nino would do it, if we asked. He named his price. But I said to him, surely there must be another way to keep him off the trail.

"Nino is enterprising. He's clever with the internet, and he was ready with another suggestion, where no one else has to die. He found pictures from a charity benefit in Boston. Donovan was there with a woman who was named. Nino found recent posts from her on Facebook, and it seems she is in our backyard."

Hugo reached for his computer. The others gathered around, and he showed them photos of Jessica Nelson drinking champagne on a plane, eating lobster on a hotel terrace, lounging on the sand, and splashing in the impossibly blue waters of Taormina.

The meeting came to an end, and as the men were filtering out, Hugo called to Christopher, "Could you stay for a few minutes longer? There's something I wanted to ask you."

The book by Charles Graves was waiting for Cal when he returned to the hotel. His room, with its dark-purple wallpaper and drapery, was no less Belle Epoque than the lobby. He flopped onto a bed with a purple headboard the shape of a fleur-de-lis, and, turning to a random page, he reaffirmed his opinion that the priest's prose was turgid. He blanched at the thought of reading it closely. It occurred to him that two things could make it more somewhat more palatable—steak and vodka—and he called for room service.

The book was organized into three sections: the first, a re-hashing of the miraculous events at Fátima during the summer of 1917; the second, a biographical sketch of Lúcia from childhood to old age; the third, a discussion of the relevancy of Fátima for people of faith. It was, as he had recalled, a minor piece of scholarship and theology, devoid of footnotes or references and aimed at a general audience. Its only interesting offerings, as far as Cal was concerned, were Lúcia's personal anecdotes and reflections on her life. By the time he reached the end of the third section, the steak and a good quarter bottle of vodka were gone. He absently turned the last page, expecting the back cover, but instead found a brief afterword.

The author wishes to thank several people who made this book possible. His Eminence Joseph Wright, archbishop of the Diocese of Westminster, gave me leave to pursue the project. Bishop Joaquim Pereira of the Diocese of Leiria-Fátima arranged for my visit to the Convent of Santa Teresa in Coimbra, Portugal. The Mother Superior of Santa Teresa, Sister Madalena, graciously hosted my visit to her sanctuary. And, finally and most importantly, I wish to express my heartfelt gratitude and appreciation to Sister Lúcia, the seer of Fátima, for allowing me to spend a precious day in her presence and for bestowing upon me a truly wonderful gift I will treasure for my remaining days.

Graves's writing style was flowery and overblown, and Cal's initial thought was that the gift was of a spiritual nature, but as he reached for the vodka bottle, a thought froze his motion: *What if it wasn't spiritual?* What if Lúcia had given him an actual gift?

It was almost nine. He did a quick search on his laptop and then found Elisabetta still at her office number.

"Tell me what you think about this," he said, reading her Graves's afterword.

"She gave him a gift," she said.

"Metaphorical or real?" he asked.

"I want to believe it was a physical object."

"I do too."

"You'll need to speak with Father Graves," Elisabetta said.

"That might be difficult," Cal replied. "He died eighteen years ago."

11

London, 2001

R ev. Charles Graves sat on his unmade bed, surveying the sorry state of his room. There were books scattered everywhere, many owned by him, although he had been borrowing heavily from the library of late. His desk was impossibly cluttered with folders and notebooks, and underneath it were dozens of crumpled balls of paper. He was unsure when he last did his washing. His laundry basket was overfilled and surrounded by dirty socks and shorts. He had never been a late-night snacker, but in recent months he had developed a sweet tooth, and there were candy wrappers, empty tins of biscuits, and crumbs—lots of crumbs—that were attracting ants.

The phone startled him. It was the reception desk informing him that his brother had arrived.

On the way out, he used the mirror to straighten his clerical collar and noticed a smudge of jam on the front of his shirt. A wetted towel fixed it to his satisfaction, and he donned his jacket.

The Allen Hall College was the seminary for the Diocese

of Westminster. Some forty men studied for the priesthood on a campus in Chelsea, hard by the Thames, on the site of an estate once owned by Saint Thomas More. More's house was no more, but one of the mulberry trees he had planted five hundred years earlier was thriving in the walled garden of the seminary.

Charles was sixty. He'd been at the college for almost thirty years and had the longest tenure of any teacher. "I've been at Allen Hall almost as long as that mulberry tree," he would say to the students. Over the years, he had taught a variety of subjects, from philosophical ethics to catechism to the Gospels to a survey course on canon law.

More recently, his rector had reduced his teaching schedule to a single class in each of the fall and spring semesters. Rather than protest the cutbacks, Charles professed delight at the lightened load, as it freed up time for travel and the book he had begun to write.

He was a small man with tiny feet, who perambulated with mincing footsteps that students imitated when they wanted to crack each other up. His nervous, darting eyes were dark and rodentine. When his hair first grayed, he began dyeing it black, but of late his expertise had faltered, and the morning after an application, he walked about with smudges behind his ears.

His brother, John, greeted him in the lobby with a formal handshake. He was a decade younger but cut from the same genetic cloth—smallish stature, black hair, similar widow's peak. He was smartly attired in a double-breasted suit and carried an expensive portfolio under his arm and a closed umbrella dripping onto the floor.

"I was surprised to get your message that you were coming today," Charles said.

"Bit of a last-minute affair," John replied. "What do you say we get a coffee?"

"There's a good café nearby. You know the one."

"It's pissing down rain. Your commissary will do nicely."

The second period had just begun, and the commissary was nearly empty. The brothers sat by a window overlooking the garden and watched the branches of the mulberry tree move in the wind.

"So how goes the war?" John asked.

"The Christian soldier in me goes onward," Charles replied.

"Good, good."

"How is Ann?"

"She's well. Breaking in a new horse. Cost a pretty penny, but she's a looker. The horse, I mean."

John Graves had an estate in Norfolk of several hundred acres of meadows and farmland that had been in the Graves family since the eighteenth century. He had trained in business and worked in the City when he was younger, retiring to manage the estate and inheritance when their father died. There were just the two siblings, and Charles had forsaken all things material. "Suits me," he had said when his brother announced he was becoming a priest. "I'll enjoy spending your money."

"What brings you to London?"

"My bookseller has put some items aside for me. Some of them are pretty tasty, but I'm old-school. I won't buy unless I've pawed over them."

"Any room left in the library?"

"We'll squeeze them in."

His wife spent her money on horses, he on antiquarian books. There were well over fifteen thousand, with some notable standouts: a good Second Folio and first editions of *Paradise Lost*, *On the Origin of Species*, and *The Canterbury Tales*, to name a few.

"I'm going to get a bun," Charles said. "Want one?"

"No, not me. You've become plumper, haven't you? I don't recall you having a paunch."

"Do I?" Charles said. "I hadn't noticed."

When he returned with his cream bun, his brother said, "How's that book of yours coming along?"

There was already a dusting of icing sugar on his black shirt, drawing his brother's uncomfortable stare. "It's been a slog, but I've got two-thirds of it done. I told you what it was about, yes?"

"Of course you did, don't you remember? That Fátima thing."

"Bit more than a thing," Charles said. "Only one of the most consequential events in Christianity."

"Do you have a publisher?"

"A small press has expressed an interest, with the proviso that I gain an interview with Sister Lúcia, the seer of Fátima. Fortunately, I've recently secured this interview, no small feat, given that she lives in a cloistered house. I travel to Portugal in a fortnight. The publisher has purchased a ticket for me in lieu of an advance."

"How did you finagle the interview?"

"One of the seminarians here, a year-three lad, is half-Portuguese, half-English. His father's rather a bigwig—he's the Portuguese ambassador to Britain, if you must know. I befriended the young man, partly because he's got a sunny disposition and partly because I wanted to practice my Portuguese. I mean, it's been yonks since I did my mission work in Brazil. Anyway, it all panned out, because the ambassador got the patriarch of Lisbon to get me inside. Happy days."

"I see. Are you going on your own?"

"Who else would I go with?"

"I mean, is it safe for you to travel solo?"

"I don't know what you mean."

John pulled away from the table enough to cross his legs. "Look, Charles, let me level with you. I do have an appointment with my bookseller today, but I'm also here at the behest of your rector."

"You've spoken with Reverend Jones?"

"He rang me, yes. He's concerned about you."

"Well, he needn't be," Charles snapped.

"He tells me you haven't been taking very good care of yourself." He sampled the air. "Some hygiene issues, apparently. And you haven't been letting the cleaning lady into your rooms. There's signs of infestation."

"Few ants, nothing else. Can't imagine Jones getting his knickers in a twist over that."

"That's not the biggest concern, brother mine. He tells me you've been seeing things."

"Just what did he say?"

"You've told people you've had visions."

"And so I have. Men and women of faith have been touched by visions over the centuries, and I, too, have been blessed."

"Who is it you believe you see?" his brother sneered.

"You should have a look at your face, John. I'm not going to respond to your question. You'll only use my answer for ridicule.

We share blood, and you are undeniably a Catholic, but you are not a man of faith. You worship money, not God."

His brother let Charles's anger dissipate before saying, "Your rector wants you to see a doctor. He says you've refused to go. Let me ring your GP. I can accompany you to his surgery if we can get an appointment tomorrow."

"There is absolutely nothing the matter with me."

"Let the doctor decide. Perhaps you only need to take a pill or two."

"Toward what end?"

"To stop your bloody hallucinations!"

Charles abruptly got to his feet and said, "They are visions, not hallucinations, and the last thing I want is for them to stop."

When Charles's taxi pulled up to the Convent of Santa Teresa in Coimbra, he was so nervous he forgot to pay the driver.

"Father, I don't work for free," the driver said.

"No, of course you don't."

He signed his name in the visitors' book and was taken to the Mother Superior, Sister Madalena, who was stern and reserved in her welcome. She told him that his request to visit with Sister Lúcia was highly irregular, as it bypassed the usual chain of approval that lay with the bishop of Fátima-Leiria.

"Ever since the Holy Father revealed the Third Secret a year ago, the bishop has been flooded with requests for an audience," she said. "He turns them all down."

"Does he?" Charles said, blinking in discomfort.

"You must know some influential people," she said.

"Only one. I hope I'm not causing too much of a fuss."

"A fuss? No. We don't fuss here. We contemplate. We pray. Are you aware of Sister Lúcia's condition?"

Charles rocked himself slightly in his chair. "No, I'm afraid not."

"She is not so well. She is mostly in bed. Fortunately, last year she was able to meet with the Holy Father when he came to the Shrine of Fátima to beatify Jacinta and Francisco. Since then, there has been a decline. She has good days and bad days. She is ninety-four."

"Is this a good day or a bad day?" he asked

"Somewhere in the middle, I'd say."

"Does she know of my appointment?"

"She forgot it yesterday. Today, she remembers. Come. The quicker you start, the quicker you finish."

The door to Lúcia's cell was the only one in the dormitory that was open so that other sisters might hear the clang of her bell if she needed something. Charles held his breath and even closed his eyes for a moment as he crossed the threshold, in a fleeting prayer of thanks. Sun streamed through her window and glanced off the white walls, forcing a squint.

Sister Madalena clucked and half pulled the curtains, and only then could he see the elderly nun in bed, swathed in heavy bedclothes tucked to her chin. Her hair was covered by a bonnet, with a few wisps escaping. Her face was wrinkled and compressed, her jowls bulging like squirrel pouches, giving Charles the impression of a pumpkin left to go soft in the elements. Frown lines, so deep one could lose a penny in them, had transformed that downturned mouth of hers, a trademark since childhood, into a permanent feature.

"Sister," the Mother Superior said, "your visitor is here."

Lúcia raised her lids, and her eyes came to life behind round glasses.

"Who is it?"

"It is Father Charles," Sister Madalena said. "The English priest who has an appointment to see you. Do you remember?"

"Of course I remember," she said tartly. "But I do not speak English."

"He speaks Portuguese."

Charles was standing near the bed, his hands clasped. He said, "My dear Sister Lúcia, it is my greatest pleasure to meet you."

"Come closer and sit," she said. "You're too far away."

He got the chair from her desk. Her Olivetti typewriter and a pile of books caught his eye.

"That's better," she said, scrutinizing the priest.

"I'll leave you now," Sister Madalena said. "If you need anything, ring that bell, Father, and one of the sisters will hear."

He waited for Lúcia to speak first, and she did. "Your accent is funny."

"I learned my Portuguese in Brazil."

"That explains it. Why are you here, Father?"

"I'm composing a book about Fátima. I've already written about your apparitions, and a small treatise on their spiritual lessons. To make the book truly special, I wanted to meet with you and learn from you."

"What can I possibly teach you, Father? You are a priest."

"So much, dear Sister. You are a woman of great holiness. I am humbled to be in your presence."

She asked for another pillow, and higher in bed, she seemed better able to see him. "You remind me of someone," she said.

"Who, Sister?"

"Let me think." Her eyes opened wider. "Yes! You remind me of Francisco. He was taken to heaven at such a young age, but I can see him in your face. You are dark like him. Your features are small like his. And look at your straight mouth and full lips. If he had lived to your age, he would look like you."

His eyes filled. "That is the most wonderful thing anyone has ever said to me. I beg of you, I would like to hear about your memories of Francisco. I would like to hear about those early years in Fátima, the years of your childhood."

"Ah, my childhood," she said, her voice sounding more youthful. "It was marvelous. Everyone only wants to hear about Our Lady's secrets. No one asks about my childhood."

As she talked, Charles filled pages of his notebook, fearing his fingers would cramp. Turning her head toward him seemed to tire her. Instead, she spoke into some dreamy middle space between the wall and ceiling.

"I remember being rocked. I remember falling asleep to the sound of lullabies. I was the youngest child. I remember how the others used to squabble because they all wanted to hold me in their arms and play with me.

"The first thing I learned was the Hail Mary. While holding me in her arms, my mother taught it to my sister Carolina, the second-youngest. That's when my mother found out that I could repeat everything I heard like a parrot.

"My parents were popular in the village. They attended every festival and every wedding, and that is how I learned to dance. At the weddings, the dancing went on from after the banquet until well into the next morning.

"Since my sisters had to have me always with them, they took as much trouble in dressing me up as they were wont to do for themselves. One of them was a dressmaker. I was always decked out in a regional costume more elegant than that of any other girl around. I wore a pleated skirt, a shiny belt, a cashmere kerchief with the corners hanging down behind, and a hat decorated with gold beads and bright feathers. It was as if they were dressing a doll rather than a small child!

"At the dances, they deposited me on top of a wooden chest or some other tall piece of furniture, to save me from being trampled underfoot. Once on my perch, I sang songs to the music of the guitar or the concertina. Amid the warmth of such affection and tenderness, I happily spent my first years. To tell the truth, the world was beginning to smile on me, and above all, a passion for dancing was already sinking its roots deep into my poor heart. And I must confess that the devil would have used this to bring about my ruin, had not the good Lord shown his special mercy towards me."

Lúcia closed her eyes and went still, and Charles wondered if she had fallen asleep, but when he saw her smile, he concluded she was happily reliving scenes from her childhood.

"You say I remind you of little Francisco. What was he like?" he asked.

Lúcia sprang to life. "Ah, Francisco, what a lovely boy he was! He was a child in love with God. He loved nature, the birds, the sun. He felt a special attraction to be alone and to be filled with God's presence. He would spend hours in front of the Blessed Sacrament, immobile, praying in the same position.

"Francisco did not seem to be Jacinta's brother. She was capricious and vivacious. He was quiet and submissive by nature. When we played a game and he won, if anyone claimed he did not win, he would yield and say, 'You think you won? That's all right. I don't mind.'

"Jacinta liked to dance. He did not. He preferred playing the flute while the others danced."

Charles paused his pen and said, "Much has been made how you little seers received the Virgin's message in different ways. At first, Francisco could not see her. Then he could see her but could not hear her. You could see, hear, and talk to her. Jacinta, on the other hand, could see and hear her but never spoke to her. Some say that it seems that Francisco was the least favored. Was that your impression?"

The nun turned her head to answer. "For him, that was not a problem. He did not feel devalued. Each of us had a role in the apparitions. Each one of us accepted our condition with joy and humility."

Charles said, "I've read that little Francisco also accepted his own death with joy and humility."

"That is so," she said. "He was so very ill with the influenza. I asked him sometimes if he was suffering a lot. He said, 'Quite a lot, but never mind! I am suffering to console Our Lord, and afterwards, within a short time, I am going to heaven!' Can you imagine these words coming from the mouth of one so young?"

"It is quite amazing," the priest said.

"The day before he died, he said to me, 'I am very ill. It won't be long now before I go to heaven.' I remember leaning over his bed and telling him that, once he got there, he should not forget to pray a great deal for sinners, for the Holy Father, for me, and for Jacinta. Would you like to know how he replied?"

"I would, Sister."

"He took my hand and said, 'You'd better ask Jacinta to pray for these things instead, because I'm afraid I'll forget when I see Our Lord and then, more than anything else, I want to console him.' In his final hours, he worried more about comforting Our Lord than his own mortality.

"He took his flight to heaven the following day in the arms of his heavenly mother. I could never describe how much I missed him. This grief was a thorn that pierced my heart for years to come. It is a memory of the past that echoes forever unto eternity."

Charles began to sob so violently that the notebook slid from his lap. Lúcia reached for his hand, and he stood to accept it.

"Why do you cry, Father?" she asked.

"Because I am moved to be in the presence of a woman as holy and wise as you, dear Sister. May I tell you something?"

"Yes, go ahead."

"In a small way, I am like you."

"How so?"

"I, too, have visions."

Her grasp grew tighter. "Tell me about them."

"The first was nine months ago. I was visiting the Shrine of Fátima. It was not my first visit. Each time I have gone has had a great effect on me, but this time, as I was praying, I looked up, and I saw the Virgin, just as you had seen her."

"How did she look?"

"She was in white, a color pure as new snow. She looked sad, as if she were bearing all our sins."

"Did she speak to you?"

"She told me to spread the word about the message of Fátima, how we must commit ourselves to her Immaculate Heart and pray the Rosary. It was then that I decided I had to write this book."

"That is good. Have you had more apparitions?"

He gulped. "I have seen the Virgin many times."

She let go of his hand to cross herself. "We are the fortunate ones, Father. We are the blessed ones. Over the centuries, Our Lady has honored but a few mortal souls with her presence and her teachings. She appeared at Guadalupe. She appeared at Lourdes, at La Salette, at Fátima. She appeared many, many times to the Franciscan sister the Venerable Mary of Jesus of Ágreda to dictate her divine plan for the salvation of souls set forth in her miraculous book, *Mystical City of God*. I knew you were like Francisco. I knew it. Do you know how special you are, Father?"

Charles began to wobble on his feet, and his legs turned to mush. His lips began to move, but all that came out was, "I-I-I-" and then he collapsed onto the cool resin floor, convulsing and frothing at the mouth.

He couldn't hear Sister Lúcia ringing her little bell and shouting for help.

Charles awoke in confusion on a bed that was not his own. He was in an unused cell down the hall from Lúcia's, surrounded by nuns and a doctor who had been summoned from a nearby clinic. The doctor was shining a penlight into his eyes. There was an uninflated blood-pressure cuff on his arm.

"Good, you're awake," the doctor said.

Charles blinked in bafflement and touched his sore, swollen lip, which he had bitten during his fit. His head was throbbing. "Where am I? What happened?"

"You've had a seizure. You're at Santa Teresa. Do you have epilepsy, Father?"

"I don't think so. Can I get up?"

"Not yet. Do you take any medications or have any medical conditions?"

"No."

"Did you suffer any recent blows to the head?"

"No."

"I'd like to take you to the hospital for some tests."

"No, no, I couldn't do that. I have a flight to catch this evening. I teach in the morning."

"In London."

"Yes."

"Well, you will probably be fine to travel. Sometimes people have one seizure, and they never have another. Time will tell, but I advise you to see your doctor as soon as possible."

"Yes, yes, of course. Thank you."

The doctor checked his blood pressure one more time and said, "Please stay still for a while longer."

Sister Madalena came forward and said, "When you are able, Sister Lúcia would like to see you before you depart."

Charles waited until he could confidently stand. Then he went down the hall to knock on Lúcia's open door.

She was sitting in her bedside chair with a heavy throw over her legs.

"Have you recovered?" she asked.

"I believe so."

"You are a sensitive soul, like dear Francisco. You will go to heaven, Father, but not yet. Our Lady wants you to write your book about Fátima, and you must do so in all haste. We will not see each other again, because soon I will go to heaven myself.

"Meeting you was a great gift," she continued. "You led me back to my childhood, which was the happiest time of my life. For that, I would like to give *you* a gift." She peeled back the throw to her waist, where the gift rested on her lap. "Here, take it. When you look upon it, I pray you remember me."

He reached for it with both hands and showed his gratitude with an outpouring of tears.

12

It was a hot, windless day, and the sea was utterly tranquil. The boats hardly moved on their mooring balls, their lines slack. The absence of kinetic energy and the oppressive heat had an effect on all manner of creatures. Up in the sky, there were few gulls. Those that were on the prowl soon abandoned their efforts, lacking good thermals for effortless flight. Lizards lay motionless for hours on hot, flat rocks. Down on the beach, the hotel staff moved at half speed, sluggishly laying out chaise lounges and towels. And on the hotel terrace, waiters moved at the pace of a slow waltz, serving guests who sipped cappuccinos and orange juices while they stared, mesmerized, at the immobile seascape.

The three Americans were uncharacteristically laconic. They had overdone it the night before, and they were paying the price.

Carrie was the first to stitch together a whole sentence. "Anyone have aspirin in their purse?"

Jessica had acetaminophen, and Carrie drank down a couple.

"What do you want to do today?" Carrie asked.

"Die," Jessica said. "I want to die."

Margo said, "Did we learn nothing in college? You don't mix wine and tequila."

"You can't die," Carrie said. "A tour guide's taking us to the Teatro Antico di Taormina."

"It's so hot. I'm so hungover," Jessica moaned.

"You want me to cancel?" Carrie said.

"We could go tomorrow," Margo said.

"Decision made," Jessica said, scrolling through her Twitter feed in a desultory way.

Margo suddenly perked up and pulled her sun hat down as she whispered, "Do you see what I see?"

"What?" Carrie said.

"Behind us, two tables away—we're being checked out. For God's sake, don't look."

"What are we not looking at?" Jessica said.

"Two guys. They're ogling us."

"Are they cute?" Jessica asked.

"Oh yeah, they're cute."

Carrie couldn't resist a peek. She accomplished it by dropping her napkin. "They're totally staring at us," she said.

"Jeez," Jessica said. "This is like middle school."

"They're coming over!" Margo said. "It's because you looked at them, Carrie."

"Don't blame me."

The two men were tanned and muscular. Biceps and triceps bulged under the sleeves of designer polo shirts; quads bulged under tight jeans. The taller one had long hair splashing over his collar. The shorter one sported an undercut, buzzed at the temples. They were both in their thirties—maybe just.

"Ladies," the taller one said in heavily accented English, "we heard you speak. You're Americans, no?"

Jessica was flip with them. "How do you know we're not Canadians?"

"Because Americans are more confident. You seem like confident women. Do you mind if we join you for breakfast?"

The taller one was Cesare. His friend was Vittorio. They said they were modeling scouts from Milan on a short holiday to the beach.

"We're too old," Carrie said, "and too short."

"No, no, all of you are perfect," Cesare said. "You can go straight to the magazine pages. You'll make us rich."

The women laughed at the flirtation.

"What do you do in America?" Vittorio asked.

Margo said, "I do some TV news. This lady saves lives—she's a heart surgeon. She puts us all to shame. And this lady—what is it you do, Jess?"

Jessica laughed. "I used to be a scientist."

"We are very impressed," Cesare said. "So, what are you ladies planning for this beautiful, sunny morning?"

"We were supposed to have a guided tour of the Teatro Antico di Taormina," Margo said.

"Supposed to? You're not going?"

"It's too hot," Jessica said. "We're going to cancel. Carrie, you'd better let the concierge know."

"I'm telling you, you should go," Cesare said. "We went yesterday, and the ruins, they were amazing. You don't need a guide. They overexplain everything. In fact, there was so much to see, Vittorio and I discussed going back again today. We can take you."

"Frankly," Jessica said, "we had a little too much to drink last night."

"There's only one solution for that," Cesare said, summoning the waiter and ordering five Bellinis. "You must fight fire with fire."

The women went with the flow, and after a second round of cocktails, they broke down and agreed to accompany the men to the ruins of the theater, built in the third century BC. Cesare and Vittorio went off to get ready. But as the women walked back to their rooms, Carrie, the most practical among them, said, "What the hell are we doing? These guys are nearly half our age."

"They are not," Margo said. "Besides, there's a double standard. Men go out with younger women all the time."

"The lady's got a point," Jessica said.

"This is all very much in the spirit of Operation Cancel Cal," Margo added.

"What were their names again?" Carrie asked.

Margo said, "I'm calling the taller one Cutie and the shorter one Pie."

They met the men on the hotel drive and climbed into the cramped back seat of their Fiat. As they drove off, Carrie complained about the smell of cigarettes and cracked a window.

"I'm sorry," Cesare said. "I smoked a little bit. It's a rental car—I know you're not supposed to."

Jessica told him cheerfully that, if he lit up around Carrie, she'd cut his heart out, that she knew how to do it.

Carrie made a face. "Your car looks pretty grimy for a rental," she said.

"What is 'grimy'?" Cesare said.

"Dirty, filthy, gross."

"Ah, we complained about it. There were no other cars available. They offered to clean it, but we wanted to get going."

In a few minutes, they passed a sign for the Teatro Antico di Taormina, and Jessica told them they'd missed the turn.

"Yes, we know," Cesare said. "We had a little surprise for you first. There is a small town only a few kilometers away called Castelmola. It's very high up, and it has incredible views of the sea."

"I think we should stick to the plan," Carrie said.

"I promise you, we'll be back to the teatro in twenty minutes. You'll be very happy to see it and take some amazing pictures."

Carrie grumbled as they took the switchbacks and climbed the mountain. After several minutes, Cesare took an abrupt turn down an unmarked lane.

The women exchanged worried glances. "Why are we turning?" Carrie demanded.

"It's just up here."

The surgeon was on her phone, checking their map location. "No, it's not."

"Maybe I took a bad turn," he said, pulling onto the grass.

Suddenly, Vittorio, a man of few words, pointed a small silver gun toward the back seat.

Margo began to whimper, but Jessica and Carrie kept their composure.

"What do you want?" Jessica asked, her voice as sharp as one of Carrie's scalpels.

Cesare put the car in gear and kept going down the narrow road.

"Hand over your phones," Vittorio said. "Come on, hurry."

He collected them and tossed a pair of plastic handcuffs and a pillowcase onto Carrie's lap.

Cesare pointed at Jessica and said, "Do her hands behind her back and put the hood over her."

"Why me?" Jessica demanded.

"Shut the fuck up. Just do it," he told Carrie, "or it will be bad for you."

"It's okay, Carrie," Jessica said. "Do what he says."

"Tighter," Vittorio said, prodding Carrie to ratchet the ties. "Okay, now the hood."

Cesare drove for several more minutes down the single-lane road. It was paved, but that was the only sign of civilization. There was a sharp drop-off to their right and high scrubland to their left.

"Here is good," Vittorio said. When his partner stopped the car, he said to Carrie and Margo, "Okay, you and you, out."

"Where are we?" Jessica said from under her hood.

Margo quickly opened her door, but Carrie said, "We're not leaving her."

"Get out or we'll shoot her," Vittorio said, pointing the gun at Jessica's head.

"Why her?" Margo sobbed hysterically from outside the car.

"Out!" Vittorio shouted at Carrie, who looked at him with hate-filled eyes as she exited.

"Jess, we'll—" she started to say, but Cesare did a three-point turn and sped off the way they had come.

As Cesare drove, Vittorio climbed into the back seat and

took a couple of foil packets from his pocket. He tore the first fentanyl patch open, peeled off the plastic backing, pulled up Jessica's top, and slapped the patch on her abdomen.

"What is that?" she said in a panic.

He slapped the second one on and said, "Enjoy your sleep. If we weren't on the job, I'd take one too."

By the time Cal landed at Heathrow, Nino was already back at his flat in Rome, eating a bowl of cereal and running his clothes through the washer. He had taken an early-bird flight home, departing a couple of hours before Cal. When the time was right, he selected one of his prepaid phones. The bartender in Coimbra had snagged Cal's mobile number, and he punched it in.

Cal didn't recognize the number, but it had an Italy country code, so he answered. "This is Donovan."

Nino smiled into the microphone. He'd been following this guy for a few days now, and he enjoyed wielding power over him, the way a cat must feel playing with a mouse.

"Mister Donovan, listen carefully. We have your friend. Or I should say, your girlfriend."

Cal stopped dead in the middle of the Terminal 2 arrivals concourse.

"Who is this?"

"Someone who is not your friend but doesn't have to be your enemy. You need to cooperate, and everything will be fine."

"I don't know what you're talking about. Who do you think you have?"

"Her name is Jessica Nelson."

Cal tried to make sense of things. The caller spoke in English, but he was clearly Italian, and he seemed to be calling from Italy. Jessica was in Boston.

"You'd better explain yourself," he said.

"It's very simple. We have her. We don't need to hurt her. We don't need to kill her. All you have to do is abandon your search for this Fourth Secret and return to the United States. As soon as your plane departs, she will be released."

Cal felt his skin burn with anger and fear. "I don't believe you."

"Make some calls. Satisfy yourself. I'll call you back in an hour. Don't call me. This number no longer exists."

Nino hung up, cut the SIM card in half, and flushed it down the toilet.

Cal found a quiet area and called Jessica's mobile, and when she didn't pick up, he called her Boston office. Her executive assistant answered.

"Eleanor, this is Cal Donovan. Is Jessica around?"

"Oh, Cal," she said, clearly nonplussed. He knew Jess would have told her about their breakup, and he chalked up her tone to that. "She's out of the office."

"Do you know where I can reach her? Is she home?"

"She's out of the country, actually."

"Where, Eleanor? It's extremely important."

"She's in Italy, Cal. In Sicily. I suppose I can give you her hotel."

She was in Italy. The caller was Italian. He closed his eyes. "Why Sicily? Is she at a conference?"

"No, it was a short vacation. Her friends arranged it. You know Carrie and Margo, don't you?"

"Give me the hotel, please. And Carrie and Margo's mobile numbers."

"Cal, I don't like the way you sound. Is everything all right?"

As soon as he hung up with Eleanor, Cal glued himself to a chair at Heathrow and began making calls. Carrie and Margo didn't respond, so he rang the hotel in Taormina and asked for Jessica's room. No one picked up, and he routed himself back to the front desk and asked for Carrie, whom he considered the more reliable of the two friends, and then Margo. When no one answered, he demanded to speak to the manager.

He began to explain the urgency of reaching these guests when the manager said, "I must tell you, sir, Miss Thorn and Miss Weinstein are here, being interviewed by the Carabinieri."

He knew why but he asked anyway. "What happened?"

"I cannot say. I can check if one of them is able to speak with you."

In a few minutes, Carrie came on the line and asked, "Who's this?"

"Carrie, it's Cal Donovan. Tell me what happened."

"Cal, how did you know?"

"I got a call from someone involved in the kidnapping."

Her distress was palpable, her speech pressured. "Why you? What did he say? What do they want? Does this have anything to do with you?"

"They're using her to stop me from doing something. I can't say more right now."

"Then stop doing whatever it is," Carrie said. "This is Jessica, Cal. I'm scared shitless for her."

"I will. We'll get her back," he said. "What are the police doing?"

"They're interviewing us. We've given them descriptions of the two men and the car they were driving."

"Do you have confidence in them?"

"Christ, I don't know. I'm not exactly an expert in Italian police procedures."

"Why the hell were you in Sicily, Carrie?"

Her surgeon's steeliness cracked, and she began to cry. "We took her here to help her forget about you."

Nino had been watching the clock, and exactly an hour later, he called Cal again on a different phone. "You believe me now?"

Cal had been struggling with a witch's brew of emotions, and the caller's smugness made him erupt. "Don't you fucking hurt her. I swear, I'll find you and I'll kill you."

"Big words." Nino laughed. "You're a teacher, not a tough guy."

"You have no idea what I'm capable of."

"Fine, you'll kill me. Let's deal with the situation, eh? When are you going back to your nice, comfortable home?"

"I'm not going anywhere until I've spoken with her."

"You want proof of life, just like in the movies."

"Put her on the fucking phone!"

"The mouth on you! Okay, you can talk to her, but not now. I'll call you tomorrow."

"Why not now?"

"Tomorrow. And stop looking. If you find the secret, she's dead."

Cal stared at his disconnected phone. He was still at Heathrow, and though it was morning, the bars were open. He hesitated outside one and then took off for the nearest ticket sales counter. Along the way, he called Elisabetta.

"Are you in London?" she asked.

"Yes, but I've got a big problem."

⚓

The long-haired man drove through a grotty industrial zone and pulled into the forecourt of an auto-body shop.

"You sure she's asleep?" he asked.

His partner assured him she was out cold.

They had driven around for an hour until the narcotics took hold. Jessica was lying across the back seat, breathing deeply and slowly. The long-haired man honked his horn, and the garage door opened.

A young guy in greasy overalls with his name, Andrea, stitched onto a pocket, wiped his hands with a rag and waved them in. The men got out of the Fiat and smiled.

"How'd it go?" Andrea asked.

"Good. No problems. Where can we put her?"

"In the office."

"Just so you know, if she wakes up, we used different names. I'm Cesare. Augustu is Vittorio."

"They're better than the originals. Especially yours, Donato."

Donato laughed. "Go fuck yourself."

They carried Jessica through the garage and into the office and laid her on an old sofa.

"What'd you give her?" Andrea asked.

"The good stuff."

"Maybe you'll give me some as a bonus."

"Yeah, maybe."

"How long are you going to keep her here?"

"Until it's night. We don't want to move her until it's dark."

Donato dropped his cigarette in Andrea's ashtray, a plastic cup half filled with water, and announced he was going out for food.

"What if she starts waking up?" Augustu asked.

"Stick another patch on her."

When Cal landed in Rome, an officer of the Vatican Carabinieri met him at the gate and drove him to the Vatican, blue lights flashing, where Emilio was waiting for him in Elisabetta's office.

"Cal, I'm so sorry this has happened to you," Elisabetta said. "We are terribly concerned. The Holy Father is terribly concerned."

Cal's nerves were shot, and he wasn't interested in sympathy. "What do you know, Emilio? Have there been any developments?"

"I told you I'd be getting in touch with the authorities in Sicily, and I've done this. Given the high-profile nature of the case, the local police quickly got the Carabinieri involved, and after I inserted myself into the conversation, the ROS was given jurisdiction."

"The ROS?"

"It's the Raggruppamento Operativo Speciale, the special operations group of the Carabinieri. They deal with organized crime, anti-terrorism, and the like. Think of it like your FBI.

"Here's what we know," Emilio added. "The men who took Miss Nelson and her friends were not guests of the hotel. They came only for breakfast. The women were supposed to have a tour of some ruins nearby, but they canceled the guide and went off with the men."

"Willingly?" Cal asked.

"Yes, willingly. Her friends, who were released, thought the men were tourists from Milan who were going to the ruins themselves, and they agreed to go with them. We have good descriptions and artist sketches already, and a few frames from hotel video cameras that are not so helpful. The men paid for their breakfast with cash.

"One of the women got a few numbers of the registration plate after they were let go. The plate was covered in mud, they said, but maybe some fell off. It matched a Fiat reported stolen yesterday in Palermo. A highway camera picked up the vehicle on the way to Messina, and then it vanished. Of course, the police are still searching for it."

Cal was aware that Elisabetta was watching him closely enough to notice his hands shaking when he lifted a coffee cup to his lips. Her lower lip quivered, as if in empathy.

"Tell me what happened. The details," Cal said.

Emilio seemed reluctant to put him through the trauma, but he relented. "The women were in the rear. They started getting nervous when the turn to the ruins was missed. The guy in the passenger seat, who called himself Vittorio, pulled a gun on them and had them handcuff Miss Nelson and put a sack over her head. The driver, who called himself Cesare, drove for a while down an isolated road between Taormina and Castelmola, took their mobile phones, kicked the other two out of the car, and drove off. They had to walk back to the main road, where they got someone to stop for them and called the police."

"Jessica must have been so scared," Cal said.

"The police will find her," Emilio said. "Have faith."

The notion had started to percolate on the flight from London, and now it jelled. "I'm going to Sicily," Cal said.

"What's the benefit in going there?" Emilio asked. "Now that I'm in the loop, the ROS will give me updates, and you'll know what I know."

"She's in trouble because of me. I've got to go."

"Cal," Elisabetta said gently, "there's nothing you can accomplish as a private citizen. The police know what to do."

"Maybe it's not rational. I really don't care. I'm going."

Elisabetta carefully smoothed her habit over her lap, something Cal had seen her do when she was nervous, a tell.

"Perhaps you could do the greatest good for Miss Nelson by complying with the kidnappers' demand and returning to Boston," she said.

"I thought about that, and maybe I'll cave in, but there's no way that's going to happen before I get proof she's alive. Even if I leave, they might kill her. You know it's a possibility."

Emilio said, "No, no, Cal, don't think like that. These kidnapping gangs prefer not to have murder charges hanging over them. They get what they want, they release the victim."

"These people already have blood on their hands. They

murdered Ramiro Loureno, a complete innocent. A young woman, Chloé Loureno, lost her father. These are killers, Emilio."

There was a knock on Elisabetta's door, and Cardinal Da Silva burst in. His cheeks, normally apple red, were ashen.

"Cal, my dear man, I'm crushed by what has happened. The agony you must be going through. We must do everything we can, mustn't we, Colonel Celestino?"

"I'm assured the best people are on the case," Emilio said.

"Thank you, Rodrigo," Cal said. "Your support means a lot to me."

"Cal was just telling us he intends to go to Sicily to be closer to the situation," Elisabetta said.

Da Silva said, "You should go where your heart tells you to go."

"I'll be honest," Cal said. "This is tearing me up. It's only four days until the canonization, and I'm here, abandoning our last lead. The kidnappers have already won."

Elisabetta said, "We don't even know that following the Charles Graves trail would lead us to the Fourth Secret. It's likely to end at a blind alley, like the others."

"It's all very confusing to me," the cardinal said. "Someone *wants* us to find the Fourth Secret. At the same time, someone is desperate for us *not* to find it and is resorting to brutal tactics. Can anyone explain this?"

No one could.

"Please get the Holy Father to cancel, or at least delay the Mass," Cal said. "Find an excuse. Blame it on a sudden illness."

"Believe me, we've tried," Da Silva said. "He's as stubborn as a bull."

"Will you let me try?" Cal asked.

"There's no harm in it," Da Silva said. "He wants to see you, in any event."

"Is he available? I booked a three o'clock flight to Catania. I need to get back to the airport."

Elisabetta checked Celestine's calendar and told Cal that he was in a meeting, but she could get him an audience in a few minutes. The cardinal said he had to rush off to an appointment and asked Cal to call him that evening to let him know how he was getting on.

Emilio had become disengaged from the conversation. Head down, he had been texting furiously until he stopped, pocketed his phone, and told Cal, "You're not going to the airport."

"Why not?"

"Because I've arranged to have the Vatican helicopter take us to Catania."

"What do you mean, us?"

"If you go alone, the police won't give you the time of day. If I'm there, it will be different."

"You can't leave," Cal said. "Celestine needs you."

"Everything is set. My team knows what to do, and I'm sure I'll be back in time for the Mass. Really, I insist." He made for the door, stopping to kiss his sister. "See you at the helipad in one hour."

Cal was left alone with Elisabetta, and all he could do was stare at his shoes.

She broke the ice by asking, "Are the two of you very close?"

He raised his head at the question. "Jessica and me? We were close. Not anymore. We broke things off a couple of weeks ago."

"Oh, I see."

"That's what makes this especially difficult for me. I—"

"I don't need to know more." She shifted in her chair.

"It's okay. I want to tell you. Jessica's a brilliant, accomplished, and beautiful woman. Unfortunately, she wanted more than I could give. I broke things off. I was an ass. She didn't deserve to be treated the way I treated her, and she sure as hell didn't deserve becoming a pawn in this Fátima business. I've had some darkness in my life, Sister, but this is the blackest pit I've ever been in."

"Eli," she said. "My friends call me Eli." She glanced at the buttons on her phone and said, "He's off his call now. Come. Oh, and it's a small thing, but I meant to tell you that Maurizio Orlando's further archival research came to nothing. There was no correspondence in subsequent pontificates that shed any light on our quest."

"I'm not surprised," he said dully.

Celestine was at his desk, and when he seemed to struggle to stand, Cal came to him for their greeting.

"Any news?" the pontiff asked. "Have our prayers been answered?"

"Not yet. I've decided to go to Sicily to be closer to the investigation. Unfortunately, that means I'll have to suspend the search for the Fourth Secret."

"It is the correct decision, Professor. You must go. Your friend will know you did everything in your power to help her. I will pray for her, and I will pray for you. The power of prayer is not to be underestimated."

"Before I leave," Cal said, "I want to beg you to heed the warning."

"They want me to resign! Do you think I should resign, Professor?"

"Absolutely not, but I think it would be prudent to postpone the Mass."

"No, we cannot do this."

"Then Cardinal Da Silva could officiate in your absence."

"Professor, please. This is for Fátima, this is for Lúcia, and I am the pope."

"Forgive me for saying this, Holy Father, but you are a stubborn man."

"Let me tell you something, Professor. I grew up in a difficult neighborhood. I was good at football and quite strong, and it was assumed I would hang out with the tough kids, who stole and dealt in drugs. My parents would not allow it, and even if they had not been strict, I had no affinity for these boys. I knew right from wrong.

"The price I paid for my resistance was to be bullied. One thing I learned, Professor, is you must never back down from a bully. I am not saying that you should fight them with fists, but you must never bend to their will. Go to Sicily. God willing, you will bring your friend home. I will say Mass for Blessed Sister Lúcia, and I will accept with grace whatever the Lord has planned for me."

13

―――――――――

The white AgustaWestland AW139 helicopter lifted off from the Vatican helipad and deposited Cal and Emilio at the Catania airport two and a half hours later. During the trip, the chopper hugged the shoreline. Emilio, facing west, looked toward the sea, while Cal, facing east, took in cities and farmland.

The commanding officer of the ROS in Sicily, Colonel Marco Arena, was based in Palermo. A subordinate had initially been assigned to the case, but when the US ambassador to Italy and the commander of the Vatican Carabinieri got involved, Arena personally assumed control, telling the officer he replaced that if something went wrong, his neck was going to be stretched, so he might as well put it in the noose himself. He had agreed to meet Emilio at Jessica's resort in Taormina, and he was waiting in the lobby when Cal and Emilio arrived. While Emilio wore a business suit, Arena was in full military uniform: black gabardine jacket and trousers with red piping, white braiding, insignia, and medals. Cal found the uniform more imposing than the mousy man with a gray painter's-brush mustache. Absent the uniform, Cal would have taken him for an accountant.

Greetings were perfunctory. Arena asked Cal if he'd received a call from the kidnapper.

"He said tomorrow," Cal said.

"We should have the call recorded. There's an app you need to download onto your phone. I'll show you."

"Have you located the Fiat?" Emilio asked.

"There's no sign of it. It was stolen in Palermo, so we might assume the kidnappers are based there, and perhaps they've returned there, feeling safer on home turf. However, if they did return, they must have changed vehicles, because we would have found the Fiat on CCTV cameras. These kidnapping gangs used to be quite common in Sicily, but not these days, and this isn't a caper for money, at least not on the face of it. From what you've told me, Inspector General, this kidnapping was for leverage, not loot."

"That is correct," Emilio said.

"It would be helpful to know more," Arena said.

"They want Professor Donovan to stop the work he is doing on behalf of the Holy Father and return to the United States."

A waiter interrupted, and they ordered coffees. When he was out of earshot, Arena asked, "If I might inquire, what sort of work?"

"It's a delicate and time-sensitive matter," Emilio said vaguely, and Arena shrugged deeply, demonstrating that he understood there was no point in pushing for more.

"Professor, do you intend to stop this work?" Arena asked instead.

"I suspended my activities when I heard about Jessica. If I have to return to Boston to save her life, I will."

"She is your friend? Your fiancée?"

"We were close. Now we're not."

"I see."

Emilio asked Arena, "Can you tell us more about how you are conducting the investigation? How many men are involved, what are your tactics?"

"We have over thirty officers involved from Palermo, Catania, Messina, and other locations. In addition, we are working closely with the Polizia di Stato, and this is a huge force multiplier for us.

"We have put out information to the public about the car, and Jessica's photo has been released to the media. I've just learned that her company has posted a generous reward for information leading to her safe return and the capture of the criminals. Beyond that, we must wait for leads to develop and for your call from the leader of the gang. You'll be staying at this hotel, I understand?"

"We have rooms," Cal said. "This is where she'll come when they let her go. I want to be here to tell her I'm sorry."

As Cal was checking in, he felt eyes on the back of his head and heard, "He's here."

He turned like a man expecting a bullet. Carrie and Margo were staring at him with tired, angry eyes. He asked if they were okay.

"No, we're not," Carrie said. "Why are you here?"

"How could I not be?" Cal replied. "This is Colonel Emilio Celestino of the Vatican Gendarmerie. He's here to liaise with the police. Emilio, these are Jessica's friends, Carrie Weinstein and Margo Thorn."

Emilio bowed. "I'm pleased to meet you and sorry for your ordeal. I'm sure you've told your story multiple times already, but perhaps we could talk after I put my bags in my room?"

Cal went to the veranda with them. It was just getting dark, and the fairy lights on the trellis were lit. A wind was blowing from the shore, and the heavy air was scented with sea brine and jasmine from ornamental pots.

Carrie made no attempt to conceal her anger. "You said they were using her to stop you from doing something."

"That's what I was told."

"What exactly are you doing, Cal?" Margo asked, using her on-air-reporter voice.

"It's a special project for the Vatican. I can't tell you more. It's the reason that Colonel Celestino is involved."

"How are you supposed to prove you've stopped?" Margo asked.

"By getting on a plane back to the States."

Carrie shook her head fiercely enough to set her hair in motion. "And here you are. You're not stopping. You're putting Jess's life in danger instead."

"I'd never do that. The guy who called me this morning told me he'd call tomorrow and let me speak to her. Once I know she's okay, I'll do what they ask."

"I'm sorry, that doesn't wash," Carrie said. "If you were on a plane right now, maybe Jess would be released right now."

Cal wished he could tell them the whole story and explain

himself. But he couldn't, so all he said was, "They're not expecting me to leave until I've heard from her. That was the deal."

They were still unsatisfied and showed it. Margo announced that they were taking a walk on the beach, but before leaving, Carrie said, "She was in love with you. Did you know that? You broke her heart, and now you've put her life in danger."

He let out a stuttering breath and looked at the waves.

Margo added her dagger thrust. "We kept telling Jess you were no good for her. You're poison, Cal. You're nothing but poison."

Cal was on his third vodka while Emilio sipped a soda. Although he wasn't officially on duty, he was there on official business, and he was a stickler for the rules of the game. Before dinner, he interviewed Carrie and Margo, but he had learned nothing new. He told Cal, "They're quite unhappy with you."

"I'm aware."

"Their anger will fade. They'll come to understand that this was no fault of yours."

Cal bowed his head to answer. "If it weren't for me, she wouldn't have been kidnapped. I can't absolve myself so easily."

"I think you're being hard on yourself. My sister agrees. I spoke with her tonight."

They were in the lounge under a picture window that during the day framed an azure sea, and at night a canvas of pure black.

"I envy you, Emilio."

"Why?"

"You have a marvelous family. I appreciated the invitation to your father's."

"We fight a lot, but we love a lot. You don't have this with your family?"

"I don't have a family. My parents are gone. I was an only child."

"That's too bad. I'm sorry for you. Life is bigger with a family. That's my opinion."

"Can I ask you something?" Cal said. "Was your father disappointed that Elisabetta became a nun?"

"Oh my God, yes, but it was hard for him to express himself openly. You see, we had almost lost her to violence, and her recovery took a very long time. When her health was restored, he was so grateful he almost thanked God. Almost. He's not a religious man. He believes that everything can be explained by science and the laws of mathematics. God is for superstitious people, he says, people who take the easy road rather than trying to understand the complexities of existence.

"But maybe my mother rubbed off on him a little during her time on this earth. She was deeply religious, so God couldn't be banished from our house without banishing my mother. The first Sunday after Eli was discharged from the rehabilitation hospital, he agreed to come to Mass with the rest of us. Afterward, at lunch, she made her big announcement. I remember his face. He wanted to say something mean, which is his usual way, but how could he? He had his daughter back from the jaws of death."

From across the room, Cal noticed Carrie and Margo

returning from dinner on the veranda. They didn't seem to see him, and he was glad.

"Is she happy?" he asked.

"Eli? Happy? I would say she's satisfied. She was never a happy person in the way that our sister, Micaela, is happy. Being a nun suits her personality. She doesn't have to worry about taking care of children, taking care of a husband, and balancing these chores with a job. She has her faith, and she has her work. She likes the simplicity."

"Nothing about her job is simple," Cal says. "As the highest-ranking woman in the history of the Vatican, she's a lightning rod for conservatives, especially since she had a prominent role in the art divestiture."

"Maybe, but Eli is tough. She can take it."

"Her toughness is an asset. The Holy Father needs tough people around him, now more than ever," Cal said. "She told me you admire Commander Studer."

"Why mention him?"

"She didn't tell you?"

"About your suspicion of Studer being the leak? I told her it was absurd. Studer is a dedicated professional."

"What about his politics?"

"I don't know, and I don't care. He's a military man. He took an oath to the Holy Father and the Church. That's good enough for me."

Cal waved his empty glass at the waiter. "If it's good enough for you, then it'll have to be good enough for me."

Jessica became aware of a fan with a loose blade clicking rhythmi-cally overhead and the noisy rumble of a window-mounted air conditioner. Her eyelids hadn't been open for hours, and with effort, she overcame the secretions that had glued them shut and tried to take her bearings. She was in a dark room, but a little light was leaking from under a door, and she could hear the sounds of a television. Her hands were bound behind her back, and with effort, she rocked herself across the bed and got her feet onto the floor. Her mouth was bone-dry, and her bladder ached.

"Hello? Is anyone there?" Her voice lacked steam.

The door opened, and Donato, the one Jessica knew as Cesare, called to his brother, "She's awake."

"Where am I?" she asked.

"In a nice, cool room. How was your sleep?"

"How long have I been here?"

"Not so long."

"I'm thirsty. I need the bathroom."

"Sure, no problem."

"My hands."

Donato cut the ties with a flick knife. "There. It's en suite. Only the best for our guest."

When she wobbled out of the bathroom, Augustu was in the room, holding a bottle of apple juice. Jessica drained it in a series of gulps, leaving her panting.

"I need to put new cuffs on."

"Please don't."

"It's not a negotiation. Cooperate or we'll hold you down."

She opened one of her hands to show them the patches she had peeled off her abdomen. "You gave me these. You could have killed me."

"As you see, you're alive," Donato said. "Lie down on your side."

She felt the ratchets binding her wrists.

"We're not going to feed you."

"Why?"

"We don't want you to vomit in your sleep."

"I'm not going back to sleep."

Augustu held up another foil pouch of fentanyl.

"Please, no more," she begged. "I'll be quiet."

"Again, it's not a negotiation."

She tried to shout, but her voice was too weak. "Why are you doing this? Is there a ransom?"

"We looked you up. You're a wealthy woman. We really should be asking for money, but it would complicate things. This isn't about a ransom."

"Then what's it about?"

"I think it's got something to do with a friend of yours, a guy named Donovan."

The next morning, Cal woke up obsessed with his phone. He turned the ringer to maximum and took it into the bathroom with him. When he showered, he kept the door open, and when he had breakfast with Emilio, he set it next to his plate.

"Staring at it won't make it ring," Emilio said.

"When do you talk to Arena again?"

"Midmorning. That was what we agreed. Of course, if he has new developments, he'll call immediately."

As the morning dragged on and the twenty-four-hour mark

passed since his last contact with the kidnapper, Cal grew increasingly despondent. He sat in the lounge, facing the irresistibly blue sea, a sea that he fantasized would crash through the window in a tsunami wave and sweep him and his agonizing guilt away. His phone, which was lying next to his endless cup of Americano coffee, was nothing more than a black mirror that reflected his haggard face. At noon, Margo approached his table while Carrie held back at the lounge entrance.

"Anything?" she asked.

"Nothing."

"We're supposed to fly back in three days."

"You'll be taking her with you."

"Can you promise me that?"

His response was a sad headshake.

Emilio spent the morning working remotely with his security team on final procedures for the Mass, but he came to the lounge periodically to check on Cal. Just before 1 p.m., he asked if he wanted to get a table for lunch.

"I'm not hungry," Cal said. "I—"

The phone rang, and Cal snatched it off the table. It was an Italian number. He went through the oft-practiced maneuver to activate the recording app and put it to his ear.

"This is Donovan."

"You ready to speak to her?"

"Yes."

Emilio leaned forward, trying to hear what would leak from around Cal's ear.

Nino said, "Hold on," and conferenced in Donato's phone.

After several seconds, Cal heard him say, "You there?"

A deep male voice answered, "Yeah." Cal heard some background noise, of cars passing and people chattering.

"Donovan, you there?"

"I'm here."

The deep voice was on a speaker, saying, "Talk to him."

Jessica sounded far away and out of focus. "Hello?"

"Jess, it's Cal," he said urgently.

Emilio leaned in closer.

"Cal?"

"Are you okay? Did they hurt you?"

Her confusion was palpable. "I don't understand. Cal?"

"Yes, it's Cal. We're going to get you home, Jess."

"I want to go home. I don't know where I am. I think—"

"That's enough," the deep voice said, and Cal could no longer hear her.

Nino spoke up. "Okay. You've got your proof of life. Now you've got a choice to make. You go back home, or we cut her throat. You understand?"

"Yes."

"I know you're in Sicily."

"How do you know that?"

Nino ignored the question. "You won't be able to get a flight from Rome to Boston until tomorrow morning. That's your deadline. You take off, she lives. You don't, she dies. You understand?"

"I understand."

The line went dead, and Cal looked at the phone in his sweaty hand.

"Let me check the recording," Emilio said.

Cal handed him the phone, and his gaze returned to the sea. "She sounded out of it, maybe drugged."

203

Emilio listened on playback and said, "Come on, we're going to Catania. I'm emailing Commander Arena the file. He needs to hear this immediately."

Commander Arena had a war room set up at the Carabinieri command center, located in an industrial zone in Catania, behind walls topped with razor wire.

When Cal and Emilio arrived, the phone conversation was playing on a speaker.

"How the hell do they know you're in Sicily?" Arena asked.

"We have no idea," Emilio said. "It's quite disturbing."

Cal kept his mouth shut. This wasn't the time or place to raise suspicion about the commander of the Swiss Guards.

"Did you hear the sound when the first guy says, 'We cut her throat'?" Emilio asked.

"I heard it," Arena said. "It sounded like a ship's horn. Play it again."

One of Arena's men found the spot.

"Definitely a ship's horn," Arena said. "And the earlier background noises," Arena said. "It's like they were on the street."

"More likely an open window," Emilio said.

"Play it again," Arena said. "Can you make it louder?"

The officer maxed the volume setting and repeated it.

"There. Stop there," Arena said, just after they heard the man with the deep voice answer "Yeah" to the question "Are you there?"

"What *is* that?" he asked. "It's not Italian. Go back a little."

The clip was rewound and played again. Cal listened to the second-long segment intently. "I think it's Arabic," he said.

"Are you sure?" Emilio asked.

"I'm not sure, but I think it is."

"You know Arabic?"

"Some."

"Why?"

"I'm an archaeologist. I dig in the Middle East."

"Try to make out the words."

Cal strained and listened. "I really don't know. I think one of the words could be '*hayaa*' — 'come on.'"

Arena told one of his officers to see if there were any Arabic speakers in the command center. The man rushed off, and a few minutes later, he returned with a swarthy young man in tow, a junior carabiniere who had emigrated from Egypt as a child.

"Listen to this," Arena told him. "Is this Arabic?"

"Yes, sir, it is."

"Can you make out what the fellow is saying?"

"I believe it is '*Hayaa, sawf nata'akhara.*'"

"What does that mean?"

"It means, 'Come on, we're going to be late.'"

"That's it? Anything else?"

"That's all I could make out."

"Well, that's not very helpful, someone saying to someone else, 'We're going to be late,'" Arena said, dismissively. "You can return to your duties."

The young man saluted and started to leave when he turned to say, "Excuse me, am I permitted to ask the time of the recording?"

Cal said, "A minute or so after one p.m."

The carabiniere took out his phone, opened an app, and smiled. "I thought maybe, and it seems so."

Arena seemed irritated. "What are you talking about?"

He showed them the screen. "These are the salah times for Sicily, the five daily prayer times. For today, the Dhuhr, the midday prayer, started at one-oh-six p.m. I think these people are rushing to get to a mosque in time for Dhuhr."

Arena told him, "You're seconded to the ROS until told otherwise. Bring me a list of all the mosques in Sicily."

"All of them, sir? There are quite a few."

Cal found the spot on the recording and played it again. The ship's horn sounded a long, sonorous beat. "Not all the mosques," Cal said. "Only the ones near a port."

An hour later, Commander Arena reconvened his team for a status report and called in Cal and Emilio, who were waiting in a cubicle.

The young Egyptian officer's name was Jabari Ahmed, and he brought in a couple of large map rolls, which he unfurled on the table.

"Two mosques on the island are close enough to ports to capture a ship's horn as loud as the one we heard," he said, pointing at spots on the maps. "They are the Masjid Ar-Rahmah in Catania, here, and the Moschea di Palermo, here. Masjid Ar-Rahmah is seven hundred fifty meters to the Catania Cruise Port, and the Moschea di Palermo is less than two kilometers to the Palermo Cruise Terminal."

"Are we sure the horn was from a cruise ship?"

Another officer said he had played the clip to multiple people at the command center, and the consensus was that a cruise liner was more likely than a cargo vessel.

"Hardly proof," Arena sniffed.

Ahmed grinned and read from his notebook. "I have relevant information. At approximately one p.m. a Royal Caribbean ship, *Vision of the Seas*, departed the Palermo Cruise Terminal for Barcelona, Spain. And at the same time, a Celebrity cruise ship, *Infinity*, arriving from Athens, docked in Catania."

Arena said, "Good work. What was your name again?"

"Jabari Ahmed," the officer said proudly.

"Ideas?" Arena asked the room.

Emilio volunteered his opinion. "It would be good to obtain feeds from CCTV cameras on the streets near the mosques in Palermo and Catania. I would say from midday yesterday until midday today—but probably after dark—looking for a woman who was with one or more men entering a building."

"She sounded drugged," Cal said. "We don't know if she was able to walk on her own or had to be carried or dragged."

Arena said, "There's one piece of good news, I'd say. The ROS has been vigilant about monitoring extremist activities centered at mosques on the island, and I can guarantee you that we have good CCTV coverage in those areas."

"Palermo or Catania?" Emilio said. "Which is more likely?"

"The car was stolen in Palermo," Arena said, "and that tells me that they are from Palermo. The criminals will have their support structure there. This is where they would return. It's only a three-hour drive from Taormina on interior roads, less than four hours on the coastal highway. They could have switched cars and traveled with impunity."

Emilio said, "On the other hand, Catania is just down the road from Taormina, so their exposure would be minimized."

"I'll assign two teams," Arena said. "One to collect and review CCTV footage from Palermo, one from Catania. We'll meet back here at six."

When they got back to the hotel, Cal reached out to Margo and found her in her room.

"Is there news?" she said.

"They called. I spoke with her."

"Is she all right?"

"She sounded tired. She said she hadn't been hurt. It was only a few seconds."

"What now?"

"They want me to go back to Boston. I booked a flight for tomorrow morning."

"Thank God you're doing what they want. We'll be here for her when they let her go. They *will* let her go, won't they?"

"Yes, they'll let her go."

Later, driving back to the Carabinieri compound, Cal asked Emilio, "Did you let Studer know I'm leaving for home tomorrow?"

"I told him."

"If I'm right about him, the kidnappers know too."

"Please, Cal, you know what I think about your theory. Lying to Studer stinks. I'll humor you, but that's as far as I'll go."

The six o'clock meeting didn't start until seven fifteen. The holdup was the sheer volume of CCTV footage that needed to be reviewed. When they were ready, Arena dimmed the lights and said, "I think we've got the bastards. This is from Palermo, last night at two a.m."

On the monitor, they saw a dark street, not much wider than an alley. Cal reckoned a small car could just about squeeze through. The night-vision mode had the image in black-and-white.

One of Arena's officers sat at a laptop, narrating and pointing with a mouse. "This is Via del Celso, just around the corner from the mosque. Wait a few seconds and you'll see them coming into view. There, walking away from the camera. Two men and a woman. This guy has his arms around the woman's waist. This guy takes out a key, unlocks the door, and in they go. That's it. We've looked at this camera feed right up till two hours ago, and we don't see them leave."

"What do you think, Cal?" Emilio said. "Is that Jessica?"

Cal wanted to see it again and said, "Can you zoom in?" The image got grainy. "I don't know," he said. "It could be. It's impossible to say."

"She was wearing a dress when she was taken," Arena said. "This woman is wearing a dress. And if she was indeed drugged, see the way this man is supporting her. I think this is it. But, okay, to be thorough, here is the best we could come up with in Catania."

The officer on the laptop clicked on another file and said, "This is very close to the Masjid Ar-Rahmah mosque—Via

Porta di Ferro, twelve eighteen a.m." It was a wider street than the last, better lit, with four-story buildings on either side and steady foot traffic. "Here we can see a group of maybe a dozen people walking down the street away from the camera. We have men, we have women, there's someone walking a dog. It could be one group of acquaintances or multiple strangers—there's no way to tell. You see this woman in the light-colored dress? We lose her in the group right here. What happened to her?

"This is from another camera positioned on a restaurant maybe thirty meters farther down the road. We have a nice view of all the people passing in profile. The woman in the light-colored dress isn't there. She must have entered the building, where we last see her. That's it. That's all we have."

Again, Cal was asked for his impression about the woman in the video, and again, he couldn't be sure.

"What's your plan, Commander?" Emilio asked Arena.

Arena pinched his mustache between his thumb and fore-finger. "We have to hit both locations tonight. But Palermo first. My money is on Palermo."

Two tactical teams were hastily assembled, one consisting of ROS officers from the Palermo barracks, the other of Catania-based men. The architectural plans for the target buildings were obtained from the local authorities. There were four flats to cover in the Palermo building, two in Catania. Palermo would be hit at midnight, Catania an hour later—but only if Palermo was a dud.

The operations room was unlike any Cal had seen in the

movies. There were no wall screens transmitting real-time infrared images from tactical-team body cameras, no moving dots on projected maps. No countdown clocks. This was an ordinary conference room with paper maps on the walls, a speakerphone, and a military radio. He arrived with Emilio an hour before the Palermo raid and sat against the wall while Arena's team communicated with field commanders. His skin was crawling. It was long past vodka o'clock, but this night would be dry.

Precisely at midnight, Arena gave the order to commence the Palermo operation. Four four-man squads entered the apartment building on Via del Celso and quietly made their way up the stairs to the landings. Each squad leader was patched into the radio of Arena's operations room and Cal could hear a mélange of boots on stairs and heavy breathing, and then four confirmations of "Ready."

Arena barked a "Go" order.

The radio came alive with banging on doors and shouts of "Police! Open up!" and then repetitions of their commands with threats that doors would be broken down. Confused voices of residents. The crack of wood as a door was breached. Officers moving through apartments, shouting instructions to one another. And finally, minutes after it began, four sets of stand-down orders, and the team leader coming on the line with, "She's not here."

Arena grunted and told the officer to make amends with the apartment dwellers and send a carpenter to repair the busted door. "Okay," he told the people in the operations room, "Catania is next."

Cal asked Emilio, "How far is it?"

"Not far. Why?"

"If she's there, I want to be there."

"I don't have a problem, but let me clear it with Arena. If he says okay, we can ride with the men."

Arena seemed happy to have the outsiders leave his command center, but he cautioned Emilio to keep Donovan out of the way. In the parking lot, the tactical team was getting ready to embark, and space was made for Cal and Emilio in the trailing ambulance. It was a short drive to the old center of Catania.

Via Porta di Ferro was too narrow for their large vans, and they would have been too conspicuous. They drove past the dark Masjid Ar-Rahmah and rolled to a stop at the deserted Piazza Cutelli, just around the corner from the target.

When the hour was nigh, the van doors opened and men spilled out. Cal and Emilio started to follow the black-clad officers, but the team leader gave Emilio a sign with his palm to get back inside the ambulance.

"We have to wait here," Emilio whispered.

At 1:00 a.m. on the dot, Arena gave the order, and the two squads and their commanding officer made entry.

Over the ambulance radio, Cal heard the same choreography as in Palermo—banging, shouting, commands, a door smashing, more shouting. But this time, another sound pierced the night—the sound of pistol fire.

Over the radio, they heard, "Shots fired! Shots fired! We need the medics! First floor."

Cal tasted panic in his mouth—a dry, metallic taste—and when the medics spilled from the van, he ran with them, ignoring Emilio's calls to stop. He followed the medics into the building and up the stairs, where officers crowded the landing. A door was open wide, and one of the officers had to physically restrain Cal from entering. Emilio pulled him away before things escalated.

"For God's sake, find out if she's there," Cal yelled. "Find out if she's hurt."

Emilio wedged his way inside. The front room was still hazed blue with gunpowder, and three medics were working on a tall man with long hair who was lying on the floor. His shirt was ripped open. A gauze pad, pressed against a chest wound, was soaked through with blood. A second victim lay beside him, but this man, shorter with a buzzed haircut, was beyond saving, the side of his head hollowed out.

Emilio heard an officer calling from a bedroom. "Can one of the medics come here?"

He followed the medic inside and saw Jessica lying motion-less on the bed.

"See to her," the officer told the medic. "She doesn't look too good."

"Was she shot?"

The officer held up a couple of empty fentanyl foils. "No, this."

"Christ!" the medic said, shouting into the other room. "Did anyone bring naloxone?"

"In my kit box," was the reply.

Emilio watched them push the injection. He looked for signs of life as they worked on the woman. He was more religious than his father, less religious than Elisabetta, but he prayed as hard as she might have, and he kept it up for a good two minutes until Jessica gasped for air and opened her eyes.

He went to find Cal on the landing, gripped him hard by the shoulders, and said, "We've got her. She's okay."

14

Cal rode with Jessica to the Garibaldi Centro Hospital. She was in a stupor, going in and out of consciousness, and he didn't think his presence had registered. In the emergency department, he was consigned to the waiting room, where he did what was expected of him—he waited.

It was a long while until a doctor came to speak with him. Cal sprang up when called and pounced on him, way too aggressively for the mild-mannered fellow.

In rapid fire, Cal asked, "How is she? Is she awake? Tell me, was she injured or abused?"

The doctor offered a benign smile and said, "You are her husband?"

"No, a friend."

"I see. Look, as a nonrelative, I shouldn't give you details of her condition, but I understand the circumstances and I'll make an exception. She is fine. She is responding to treatment. They kept her sedated with a powerful narcotic. They easily could have crossed the line of tolerability and killed her.

214

She was lucky. She required another dose of the anti-narcotic naloxone, to reverse the effects, and now she is fully awake. But, given her ordeal, she is understandably fatigued. And, no, she has no physical injuries or signs of abuse. She was a little dehydrated, and we gave her some fluids."

"Can I see her?"

"Maybe soon. The police are speaking to her now. I'll make sure they don't make her too tired."

When Cal was permitted to enter the ward, he stood at the curtains, steeled himself for a moment, and parted them.

"Hey."

Jessica was seated in bed under a thin blanket, staring at him in confusion. "Cal? What the hell are you doing here?"

"I rode in the ambulance with you."

"You did?"

"You were pretty out of it."

"I don't understand. Why are you in Italy?"

"I was in London when I heard about what happened to you. I came to see if I could help."

She looked confused, scrunching her face in deep thought, and said, "They mentioned you, I think."

"Who?"

"The assholes who took me."

"What did they say?"

"I don't remember. Why would they mention you? Or maybe I was dreaming."

"Are you sure you want to talk about this now?"

"I'm damned sure." She was angry, and in a way, he was glad for it.

"They took you to get at me," Cal said. "They wanted me to

stop doing a job for the Vatican. For the life of me, I don't know how they knew we were friends, or that you were in Sicily."

She shook her head in disgust. "Probably Facebook. I've been posting stupid holiday pictures. I'm deleting my fucking account."

He laughed, and, thankfully, she joined in for a few seconds until she turned serious again. "Did you? Stop?"

"I did. I was going to go back to Boston tomorrow."

"And now you won't."

He hadn't thought about it. "Yeah, now I won't. It's important, a life-and-death thing."

"Like my life or death? They gave me fentanyl. I could have died."

"I'm so sorry, Jess. There was no way I ever imagined you'd get caught up in this."

She glowered as only she knew how to glower, like a death ray. "Yet here I am."

Pangs of remorse made him look away. "I called Margo and Carrie to tell them you're okay. They're on the way."

"They're still in Taormina?"

"They weren't going to leave you."

She teared up and looked for a tissue. "They're good friends. What happened to those fuckers?"

"The police didn't tell you?"

"They wouldn't."

"One was killed at the scene. The other died later in surgery, I was told."

"Good."

"I can't muster any Christian sympathy either. I'm feeling more Old Testament."

"The doctor told me I could travel in a day," she said. "I want to go home."

"Margo and Carrie will take good care of you."

She caught him with hard, glaring eyes. "You know I never want to have anything to do with you ever again, right?"

"Yeah, Jess, I know."

Cal awoke after a grand total of two hours of sleep, and he drank room-service coffee until it was a respectful time to call Elisabetta.

"Emilio called me late last night and told me what happened," she said. "I didn't want to wake the Holy Father, but I informed him at breakfast. He is very relieved, as you can imagine. Emilio said you went to the hospital with your friend. How is she?"

"Making a good recovery. There will be scars, but they won't be physical."

"Yes, I'm sure. And how are you?"

"I'm fine—well, maybe a bit tired. I want to go back to London on the next flight."

"You don't have to do that, Cal. Perhaps you should return to Boston with Miss Nelson."

"I think that would interfere with her recovery."

Elisabetta went quiet, and Cal imagined she was processing the best way to respond. She finally said, "What I meant to say is that after this ordeal, perhaps you should abandon the search. The canonization is the day after to-morrow."

"There's still Charles Graves. I have to keep trying."

"If that's what you wish, we will make the travel arrangements. I'll notify the Diocese of Westminster that you'll be arriving this afternoon."

"Thank you. I haven't seen Emilio yet this morning."

"You'd better hurry. He'll be leaving the hotel shortly for his flight to Rome. He's anxious to personally supervise the final plans for the Mass."

"I'm very glad to hear that. I'll look for him."

"Cal, please call me later when you've met with the rector."

"Thank you, Eli." It was the first time he had used her informal name, and it had a soothing effect, like applying aloe to a burn.

Cal caught Emilio as he was leaving the lobby with his bag slung over his shoulder.

"I was going to call you from the airport," Emilio said. "Are you all right?"

"Yeah, I'm fine. I'm going to London."

"Really? I thought you'd be leaving us for America."

"Not yet. I can't ignore Charles Graves. Do you think the guy who called me in London was one of the ones from last night?"

"I don't think so. These guys were local muscle from Palermo—so in that sense, Arena was correct. The fellow you spoke with was higher up."

"I'm glad you're going back," Cal said. "You'll be at the Holy Father's side on the day."

"Studer seemed pleased as well. It takes some of the pressure off him."

"Don't tell him I'm going to London. Tell him I'm still headed back to the States."

Emilio showed his exasperation. "This again?"

"Yes, this again. Please. I know I've asked you to lie to a colleague, but if he's got nothing to do with this, it's not a consequential lie. I'll feel safer."

Emilio nodded. "Okay, I'll do it."

"And tell Eli not to let Studer know where I'm going."

"Ah, you're calling her Eli now. That's great."

Hugo limped across his sitting room and seized the ringing phone lying atop an old family Bible.

"Did you find out what happened?"

Nino said, "Not everything. I don't know how the cops found them. Both the brothers were shot dead. Donovan's friend was rescued. Game over. We tried."

"Three dead now. What about your pledge? No violence, you said."

"Let me tell you something, my friend. This is your game, and it's a dangerous game. If you want me to stop, I'll stop. I've got other jobs waiting. But I'm keeping my full fee."

Hugo was gazing out his window onto his local park. Some children were kicking a football around. Mothers pushed strollers. A dog lifted a leg. It was all so ordinary and peaceful and wholly unlike this hell he had brought down upon himself. "I don't want you to stop."

"Fine. If this is going to go on much longer, you'll need to pay me more."

Hugo sounded a doleful note. "Two more days. That will be the end of it, one way or another."

"Don't be so gloomy. The good news is you won't have to pay the Palermo brothers now."

"Two men have died, for God's sake."

"I'll light candles. Where's Donovan going next?"

"Back to London," Hugo said.

"Do you have his flight?"

"Yes. I'll text you."

"Then I'd better leave for the airport."

Hugo sat at his desk and switched on his lamp. He had long recorded his most intimate thoughts in a diary. Some days, he thought he would destroy it; on others, he fantasized it might be published and widely discussed. On the chance it would be the latter, he penned a detailed entry, and then made himself a cup of tea.

The London weather was changeable. Strong winds propelled towering cumulus clouds across the sky, blotting out the sun for a few minutes before it shone through the gaps. Pedestrians strolling along the Chelsea Embankment alternated between putting on sunglasses and taking them off. Cal was one of them. He had a little time to kill before his appointment with the rector of Allen Hall College, and it did him good to lose himself in contemplation of the rough waters of the Thames.

It was July 11. Lúcia would become a saint on July 13. In

the future, what else would that day come to signify? What was sealed by fate? And what did he, a mere mortal, have the power to change? These were unanswerable questions, but he silently posed them to the murky river, as if God were lurking under the surface.

And what of July 14? Whatever happened, he would return home with the knowledge that he had done damage to a fine woman, and that he and Jessica could never have any sort of reconciliation. And he would return home with the certainty that Elisabetta would fade away, becoming no more than a fever dream. Others would drift in and out of his life, but when it came down to it, he was destined to be alone.

A barge passed, and it took his mind back to the present and to Charles Graves. He left the river, crossed the Embankment at Battersea Bridge, and headed down Beaufort Street.

The rector at Allen Hall, Rev. Nathan Hardcastle, was surprisingly youthful. He was erudite, witty, and personable, and Cal instantly liked him.

They walked the grounds, and, like all visitors, Cal was shown Thomas More's mulberry tree.

"I like to picture More sitting under this tree, a notebook on his lap, a pot of ink on the grass, writing *Utopia* on a summer's day such as this," Hardcastle said.

"Do you have a favorite More quote?" Cal asked.

"I do, actually. 'Love rules without rules.' Isn't that marvelous? You know, Professor, I had a quick butcher's around your curriculum vitae when I got word you'd be visiting today. We have four of your books in the library. I wonder if I could get you to sign them."

"I'd be delighted."

"So you're here about one of our long-departed staff, I understand."

"Charles Graves."

"We have his book in our collection, of course. It's more a labor of love than a work of scholarship, but we cherish it, nonetheless. Not many of our staff have been published. I'm not sure how helpful I can be. He died many years before I arrived at the seminary as a teacher."

"In 2004."

"I came in 2015, so, yes, well before my time."

"Do you know when he left the college?"

"My understanding is it was 2002, the same year his book on Lúcia dos Santos was published."

"I'm looking for something that might have been in his possession at the time he left Allen Hall. Is it possible any of his belongings have remained here?"

"Personal items? My goodness, I very much doubt it. That's something that has never happened during my tenure, and I rather doubt it happened in the past, especially upon one's retirement. Retirees take their things with them. I imagine he would have done the same."

"Do you know where he spent his final years?"

"No idea, I'm afraid."

"Are there any current staff who would have been here when Father Graves was here?"

"No, no, we're all new boys, as it were."

Cal was losing hope. "Do you retain personnel records of your past staff?"

"We do, but I don't think I could possibly give you access.

Privacy issues, you know. The diocese has strict rules, as you can imagine."

"What would it take to get me permission?"

The rector laughed nervously. "I suppose the pope could have a word with Westminster Palace, and Cardinal Kincaid could have a word with me."

Cal scooped out his phone and placed a call.

"You're joking," Hardcastle said.

"I'm not."

Cal let him listen to his conversation with Elisabetta, and when he hung up, he said, "While we're waiting for this miracle of yours, let's sign those books."

Hardcastle's phone rang while Cal was admiring the library. The rector peeled away to the librarian's office, and through the open door, Cal heard him say, "Yes, Eminence," over and over. The young priest came back smiling, and not the least upset that Cal had pulled rank so spectacularly.

"I'm impressed, Professor. You certainly know people in high places, don't you? The older records are kept in the basement. I'll have Mrs. Gunderson, our bookkeeper, take you down."

The matronly woman retrieved the personnel records for Cal and hovered nearby, dramatically and frequently lifting her wristwatch to her face, sighing, and letting him know she really had to be leaving soon to collect her grandson from school. Charles Graves had been at Allen Hall for many years, the records were voluminous, and Cal was in no mood to be rushed.

"Why don't I just take these with me?" he said. "That way you can leave right away. I'll have them returned in the morning."

"Well, that won't be happening," she said.

"Give the rector a call and see what he says."

She returned, compliant but unbowed. "Be certain we get these back. These are personnel files!"

Cal took the folder to his hotel, the Draycott, a short walk down the King's Road. In his room, he collapsed into an easy chair to learn what he could about Father Graves. His file chronicled a twenty-six-year tenure at the college. He arrived at age thirty-four, having recently returned from a teaching ministry at a Catholic school in Brazil. His assessments as an educator were consistently good to stellar, year after year, with no disciplinary issues. A succession of senior lecturers and rectors noted that he was well-liked by students and colleagues, an all-around good fit for the college.

However, his career took a turn late in 2000. Notes began appearing in his file chronicling complaints about inappropriate behavior: mild at first, such as bawdy jokes told to students, and steadily more serious. Once, he missed one of his lectures, and when found in his rooms, he insisted, contrary to reality, that he had no Thursday morning classes. He sometimes wandered off after a meal in the refectory without taking his tray to the kitchen. He became increasingly tardy in marking student papers, and some of his red-ink comments were bizarre. One seminarian complained that Graves failed him on an assignment when the student, quite rightly, rejected the heretical ancient Gnostic notion that Jesus only appeared to be human but was not. Graves wrote in all caps, **NO! ALL PHYSICAL**

MATTER IS EVIL, AND IT IS UNTHINKABLE THAT THE SON OF GOD WOULD TAKE UPON HUMAN FLESH.

During 2001, his behavior deteriorated to the point where his rector, Reverend Jones, noted in his file that he was reducing his teaching load. A letter from a concerned colleague, Father Jacob George, to the rector described a profound personality change following Graves's pilgrimage to the Shrine of Fátima. The letter included the following: *While anyone would be moved by a visit to the holy shrine, Charles insists that the Virgin appeared to him at Fátima, and that She has continued to appear to him on his return to London. This, coupled with other odd behaviours, deeply worries me. Despite my status as Charles's closest friend at the seminary, he has brushed off my suggestions of seeing a doctor, but perhaps you might exert a greater influence.*

A note from the Reverend Jones, in the autumn of 2001, documented his decision to strip away all but one of Charles's classes because of "volatilities in his deportment," writing that a full withdrawal of teaching duties would, under school bylaws, require a forced retirement, a step the rector was unwilling to take at the time. The message to the staff and students would be that Charles would be devoting most of his energies to the book he had undertaken on the seer of Fátima. Cal found a letter dated October 31, 2001, from Jones to John Graves, Charles's brother, asking for help in dealing with issues of concern, namely a falloff in personal hygiene and grooming, and Charles's claims of being bombarded by apparitions.

Early in 2002, Graves's situation became grave. He had a seizure in the library and was taken to the hospital for evaluation. A brain scan revealed a tumor in one of his temporal lobes that was considered to be inoperable. He was given anti-epileptic medications and allowed to return to the college. According to copies of minutes, the college governors had a vigorous debate about what to do with him and finally opted to take away all teaching responsibilities, but they allowed him to remain in his rooms until he finished the last chapters in his book.

By March, the book was finished, and so was Graves. He filled out his retirement papers and left the school. The penultimate item in his file was a photo of a diminutive and frail-appearing priest with strangely jet-black hair, accepting a plaque from assembled colleagues. The last item was a brief death notice from 2004 clipped from a newspaper in Norwich—NORFOLK-BORN PRIEST AND EDUCATOR DEAD AT 62.

Cal had Reverend Hardcastle's card, and he rang him straight away to ask about the letter writer, Father Jacob George.

"Is he still alive?" Cal asked.

"Very much so," the rector replied. "He retired, oh, five years ago, and we keep in touch. Marvelous fellow. If you'd like to speak with him, I can give you his number. He lives in Brixton."

It was a mere six-minute train ride from Victoria Station to Brixton at the tail end of rush hour. The train was crowded enough that Cal had to straphang, rocking and swaying with the motion of the carriage. At the far end, Nino melted into the throng, facing away, watching Cal's reflection in the door to the next car.

The Prince Albert was a traditional pub, which hadn't

succumbed to gentrification. Jacob George had recommended they meet there because it was close to his flat. Cal had a look around the dim room, mostly filled with locals, and didn't spot a likely priest among them. He ordered a pint of bitter and found a table as far as possible from the jukebox.

Outside, Nino had a discreet peek through one of the windows, smoked a cigarette down, and testily flicked the butt into the street. He wanted a drink himself, but he was loath to risk going inside. He had shadowed Donovan in Portugal, Paris, and now London. He reckoned there was no one better at avoiding detection, but it was only a matter of time before he was made. What was it his employer had said? Two more days and that will be the end of it, one way or another.

Usually, when he spent so much time and effort tracking someone, that someone ended up dead. Murder wasn't part of his remit, but he had come to despise this professor. Nino came from nothing. He left school early. He got his education from the streets. He made good money when he was on the job, but work was sporadic and it was feast or famine. When he had money, he blew it on drugs and fleshpots, and he didn't put much away.

He'd done his research on Donovan. He was all over the internet. He was famous. He was rich. He was good-looking and always had beautiful women on his arm. Nino couldn't imagine the gilded life he had. The Palermo brothers, Donato and Augustu—he didn't have anything more than a professional relationship with them, but they had been good boys and because of this rich, famous guy, they were dead. He felt for the handle of the brand-new hammer weighing down the pouch of his sweatshirt, and he told himself that if given half the chance, he'd gladly bury it in Donovan's skull.

A stocky man with coal-black skin stepped into the pub. Cal spotted his clerical collar and waved him over. He had lively, sparkling eyes, and a casual manner.

"What can I get you, Father?"

"A red wine would be lovely." He was a Trinidadian, and spoke with a lilting island accent.

Cal delivered the glass and watched the priest take a pleasurable sip.

"Ah, lovely, that. So, you wish to know about my dear old friend, Charles. We were separated in age by, oh, I don't know, nearly two decades, but we got on so well, like a house on fire. I never thought I would have occasion to speak about him again. Your call was most unexpected. Why the interest, if I may ask?"

"He wrote a book about Lúcia dos Santos that's of interest to me."

"Yes, a lovely little book. So heartfelt, it was. He was convinced that, of all of his accomplishments, of all the minds he helped to educate, this book would be his legacy. The fact that an esteemed academic from Harvard University is interested would have made him so very, very pleased."

Cal drank some ale and said, "I suppose one of the unique aspects of the book is that Father Graves was one of the few Fátima writers who actually visited Sister Lúcia."

The priest nodded sagely. "Such a good point. He was overjoyed when he returned from Portugal following his audience with the Blessed Sister. Do you know how he got that audience?"

"I don't."

"One of our seminarians had a Portuguese father, a prominent chap, if I recall, an ambassador or some such thing, who pulled strings. Anyway, Charles said that Sister Lúcia had been most kind. At the time, no one knew he had experienced a seizure during the visit. He chose not to reveal that until some weeks later, when he had a fit witnessed by students and staff members. That is when the brain tumor was discovered."

"He wrote in an afterword," Cal said, "that Lúcia gave him, and I quote, a truly wonderful gift that he would treasure for the rest of his life."

"Yes, I remember reading that."

"Do you know what that gift was?"

The priest's forehead was heavily lined, and the folds deepened in thought. "I assumed then, and I assume now, that he was referring to the gift of her time, the gift of being in the presence of a holy woman."

"Not a physical gift? A memento of some kind?"

"I really have no way of knowing. I don't recall the mention of a physical gift, but perhaps I've forgotten."

"Did the two of you discuss Fátima?"

"We certainly did. After he visited the shrine, he was a devotee. I wasn't disinterested in the subject, but I wasn't on the same plane as Charles."

"I've learned that he began having visions of the Virgin Mary during his visit to Fátima."

"However did you learn of that?"

Cal didn't want to mention he had read the private letter Father George had written the rector. "I spoke to some people at the college."

"Yes, it was a matter of some concern, especially when these visions became frequent. We are in the business of miracles, Professor Donovan, so we don't dismiss these kinds of things out of hand, but once his brain tumor was discovered, a medical explanation for his apparitions became more plausible than a spiritual explanation."

"Did he talk about them, or did he try to keep them private?"

"Private? No! He was proud of them. He felt blessed to be a vessel to receive teachings from the Virgin Mary, and even Jesus! The administration of the college forbade him from speaking to the student body about them, but he would tell me about his most recent encounters in a state of high excitement."

"What were the nature of his…"

"Ha, you are struggling with what to call them. 'Visions' or 'hallucinations'?"

Cal smiled at the priest's perceptiveness. "I'll call them visions."

"If I recall, most of them were related in one way or another to Fátima. He had the notion that one of the peasant children, Francisco, was somehow living on through him. He told me that the Virgin once said to him that he reminded her of Francisco and that he possessed Francisco's deep devotion to her Immaculate Heart.

"She also told him that he would be going to heaven soon. Charles was very excited by this, and he showed me the passages from Sister Lúcia's memoirs where Mary had used precisely the same language referring to Francisco's impending death. My interpretation was that he was working on his book against a deadline of his own mortality. He had been given a diagnosis of an untreatable tumor that was going to take his life. His mind was a pressure cooker where hopes, dreams, and thoughts became manifest in the form of apparitions."

The jukebox went silent, and Cal was able to lean back to converse. "I'm sure you're right," he said. "Did he ever say that any of his visions involved the secrets of Fátima?"

"Indeed he did. He was much taken by the revelation of the Third Secret, you know. The Vatican announced it in the year 2000, I believe, and it was much on his mind. Time and again, the Virgin appeared to tell him that Pope John Paul the Second was the Holy Father in the Third Secret. You see, in Lúcia's apparition, the pope was killed, whereas John Paul was not."

"I'm aware of the discrepancy," Cal said.

"Of course you are. Silly me. Charles was quite cross at those who didn't believe that the secret was a prophecy of John Paul's assassination attempt. I say, it's my turn to buy a round. Another beer?"

Cal got up and snatched up the priest's empty wineglass. "Nonsense," he said with a grin. "The drinks are on me, Father."

When Cal returned to the table, Father George was stroking a stubbled cheek. "I've just remembered something—a manifestation, I'm sure, of how twisted his mental processes had become. These tumors of the brain are frightful things, are they not?"

"What was it?"

"He was banging on one day about his latest apparition. I think he had recently completed his book and sent it to his publisher. That would have made it shortly before he left the college. He said it involved the Fourth Secret of Fátima."

The jukebox had picked up again and Cal leaned forward so sharply he almost toppled his pint. "I'm sorry, what did you say?"

The priest lifted his voice above the music. "I said it involved the Fourth Secret of Fátima."

Cal felt his heart thumping against his sternum. "Can you remember exactly what he said?"

Father George was lounging in bathrobe and slippers in his college rooms when there was a banging on his door. Its urgency was his older colleague's calling card, and George opened the door for him.

"Charles, how are you tonight?"

The small man dressed in full clerical garb entered quickly and began pacing a tight circle in the center of the sitting room. George's nose crinkled at the indelicate smell of urine, a sign that his friend might have suffered a recent seizure.

"I'm well. I'm very well."

"Have you been taking your pills?"

"My pills? What pills are they?"

"For your fits. There's a white one you're to take once a day and little red ones you're to take three times a day."

"Yes, those. I suppose."

"We must work out a system to make sure you don't miss your doses. It's for your own good, you know."

"Yes, yes," he answered impatiently. "That's not why I came to see you. I came to tell you about my vision."

"A new one?"

"Yes, it just happened." Graves stopped talking and contorted his face while seemingly engaged in some sort of a private dialogue. "Did it just happen? I'm not sure when it happened, but, by God, it did happen."

"Why don't you sit down, old chap, and I'll make you a cup of tea. Would you like that?"

The tea had a calming effect. Graves had been sitting cross-legged, his foot fluttering at the ankle, and the tempo slowed as the tea disappeared.

"That's better," George said reassuringly. "Did you want to tell me about your apparition, then?"

Whenever Graves talked about his revelations, the wonder in his eyes made him seem more youthful, and the flush that came to his cheeks masked the sallowness of his illness. "Oh, it was miraculous. If only you could borrow my eyes and see what I have seen. I've been blessed, my friend, truly blessed. I know exactly how little Francisco Marto must have felt when he was in the presence of Our Lady all those years ago. Did I ever tell you that, on occasion, Our Lady confuses me with Francisco, calling me by his name rather than mine?"

"Yes, you've told me that."

"I gently correct her. I don't think she's offended by my impertinence, do you?"

"I very much doubt it."

"Francisco was small and dark. I am small and dark. Francisco was very pious. I am very pious. When I visited her last year, Sister Lúcia told me how much I reminded her of her little cousin. When I heard that, my heart soared."

"I'm sure it did. It's getting late, Charles. Your apparition?"

"Oh, yes. I was praying beside my bed. My knees are not

what they once were, and I was kneeling on a pillow. It would be better if I knelt on the hard floor to suffer for my sins—I know that, I do—but sometimes I am weak, and I was using a pillow. Suddenly, the air cooled around me and I saw a haze appear over my headboard. Then the haze cleared, and there she was, hovering over my bed, so white, so pure, so delicate. Her pulchritude overwhelms one. Did I ever tell you that?"

"You have mentioned it before, yes."

"She asked me if I have been praying the Rosary as she had demanded, and I told her I had been. Now that my book is finished and I have more time, I am able to pray the Rosary several times per day. She seemed pleased that I was obedient and she opened her palms to me. Shafts of light shot forth, penetrating my chest and producing a feeling of warmth and well-being."

Father George slurped his tea and told the priest he was happy for him.

"I thought the apparition would end there. Many times, they are quite brief. But not this one. Our Lady wasn't finished with me."

"Oh, no?"

"No. She told me that at Fátima, on the thirteenth day of July in the year of our Lord, 1917, Lúcia, Jacinta, and Francisco were given one more secret. There is a Fourth Secret of Fátima. Do you hear me, a Fourth Secret!"

"That's really something, Charles. My goodness. Did she tell you what it was?"

The teacup rattled on its saucer, and George took it from Graves's shaking hand.

"She did tell me, Charles."

"And what was it?"

"But I can't tell you, dear friend!"

"Why not?"

"Because she said it was a great secret, the greatest secret of them all, and I must never tell a soul. Can you imagine? There are only two living souls who know the Fourth Secret of Fátima: Sister Lúcia and me. My heart is bursting with the awe of its message and the joy of being chosen."

George got up and reached over to pull the small man to his feet. "Well, you must do as you were commanded, Charles. Now let me take you back to your rooms. Look at the time!"

Cal could barely contain himself as he listened through the blare of the jukebox to Father George's account of that night. The priest signified he was finished by picking up his glass and quaffing the rest of it, smiling across the table, and becoming quiet.

"Did he ever mention a Fourth Secret again?"

"That was the one and only time, Professor. I believe he left the college shortly thereafter."

"Not by choice."

"No, reluctantly. It was difficult for Charles to face the facts. The college was his life, you know. They treated him well, anyone would tell you. My goodness, they waited for him to finish his book before forcing his hand."

Cal asked a question he desperately hoped would bear fruit. "When he left, did he give you any keepsakes?"

"I don't believe so."

"Would he have taken all his possessions with him?"

"Undoubtedly. The college provides as many cardboard boxes as one requires for the clear-out. I had so many I had to hire a removals company! One accumulates, doesn't one?"

"Do you know where he went?"

"I do. It was a care home near Norwich—not far from where he was born, I believe. I visited him there once, probably the year he died."

"In 2004."

"Yes, it must have been 2004. I took the train. It wasn't the most salubrious of homes, but it was comfortable enough. I think I might have been a little surprised that the place was run-down and shabby, because I'd been led to believe that Charles's brother was wealthy. You know, we retired priests are largely on our own. I, myself, have very basic retirement accommodations nearby."

"Do you know his brother's name?"

"Afraid not. I must say, I don't like coming to the pub on my own, and I rarely have visitors, so this is a treat."

"For me too," Cal said quickly. "What was the name of the care home?"

George tapped his head with a long finger. "The name, the name. Something with 'heath' or 'heather' in it."

Cal did a phone search for facilities in Norfolk. "Is it Heather Grove?"

"Yes, indeed! Heather Grove."

"Father, it was a pleasure meeting you. This was extremely helpful. I've got to be getting back to my hotel now. Can I get you a taxi?'

"No, no, it's only around the corner. It was lovely meeting

you, and it did my heart good to speak about my old friend. Now that I'm here, I think I'll stay for another glass of wine."

Cal shook his hand warmly and said, "I'll have the barman bring one over."

The evening was warm and breezy, and Cal started fast-walking down Coldharbour Lane toward Brixton station with his phone to his ear.

Elisabetta answered her office line and asked how he was doing.

"I'm doing better than expected," he said.

"What do you mean?"

"Charles Graves is the missing link. He knew about the Fourth Secret. I'm going to Norfolk in the morning. The clock is winding down, but we're not out of time yet."

Nino was following Cal from Victoria Station to his hotel when his burner phone vibrated in his pocket. Only his employer had the number.

Nino grunted a "Yes?"

"Donovan is going to be on the ten-oh-five train tomorrow morning from Liverpool Street station to Norwich. Don't lose him. He's getting close."

15

The rain was beating down, and rivulets of water ran in diagonal streaks across the windows of the speeding train. The low, gray light washed the color from the landscape, and the countryside of farmland and pastures was a dispiriting monochrome. Cal usually enjoyed train travel—the pleasant jostling of the carriages, the hypnotic sound of wheels on tracks, the conduciveness to reading, but he took no pleasure in it this morning. All he could do during the journey to Norwich was stare into a vista that matched his mood, and brood on the collapsing timeline.

When he stepped on the train at Liverpool Street station, there were twenty-five hours until the Mass began. When he arrived at Norwich, there would be twenty-three hours. He was punctual—professors who taught tended not to be casual about time—although he was never compulsive. This day demanded an obsessional level of clock-watching.

He hopped off the train at Norwich with nothing but a shoulder bag. He had left his rolling bag at the hotel, with a

238

plan to return to London on an afternoon or evening train. The care home was twenty-five miles from the city, and he had a car booked. The hire company was a taxi ride away. On arrival, a royal-blue BMW 1 series was gassed and waiting, but the clerk insisted on getting Cal's seal of approval before doing the paperwork. Cal obliged, opened his umbrella against the downpour, said the car was fine, and went back inside to complete the transaction.

Nino didn't use umbrellas. It was one of his many prejudices. A fellow he knew in his game had been assassinated by someone who came at him from the side. The umbrella had blocked his peripheral vision, or so it was said. Nino's answer to the rain was a hoodie. He didn't mind getting wet—it was a warm rain anyway. He liked to keep things simple. The tools of his trade were few. Most important was his smartphone. He didn't use it for calls while on a job but to research his targets. Another was his supremely low-tech hammer. The last was his GPS tracker, a small marvel perfect for a day such as this. It was a "slap-and-track" unit with a three-month battery and a smartphone app. Planting it took no time. When Cal was in the office, Nino paid his taxi driver, found a scoop in the rear bumper of the BMW that hid the device nicely, and went for a cigarette under an overhang around the building.

When Cal had his car keys, he entered the address of the care home into the BMW's satnav and took off, wipers beating on full. Unhurried, Nino finished his smoke and sauntered into the office.

"I need a car."

"Do you have a reservation?"

"No."

"Never mind. We can probably accommodate you. What type of vehicle?"

"You have vans?" He didn't know if he'd need one, but vans were handy for bodies.

"We do."

He produced a false Italian driver's license with a corresponding false passport and paid with a credit card he used when he couldn't pay in cash. It was linked to a Corsican entity buried under an impenetrable mound of shell companies in tax havens. Nothing was completely safe, but he never lost sleep using that card.

Cal had a half hour's head start on him by the time Nino rolled out of the lot in a Ford Transit van, but the signal from the BMW was transmitting strongly. He ignored the NO SMOKING signs plastered all over the dash, lit up, and began following the red triangle on his screen.

The Heather Grove Care Home began its existence as a substantial mid-nineteenth-century private residence in the village of Costessey. By the 1940s, the property had fallen into disrepair, at which time it was purchased by a local man who had served during the war as an army medic, with the idea of turning it into a care home. It had remained in his family since.

Cal found it without any bother and pulled into the gravel forecourt. The rain was letting up, but the trees and bushes were still dripping and drooping, and the downspouts of the building were gushing.

He immediately saw why Father George had complained about the place being a disappointment as final accommodations for his friend. The stucco was bare in places where chunks had dislodged, and it looked like it hadn't seen a coat of paint in decades. The slate roof was coated by an inch of slimy moss, the landscaping around the house was the living version of threadbare, and the lawn was overgrown in some spots and bald in others.

Cal rang the bell and waited until a middle-aged woman in a pink smock answered.

"Is Mr. Entwistle in?"

"Are you expected?"

"I left a message I'd be coming."

"Do you have a loved one here?"

"No, I don't. Is he here?"

She took his name and left him in the hall. He had a look into the lounge, where residents sat in chairs or wheelchairs, watching an ironic TV show, about fixing up properties. The dining area was off the lounge, where a different woman in a pink smock was clearing the tables. The smell of cooked beef and veg hung in the air.

The owner appeared with an annoyed look plastered on his pasty face. He was in his fifties, with a bulbous nose and a generous paunch that bulged beneath his butter-colored shirt and lime necktie. He possessed one of the more ill-fitting and obvious toupees Cal had ever seen.

"I'm Peter Entwistle," he said.

"Pleased to meet you. Cal Donovan. I left you a voicemail last night."

"Yes, I listened to it this morning. If we had spoken, I would have advised you not to make the journey, Mr. Donovan. You see, I know nothing of the former resident. Mr. Groves, was it?"

"Graves."

"I see."

"As I mentioned, he passed away eighteen years ago."

"Before my time, you see."

"Are there any present staff or residents who were here when he died?"

Entwistle let out a wet guffaw. "You must be joking. The residents completely turn over every ten years or so, and I'm lucky if I can get aides to stay with me half as long. So, no, I won't be able to help you with your inquiries."

An elderly woman approached from the lounge on a cane and began accosting the owner about a dripping tap in her room that was driving her batty.

"I said we'd sort it, Mrs. Davis, and we will. The plumber has been remiss in getting back to me."

When the old woman retreated, Cal said, "Do you think we could talk somewhere private? I've come all the way from London, and it's really very important."

Entwistle's office was untidy, with a view over the parking area. The dilapidation of the old house extended to his water-stained walls. He settled behind his desk and said, "I really don't know what more I can tell you."

"It's vital that I speak to someone who knew Charles Graves back in the day."

"As I said as clearly as I know how, no one presently at Heather Grove was at Heather Grove two decades ago." Entwistle's tone was nasal and officious.

Cal kept his cool. "Do you retain records of past residents?"

"Only for the statutory time period, which in this case is long past. His file was undoubtedly destroyed."

Cal asked what he hoped would be a persuasive question. "You don't happen to be Catholic, do you?"

"Whyever would you ask that? I'm C of E, as it happens, but what does my religion have to do with it?"

"I'm working on an assignment from the Vatican. I just thought—"

"I've no interest in papist affairs. None whatsoever."

Cal kept working on his temper. "Could I ask who was running the home eighteen years ago?"

"It was my father, RP Entwistle."

"Is he alive?"

"Very much so."

"Could I talk with him?"

"You may not. He's retired and enjoying being retired. This is my shop now, and I have a busy schedule. So good day to you."

Cal had been relying on the Vatican opening doors for him, but the pope's card wasn't accepted on these premises. "What if I made a donation to Heather Grove? It looks like you've got some deferred maintenance issues."

Entwistle's puzzled expression belied the inner conflict of a man whose pomposity wanted to have him say, *Get out immediately*, but whose financial desperation wanted to make him ask, *How much?* "What kind of a donation are you suggesting?" he said.

"How about five thousand pounds?"

The owner licked his lips. "What would we have to do?"

"Just let me talk to your father and any other past employees who might remember Father Graves."

Entwistle drummed his fingers and got down to brass tacks. "What form would this donation take? I don't know you from Adam. A check takes days to clear."

"Give me wiring instructions, and I'll do it right now from my phone."

"It appears we have an agreement," the owner said. "I suppose I'd better make sure my father is available. It's today you need, presumably."

Cal nodded. "As soon as possible."

The owner reached the senior Entwistle, and from the one side of the conversation he could hear, Cal gleaned that it was like father, like son. He seemed to want nothing to do with outside inquiries concerning the past. That is, until the donation was mentioned, and the phone was handed across the desk.

Cal repeated his interest in Graves and asked whether the man remembered him.

"Graves? The old priest? Of course I remember him. He wasn't with us long, but he was a handful."

"Can we meet to talk about your recollections?" Cal asked.

"I've got an appointment with my GP this afternoon. I can't miss that. It took ages to get it. I can see you at four at Heather Grove."

"Is there any way it could be sooner?"

"There is not. If you're spinning your wheels, why don't you go to Our Lady and Saint Walstan's Church and see if Father Ashton is about? He'll remember Charles Graves, all right."

The church was in the village of Costessey, set back from the road behind a brick and rubble-stone wall. A graveyard occupied a portion of its holdings. It was nothing but a co-incidence that the unpretentious Gothic revival building was erected in the nineteenth century, in almost the same year as Heather Grove.

Cal parked and entered the church. Although the rain had stopped, the sky was still as gray as smoke, but despite the dull ambience, the sanctuary seemed bright and cheerful. The stained-glass windows were done in vivid primary colors, and the paneling behind the altar and the pew kneelers was a matching bright blue.

It was deserted, but a woman soon appeared with a carpet sweeper, and, upon seeing Cal, said she'd come back so as not to disturb him.

"I was looking for Father Ashton, actually."

"I believe he's in the presbytery. Just go outside and around to the back. There's a bell."

Father Ashton was a florid, heavyset man in his late sixties, who was wearing an off-duty secular outfit of khakis and a checked short-sleeved shirt. Cal explained that RP Entwistle had suggested he talk with him, and when the mention of Entwistle evoked a certain sourness, Cal played his stronger cards: the Vatican and his Harvard professorship. The priest's demeanor changed, and Cal was invited in for tea.

"Small East Anglian villages don't often receive emissaries from the pope," he said, putting the kettle on. "How can I possibly help you?"

"It's about a former resident of the Heather Grove Care Home, Father Charles Graves."

"Gosh," the priest said, "that's someone I haven't thought about for a while. Charles Graves, that poor, dear man. He met a tragic end. Brain tumor, it was."

"Did you minister to him there?"

"Yes, I did. I call on Heather Grove, providing they have Catholic residents who wish to have my attention. It's not a large facility, perhaps a census of thirty souls these days. Sometimes there are a handful of Catholics. Sometimes, as now, there are none. Charles Graves was the only priest during my years, and that made him stand out, as you can imagine. One's heart goes out to a fellow clergyman who's fallen on difficult times."

"You got to know him well?"

"Quite well, although he was only there for two years or so before he passed. We enjoyed our chats. I took him for a tour of Saint Walstan's one day. He couldn't really come to Mass, owing to his condition. He had frequent fits, some incontinence, if I recall, and he was given to bouts of disruptive behavior that would have been difficult for our parishioners. He liked the church a great deal, particularly because an eleventh-century East Anglian noblewoman from nearby Walsingham, Richeldis de Faverches, had a Marian vision and was henceforth known as Our Lady of Walsingham. This church is dedicated to her, and to a local saint, Saint Walstan."

"I can see the attraction," Cal said. "Graves was well versed in Marian visions."

"Fátima," Ashton said. "Yes, I know. He gave me a copy of his book."

"Did he give you anything else of his?"

"No, why do you ask?"

"Because I'm looking for a document that once belonged to Sister Lúcia dos Santos that she might have given him."

"I see! The Blessed Sister. I'll be watching her canonization tomorrow on the EWTN channel. Very much looking forward to it. Ever since meeting Charles, I've had an interest in Fátima. The shrine is on my bucket list."

"Did you frequently talk about Fátima with him?"

"Frequently? I don't know about that, but we did have our discussions. He had some...well, unorthodox views."

"What can you tell me about that?"

The priest added splashes of milk and said, "Here's your tea. You can sugar it yourself. Why don't we go to the lounge? I'll tell you about the one I remember best. It was only a few days before he died."

Charles Graves had been wheelchair-bound since an accident a fortnight earlier when he suffered a seizure in his room, fell hard, and broke his hip. He would need a hip replacement if he lived long enough, but for now, a few surgical pins would have to suffice. Father Ashton came to Heather Grove as lunch was winding down. He sat with Graves as he shakily spooned up the last of his pudding and then wheeled him back to his room, where they would pray together.

"How's the leg?" Ashton asked. "Much pain?"

Charles was drooping at an angle, as if he might pitch forward out of the wheelchair. "It was howling for a time, but now it only barks occasionally."

"Lovely imagery, Charles. Coming from a writer, I'm not surprised."

Charles looked toward his bookcase and said, "Did I ever show you the book I've written?"

Father Ashton gently clucked. "You were good enough to give me a copy. As I've told you, I greatly enjoyed it."

"Oh! You've read it. Marvelous. Did I ever tell you I spent a day with Sister Lúcia?"

"I believe you did."

"An exceedingly holy woman, she is. Must be getting on in years."

"Yes, I imagine she is."

"I was fortunate to have visited with her in the aftermath of Pope John Paul II's revelation of the Third Secret of Fátima."

"Did you discuss it with her?"

Charles frowned so deeply his lips nearly touched his nose. "You know, I don't recall. Imagine not recalling something like that! Let me check in my book. Could you fetch it for me? And my readers."

Ashton found the slim volume in the bookcase and patiently waited while Charles painstakingly searched it.

Putting the book aside, Charles said, "I can't find a passage that references a discussion between the two of us about the Third Secret. However, I do have a firm recollection that I told her about my own experiences with the Holy Virgin."

"Yes, your visions certainly leave an impression. Are you still having them, I wonder?"

Charles opened his crusted eyelids wide and said, "I had one not long ago. Was it this morning? No, not then. Perhaps it was yesterday. Yes, definitely yesterday, Father. The Virgin appeared just there, where you are sitting, and told me there was a Fourth Secret. No, she did more than tell me it existed, she told me what it was."

"And what was it?"

"Now, now, Father, you know I'm not allowed to divulge that."

"Are you not?"

"It is a great secret, one of the greatest known to mankind. Sister Lúcia knows it, and she is not allowed to tell. I know it too, and I am likewise constrained. She and I will take it to our graves."

"Well, Charles, you are in privileged company. Would you care to pray with me?"

"The Rosary," Charles said, fumbling for his beads. "The Virgin always exhorts me to pray the Rosary."

Father Ashton offered another biscuit, and Cal didn't refuse it. He hadn't eaten since breakfast.

"That was the last time I saw him. He was taken shortly thereafter."

"What did you make of his claims about a Fourth Secret?"

"I don't know, really. He was, in a way, fixated on the secrets of Fátima. He did have a brain tumor. In any investigations into miracles, I first look toward temporal explanations. What do you think, Professor?"

"I think Sister Lúcia may have given him a document, a very important text. In his book, he described it as a wonderful gift."

"And that's why you asked if Charles ever passed something along to me?"

"That's right."

"Unfortunately not. Why don't you ask Charles yourself?"

Cal wasn't easily confused, but his look of bewilderment amused the priest.

"He's buried in our cemetery. Come, I'll show you his grave."

The graveyard wasn't ancient by British standards. The oldest plots dated to the 1850s. At the section that Father Ashton described as the modern bit, a simple stone marked the final resting place of Father Charles Graves, 1941–2004, with an inscription Charles had hand-picked for himself from John of Damascus: DEVOTION TO YOU, O BLESSED VIRGIN, IS A MEANS OF SALVATION WHICH GOD GIVES TO THOSE WHOM HE WISHES TO SAVE.

"I'll leave you now, Professor," the priest said. "I do hope you find what you are looking for."

An oak tree rustled overhead, and a squirrel chattered noisily.

Cal whispered to the grave, "Come on, Charles. Tell me what you did with it."

⊙────╫────⊙

Cal returned to the care home at four and found the two Entwistles in the office, discussing, presumably, whether the wire transfer had gone through. Entwistle the younger declared that it had.

RP Entwistle demonstrated what his son would look like in thirty years or so. Provided the younger Entwistle gave up his toupee, he would have the same enormous bald dome as his father, and the same large nose, subsided by time as if the cartilage had gone soft, and his paunch would greatly expand, turning his gait into a wobble.

There was a raspy gruffness to the older man's voice and a curt manner that seemed to be born of some exaggerated view of his importance. "Did you see the padre?"

"I saw Father Ashton, yes."

"Then you probably had all your queries answered. You don't still need me, do you?"

"I have a few questions."

"Five thousand quid's worth?"

Cal smiled. "Let's find out, shall we?"

The old fellow unceremoniously kicked his son out of his office and assumed the spot behind the desk that had once been his. "What do you want to know about that crazy old priest?"

"Why do you say he was crazy?"

"Because he was always causing a ruckus amongst the other residents, banging on about having visions of the Virgin Mary, Jesus, and probably half the characters in the New Testament. I was always fielding phone calls from the families whose relations were upset about his religious spewings."

"The man was a priest."

"He surely was, but this is not a religious establishment. Furthermore, we don't get all that many Catholics here. We Protestants don't get overexcited the way they do."

"Yes, we can get overheated, can't we?"

"No offense," Entwistle said.

"None taken," Cal lied. "When he died, what happened to his personal possessions?"

"I've no idea."

"What usually happens in this situation? I imagine that deaths occur with some frequency in care homes."

"Folks have wills. Possessions are bequeathed."

"Did Charles Graves have a will?"

"I doubt that very much, and I'll tell you why. The man was a priest, and priests are generally as poor as church mice. I was in his room on multiple occasions, owing to his medical problems—the fits and the like. We often had the ambulance around. He had nothing, really. His closet was mostly empty. He wore the same shabby things every day. Some books, a crucifix on the wall, a photo of a nun, I think."

"Sister Lúcia," Cal said. "Do you know what happened to the photo?"

"Likely binned. No one wants personal photos."

"And the books?"

"No clue, but I wouldn't, would I? I was in Spain on holiday when he passed. By the time I returned, there was a new resident in his room."

"Who would have been in charge when you were away? Your son?"

"He wasn't in the business then. He had a succession of useless jobs in those days. I had an assistant manageress. They can't afford one anymore. Too many health and safety regulations eating into the bottom line. Mrs. O'Hara. She was as Irish as you get. The residents liked her accent for some reason."

"Where is she now?"

"She moved up north—Durham, I think—to be with her people."

"Do you know how to reach her?"

"Tom might have it filed away somewhere. I'll have to get him." He groaned himself to his feet and went in search of his son, leaving Cal in helpless contemplation of the shrinking timeline. The Fourth Secret was slipping out of reach, and there was precious little he could do about it.

The old fellow returned with Entwistle Junior, who began spinning a Rolodex on his credenza. This was, Cal thought, a decidedly analog operation. As Entwistle worked through the stuffed wheel, his father told him that Donovan wanted to know what happened to Graves's books when he died.

"I know what happened to them," the son declared. "They were absorbed into our reading room."

"How do you know that?" his father asked.

"Because a while back, I came across his bookplate in a paperback," he said. "Do you still want O'Hara's info?"

Cal had perked up at the news, and said, "I might as well get her number if you have it. And I'd like to see your reading room."

Entwistle Senior snorted. "For five grand, you can take a few books with you."

"One more question," Cal said. "Did Graves have many visitors?"

"Not many," the old man said, zipping his windbreaker in anticipation of leaving. "A priest from London came once, I think, a Black fellow. And he had a brother named John Graves, a Norfolk man, whom I called whenever he had to go into hospital. He visited from time to time, but not often. Now, then, are we done?"

There were only a few hundred books in the Heather Grove reading room, but Cal had no choice but to pull each one out and look for the Graves bookplate. He finally found one, a paperback copy of *The Ecclesiastical History of the English People* by the Venerable Bede, with a bookplate of a lithograph of Westminster Cathedral marked Ex Libris Fr. Charles Graves.

The small library was off the lounge, and at five o'clock, a steady stream of residents filed through, sniffing the air and chattering about the shepherd's pie in the offing. By five thirty, Cal was done and dejected. The stack of twenty-one worn paperbacks that he had set aside was the sad legacy of Charles Graves. There were history books and novels (Graham Greene, mostly) and two copies of Graves's own book.

That was it. Cal was done. There was a seven o'clock train back to London. He'd see if he could get on a morning flight to Boston. Whatever would happen at the Mass would happen.

He returned the books to the shelves and, as an afterthought, called the number he'd been given for Mrs. O'Hara. It was the last stone left, and he'd be remiss not to turn it over.

She certainly did have a broad Irish accent. He explained himself to the amiable woman, who needed little encouragement to enter into conversation.

"RP gave you my number, did he? How is the old scoundrel?"

"He seems hale and hearty," Cal said.

"Has his son, Tom, run the place into the ground yet?"

"It's a little worn around the edges, but it's still standing."

"Well, that's fine. I have fond thoughts. Mostly. It's Father Graves you're wanting to know about, eh? He was a gentleman. It was lovely having a priest about. I was his favorite—probably because I was a religious woman and I prayed the Rosary. He did love his Rosary."

"I'm trying to find out if, after he died, any of his personal possessions found their way to you or anyone else."

"The answer is yes. RP was away when Father Graves passed, so I was the one who dealt with these matters. Would you like to hear about it?"

⊙═━═⊙

Mrs. O'Hara, a statuesque woman with a splendid head of wavy black hair, answered the nighttime bell and greeted John and Ann Graves, who had driven down from Great Melton in their Land Rover.

"Is he still with us?" John asked. It was near to midnight, but the man had still felt compelled to put on a suit and tie.

"He is. He's clinging on," O'Hara said. "Are you sure you don't want the doctor called?"

"It's what we discussed. I haven't changed my mind. Has he?"

"No, I believe he's ready for his Maker," O'Hara said.

"Well, then, there you have it. I suppose I'd better go to his room. Ann, do you want to come with?"

She said no, that she'd wait in the lounge.

In the wan yellow light of a single lamp, John and the assistant manager entered his room to find Charles breathing heavily, nearly upright in bed, bolstered by three pillows. His rosary beads were coiled around his knuckles. He managed to turn at O'Hara's announcement that his brother was here.

In the weakest of voices, he said, "John?"

John approached the bed, with Mrs. O'Hara carrying the chair over from the desk.

"Yes, Charles. I was called to come because you were poorly."

255

"I am. Poorly," he gasped. "It's my time."

"So I understand. Are you in any pain?"

"No pain."

"Is there anything I can do for you?"

"Do? You can pray with me."

"You know I don't go in for that," John said stiffly.

O'Hara went to his bedside and took his frail hand. "I'll pray with you, Father."

John withdrew to give her the chair and stood by the window, brooding into the darkness.

In unison, Charles and O'Hara said, "Our Father, who art in heaven, hallowed be thy name. Thy kingdom come, thy will be done, on earth as it is in heaven."

By the time they finished, Charles's grip had weakened.

"You've lived a good life, Father," she said. "You are a good man."

"Yes, a good life," he whispered. "I have but one regret."

From across the room, his brother, suddenly interested, asked, "What regret is that, Charles?"

"That I couldn't live to see the final prophecy of Fátima fulfilled. I would have—" And in midsentence, he was gone.

O'Hara wiped away a tear, smoothed the bedclothes around him, and told his brother that she had to call the coroner per their protocol.

"To save you the trip," she said, "why don't you see if you want to take any of Father's things with you? I'll let your missus know he's gone."

When she returned, she found John with a stack of books he'd placed on the desk.

"I'll have the hardbacks," John said. "I collect books. Nothing special here, but, well, there's sentimentality, I suppose."

"You sure you want nothing else? His clothes, personal effects?"

"Had a look. It's all rubbish. Bin the lot of it, I'd say."

"Do you want the picture of Sister Lúcia? Father spoke of her often."

"You have it, if you want it. It's rather late. If we're done here, I'll be going."

"So I took the picture, and John Graves took the books."

At this point, Cal's hand was clamped down on the phone. "Do you still have the picture?"

"I do. It has pride of place in my parlor."

"Can you do me a favor? Can you check the frame and backing to see if there's anything that Charles might have kept hidden there?"

She was cheerfully amenable and disappeared for a few minutes.

"Nothing. Just a photo in a thin black frame," she said. "It's not even signed, you know. But just having something that belonged to that dear man is a treasure."

Cal was on the road again, but it wasn't the road to Norwich. His phone chimed when Elisabetta returned his voicemail.

"I was in our last security meeting before tomorrow," she said.

"Was Studer there?"

"Of course."

"He thinks I'm back in Boston, right?"

"I assume so. That's what Emilio told him. I didn't wish to participate in a lie. Did you find anything?"

"Not yet."

"I'm afraid we're out of time, Cal."

"Not until tomorrow morning at ten. I've just learned that Charles Graves's brother took a bunch of his books when he died. He's agreed to let me see them. I'm on my way now. It's not far. I've got a feeling this is it, Eli. I've got a feeling we're getting close."

16

Coimbra, 2004

His favorite library, bar none, was Biblioteca Joanina, and he took the opportunity of stopping in whenever he was in Coimbra. As a university student in Lisbon, he had developed an interest in the mystical works of the sixteenth-century writer António Gonçalves de Bandarra, and he first traveled to Coimbra to examine one of Joanina's precious texts, an early copy of Bandarra's ballads. When he recently learned he was being sent to Coimbra on assignment, he rang the head librarian and asked to see the book again, and a viewing was arranged.

Contentment coursed through his body as he sat in the ornate gilded reading room with the old leather book before him. High above his head, a single bat, which hadn't yet settled in for its daytime rest, fluttered and swooped. *What a wonder this place is! One could happily spend all one's days here among the books, the painted wood, the bats.* He donned white cotton gloves and paged through the ballads, settling on passages he had included in the thesis that had earned him high honors.

After the happiest of hours, he returned the book and took a taxi across town.

Before becoming a priest, he had never been sure where he belonged in this world. His bloodline was aristocratic, tracing back centuries to feudal Portugal, where powerful families with fealty to the crown ruled the countryside. His grandfather and father had fared well during the autocratic New State rule of Prime Minister António de Oliveira Salazar. The politics of his family were in complete alignment with the Salazar government—conservative, nationalist, anti-communist—and their businesses fared well during Salazar's four decades in charge.

Then came Salazar's death and the 1974 Carnation Revolution that swept away the old guard in favor of a new, liberal democracy. The family holdings were nationalized, and they lost everything. His father shot himself while the future priest was in university, but far from being devastated, he felt liberated. He was now free to pursue his own path in life, unshackled from obligations of going into business or law. He pondered academia, although his observation of departmental politics convinced him that he didn't have the stomach for clawing himself up the ladder. Besides, he had been imbued with right-leaning philosophy since youth, and he would have been a fish out of water on a university campus in the new Portugal.

The priesthood presented itself as an option by process of elimination. His family were devout, and the rituals and teachings of the Church had always given satisfaction. For him, celibacy and sacrifice were not problematic. He was uninterested in women, and, likewise, was uninterested in men. His apathy went beyond sexuality; he didn't care for people all that much. He preferred ideas and books, art and music. Not every priest had to minister to a flock, and not every priest had to aspire to advancement through the hierarchy.

He felt there would be a place for him within the Church, and he was proven correct. After ordination, he applied for a posting to Rome. Performing unpressured research in John Paul II's anti-communist Vatican fit him to a tee. Now, on the cusp of middle age, he was satisfied with his life. What more could one want?

The reason for his visit to Coimbra was delicate, and he planned to dance around its true purpose. Sister Lúcia's condition was being monitored inside the Vatican, and John Paul II, her great patron, demanded frequent updates. She was ninety-six and in failing health. Her heart was weakening, her sight failing, and her hearing diminishing. It was apparent that the clock of her existence was winding down, and that the end was coming soon.

The Mother Superior of the Convent of Santa Teresa, Sister Madalena, sat behind her desk and declined his invitation to dance. The stern, no-nonsense woman demanded to know the reason for his visit.

"The Holy Father and others are concerned about the dear sister. They wanted a firsthand report. I am Portuguese, I know the area, they sent me."

"They only had to ask me. I am perfectly capable of giving them information concerning her health."

"Undoubtedly. Well, you know of the Holy Father's fondness for Lúcia. I am certain that if his own health were better, he would have made his own pilgrimage to her bedside. I was asked to come, and, well, here I am."

She looked over her reading glasses and said, "Why did you decline to sign the visitors' book?"

"The Vatican does not wish there to be a record of my visit. It might appear unseemly."

In a flinty voice sharp enough to slice flesh, the nun said, "Lúcia is unwell. Perhaps too unwell to see you. If your purpose for this visit is not persuasive, I am within my rights to turn you away."

Confrontation made the meek priest wobbly, but it would be difficult to return to Rome empty-handed. "Your bishop would be displeased. He participated in the decision for me to come."

"I can handle the bishop."

"Very well, Sister. Let me be frank. There are certain truisms at play. The first is that Lúcia's days are surely numbered. The second is that she has lived a remarkably holy life. And the third is that the opening of a cause for her beatification one day is inevitable. As you know, her cousins Jacinta and Francisco were beatified in 2000. With that in mind, I have been sent to perform a final interview to set the stage for a future process."

The old nun sucked in her cheeks. "All this nonsense. I give thanks to God every day that I live a cloistered life of devotion, devoid of the bureaucracies of the diocese and the Vatican. This woman, Lúcia dos Santos, is saintly. Every aspect of her life has been holy and flawless. There is not a shred of doubt she will be declared a saint. Mother Mary chose Lúcia as her instrument. Why is it necessary to jump over all these hurdles? I am a simple woman. I don't pretend to understand."

The priest opted for patient explanation. "While I agree that her eventual canonization is probably a foregone conclusion, there are inviolate procedures that must be followed. Upon her death, the bishop with jurisdiction, in this case the bishop of Fátima-Leiria, would give his assent to open an investigation as to the virtues of the sister. Usually, this phase cannot commence until five years have passed. However, Pope John Paul or his successor could waive the waiting period. Her case is extraordinary enough that I would not be the least surprised if that were to occur.

"What follows would be an examination of her writings. A detailed biography would be composed. Eyewitness accounts would be collected. The bishop would then present his findings to the Congregation for the Causes of the Saints, and, at that stage, Lúcia would be designated as a Servant of God. At some point, her body would be exhumed and examined for signs of nondecay and incorruptibility.

"When sufficient evidence has been collected, the Congregation would recommend to the pope that he proclaim her heroic in virtue, entitled to be called a Venerable. To achieve beatification, proof would be required of the occurrence of a miracle of healing through the intercession of the Venerable.

"Once satisfied, the Venerable would be bestowed the title of Blessed. To be canonized as a saint, at least two miracles must have been performed through the intercession of the Blessed after their death. Assuming all these things occur, one day, a future Holy Father will conduct a canonization Mass, and Sister Lúcia will become a saint."

Sister Madalena rose to show him the door. "To me, this woman is already a saint."

The priest was escorted to Lúcia's room, where a young African nun, Sister Ana, was tending her. The afternoon sun struck the windows in such a way that the half of the room where her desk stood was blazing in light, and the half with her bed was in deep shadow.

"This priest is here to see Lúcia," the Mother Superior said. "I hope he will not tire her before her supper."

Sister Ana surrendered her bedside chair and told him she would be within earshot of the small brass bell, should she be needed.

"You will need to speak loudly," she said. "And if you smell something bad, summon me quickly."

She was at the door when he asked, "Is she...all there?"

"All there?"

"Mentally acute."

"Sometimes yes, sometimes less so. The doctor says her brain sometimes wants more oxygen than her heart can provide. We tried an oxygen tank, but she didn't like the mask or the little prongs."

The priest approached the bed tenuously. He could hardly tell that someone was there among the pile of blankets and pillows. As Lúcia's heart problems had progressed, it was impossible for her to lie flat without fluid accumulating in her lungs, so a carpenter had built a padded incline that kept her head above her heart at all times.

When his eyes acclimatized to the shadows, he saw she was wearing some sort of knitted bonnet. She was lying so still that he thought she might be asleep, but then he realized her eyes were open wide.

"Hello, Sister," he said. "Am I disturbing you?"

When she failed to respond, he remembered the young nun's advice and spoke much louder.

"Who is that?" she answered, turning her neck. Speaking was difficult—breathy sounds mixed with faint vocalizations—and the priest had to lean over, bringing his ear within inches of her lips.

"I am a priest sent from the Vatican."

"Oh! A priest."

"Yes, Sister."

She said, "Let me have your hand."

He let her explore it.

"Smooth hands. You haven't worked on a farm."

"You're right, Sister. I never did. I work at a desk. In the Vatican."

"Oh. You must know the Holy Father."

"I see him often. I have met him personally only one time. That was just before my visit here today."

"He is a great man. A true man of God."

"He is. I wanted to tell you why I came to see you."

"Yes?"

"One day, the Vatican will want to study your life."

"My life? Why?"

"Because of Fátima."

"Yes, Fátima. Have you been?"

"Why, yes, Sister. I was born not far from the shrine. I have great reverence for what happened there."

Her breathing suddenly became noisier and more labored,

and he eyed the brass bell. He asked if she needed anything—water, medicine, Sister Ana?

"The Lord gives me everything I need," she finally said, her lungs quieting. "What were you saying?"

"That I have great reverence for Fátima."

"I was but a girl," she gasped. "Jacinta and Francisco were even younger. Our Lady gave us such a great responsibility to bear. I had to bear it longer. They were taken to heaven so young."

"Yes, they were. They are on the path to sainthood."

"They were good children. They loved Jesus with all their hearts."

"At the Vatican, people study their lives, just as one day, people will study your life. They will want to know all about what you wrote, and what you thought about your cousins, about Fátima, about the apparitions."

"Oh?"

"Yes, for sure."

"I think I wrote books. When I was younger."

"Indeed you did, Sister. I have read your memoirs. They are very beautiful."

"Are they?"

"They are. I am interested in learning of other things you may have written—unpublished memoirs, diaries, letters."

"I don't know about that."

"Are you sure? Do you keep papers in your room? Perhaps in your desk, or this chest here, or the closet?"

She closed her eyes. He feared she had drifted off, but she opened them again and said, "Do I? I don't remember."

"Would you give me permission to look?"

"Whatever you think is best. You are a priest. You know the Holy Father."

Her bedside chest was within arm's reach. Inside were old-lady's clothes, a blanket, and a few toiletries. Her desk was immaculate. Beside a typewriter was a stack of books, including her own memoirs. Standing, he thumbed through them. One day soon, they would surely become museum pieces.

The desk drawer had writing implements, India ink, and writing paper. A folded piece of paper had the beginning line of an undated letter, never finished.

Holy Father, I wish to thank you for——

The closet was more promising. Ignoring the hanging garments, he went straight for the two dozen or more shoeboxes that occupied the floor and the shelf, and, as he suspected, they did not contain shoes. Each one was filled with letters. The boxes were not arranged in any chronological order, but the letters within each were from a similar time frame. He imagined that whoever was tasked with cataloguing the letters one day would appreciate the semblance of structure. He counted the letters in a single box, multiplied that by the number of boxes, and made note of the total. He took a box with correspondence from the 1980s to the desk and began pawing through it. Sister Lúcia, motionless in her bed, was a silent presence. After a while, he found a letter of historical significance. It was written longhand on papal letterhead, dated July 13, 1981.

My Dear Sister Lúcia,

I write you on the sixty-fourth anniversary of the Miracle at Fátima, when you and your cousins Jacinta and Francisco Marto received the prophecies from Holy Mother Mary. I have had occasion to read your account of the Third Secret of Fátima. It has filled me with gratitude. I wish to thank Our Lady of Fátima for the gift of my life having been spared, and you for being her vessel.

The message of Fátima is an exhortation to conversion, prayer, especially the Rosary, and reparation for one's own sins and for those of all mankind. It is an outpouring of the love of the Heart of the Mother, who is always open to her child, never loses sight of him, and thinks of him always, even when he leaves the straight path and becomes a prodigal son. Mary's maternal love is best shown in her compassion on Golgotha, when she became the mother of all those redeemed by Christ. From that time on, the greatest concern of her Immaculate Heart has been the eternal salvation of all men and women.

Mary's apparitions at Fátima indicate that still today the Blessed Virgin desires to exercise through this same prayer that maternal concern to which the dying Redeemer entrusted, in the person of the beloved disciple, all the sons and daughters of the Church.

When I am recovered, I wish to meet with you so we might pray together and give thanks to Mary.

John Paul II

The priest returned the letter to its envelope and the box to the closet. No doubt, the world would see it published one day. For now, he had accomplished his mission. His report would delineate the wealth of correspondence in Coimbra and give recommendations for its timely preservation.

At her bedside, he drew near to her. Her eyes were open, and so watery that he almost felt the need to blot them with a tissue.

"Thank you, Father."

"You have a great many letters."

"Do I? Who wrote me?"

"Many, many people. Ordinary people of faith, bishops, popes."

"Why?"

"Because of Fátima."

She alerted to the word. "Yes, Fátima. I remember."

"I saw a letter you received from Pope John Paul, following his assassination attempt."

"A great man. Our Lady saved him as she said she would. Each of the three prophecies came to pass. I am sad I will never see—"

"See what, Sister?"

"The last of Our Lady's prophecies."

She choked on secretions and began to cough, and he was forced to put his rush of thoughts on hold to raise a cup to her mouth and place a plastic straw between her lips.

"Better?" he asked.

"Better. Where is Ana?"

"Nearby. Do you need her?"

"Soon."

"What did you mean by 'the last of Our Lady's prophecies'? Were there more?"

She looked toward the white ceiling. "Don't you know?"

"I'm afraid I don't." His excitement made him bolder. "Can you tell me?"

"I'm not sure. Can I? It may be a secret. I cannot remember."

"Have you told it to anyone?"

"Have I? I don't think so."

"As a priest, people tell me their secrets all the time."

"In confession," she said, showing a glimmer of her old, logical mind.

"Would you like to confess?"

"Yes, Father."

"Go ahead."

She freed her hand from the blanket and weakly made the sign of the cross and said, "Bless me, Father, for I have sinned. My last confession was—"

"Yes?"

"I can't remember."

"It doesn't matter."

"My sins are...I can't remember those either."

He went to the door to close it. Her hearing was so poor that everything had to be practically shouted, and he sought discretion. He leaned over her again and said, "Tell me about your secret, Sister. Surely, it's a sin to keep something so important to yourself."

"I must show my contrition before I die," she said.

"Indeed you must."

"All right, Father, I'll tell you."

Her breathing was labored, her diaphragm a weak bellows

forcing words past her dry lips. The priest listened in astonishment to her account of what the apparition of the Virgin had told her almost nine decades ago. In ordinary conversation, the nun seemed to have a diminished capacity, but her recollection of what a ten-year-old girl had experienced on July 13, 1917, was clear and precise. It was so seared into her memory that he suspected it might be the very last thing the old woman remembered.

When she was done, she closed her eyes in exhaustion, and he said the Prayer of Absolution. She was still awake and managed an amen.

"I'll leave you now, Sister. God bless and protect you."

He was at the door when he heard a loud gasp, and when he turned, her hand weakly beckoned him back.

"Father! I remember!" she said with a look of terror in those cloudy eyes.

"Remember what?"

"I promised the Virgin I would never tell a soul. I will be damned!"

"You never told anyone?"

"Never! I only—"

"Only what?"

"I think I wrote it down once. Or did I? I can't remember."

"You wrote it down?"

"That's it, yes. I hid it."

"Hid it where, Sister?"

"I don't know. It was a long time ago, and I am old now. You won't tell anyone, will you?" she asked, her eyes searching his in desperation.

"Calm yourself, Sister. Don't worry," he said, with absolute sincerity. "A priest must honor the sanctity of the confession. Your secret is now my secret. I will tell no one."

The priest meant what he said. He would never violate the confessional, but now, the burden that the Virgin Mary had given the little seers of Fátima to carry was his burden too. He rang the brass bell to summon Sister Ana and began to limp down the long dormitory corridor, lifting his paralyzed left foot high, then slapping it down hard onto the tiled floor.

17

It was early in the evening, and Elisabetta was restless and needed air. There was still some light left in the day, and the Vatican Gardens were lovely at this hour. On her way out of the guesthouse, she passed by Monsignor Cauchi's office, and through the open door, she saw he was still at work. A pang of guilt made her stop for a word.

"Father, it's getting late."

He looked up from his laptop and did his best to smile.

She thought the priest looked haggard, even more so than usual. Even though he was older than she was, his painful thinness and perennially sad countenance engendered maternal feelings. Her well of motherliness was far shallower than her sister Micaela's, but it was not nonexistent. His spiderlike body cried out for feeding, and his melancholy was in need of uplifting.

Before the priesthood, he had studied accounting in his native Malta, and a priest with financial expertise had currency at the Vatican. He was recruited into the Autorità di Supervisione e Informazione Finanziaria, the Vatican institution in charge of financial intelligence and supervision, and during his tenure at the AIF, he served on several committees that worked on Pope Celestine's initiatives. Celestine had long taken note of his competency, and as the pontiff had grown frustrated with Curial pushback on his financial reforms, he had tapped the priest to work for him as a papal secretary concentrating on fiscal matters.

"I'm almost finished for the night," Cauchi said.

"Good," she said. "You put in very long hours."

"As do you, Sister."

The source of her guilt arose from not having the time to mentor and supervise him adequately. On paper, he reported to her, yet she was only peripherally aware of the work he was doing, and when she had occasion to review the reports he sent to Celestine, she didn't fully understand them and lacked the bandwidth to get up to speed. The Holy Father himself, having commissioned various analyses, seemed too busy and distracted of late to process them, and Elisabetta saw Cauchi's unread folders become buried deeper and deeper in Celestine's in-tray. She imagined that the priest must have been frustrated by the lack of feedback, but she had done little to help the situation while the skeletal man soldiered on quietly.

"I was going to take a walk in the gardens," she said. "Would you like to join me?"

He exposed a childlike wrist and glanced at his watch. "Thank you, but I have a dinner appointment."

"Oh, good," she said, pleased to hear he had some sort of life beyond the office. "Some other time, perhaps. I would like to spend some time with you when things are a little quieter. Your work interests me. I only wish I understood it better. Perhaps you can tutor me."

"I would enjoy that," he said.

The Vatican Gardens were fragrant and in full summer bloom. The last visitors' tour of the day had long passed, and Elisabetta had much of the lush acreage to herself. Amid the lengthening shadows that dulled the greenery, she tried to lose herself in birdsong and the gurgling of fountains, but her worries about the morning Mass clouded her enjoyment. In a last-ditch effort to find some peace, she strolled to her favorite section, the English gardens, and took a bench on the edge of woodland, but it was to no avail. Her anxieties fought back to win the day, and she returned to the guesthouse feeling no better for the interlude.

At the end of the hall, she was surprised to see Pope Celestine standing at her office door. One of his Swiss Guards noticed her and spoke to him, and the pontiff turned to her with arms raised triumphantly.

"Ah, there you are!" he called out.

She picked up her pace and apologized for being unavailable.

"I'm glad I found you," he said. "I have an urgent question for you."

"Yes, Holy Father, what is it?"

"Would you like to have an ice cream with me?"

She laughed in relief. "I would love to have an ice cream with you."

"Let's go, then," he said. "Not a minute to lose."

The Swiss Guards must have alerted the cafeteria, because one of the cooks was ready with tubs of the pope's favorite flavors and toppings.

"After you," he declared, scratching his cheek while contemplating the choices.

They took a table in the empty cafeteria, and the guards gave them space for privacy. Elisabetta absorbed the lovely oddity of the moment—a nun and a pope, protected by men in medieval regalia, having ice cream in an otherwise empty cafeteria.

The pope dipped a spoon into his chocolate fudge swirl and closed his eyes in pleasure at the first spoonful. "So tomorrow is a big day," he said.

"All the preparations have been made," she said. "I feel good about where we are."

"If you feel good, I feel good," he said. "As for me, my preparations are incomplete. I've been rereading my homily, and I think it still needs some work."

She objected, telling him she thought the last draft was powerful.

"I think I can make a sharper point about the lessons of Fátima as embodied in the life of Lúcia dos Santos. I've started rewriting the middle section. With her and her little cousins, we have absolute proof of the importance of children in our faith. The Virgin could have chosen anyone to receive her messages—people with more powerful voices—but she chose tiny children, and now, all three of them will be saints. That is a wonderful thing.

"I also want to speak more clearly about the lessons of sacrifice. The Virgin told Lúcia to make sacrifices to help sinners and save them from hell. So, what did our dear sister do? When she was a shepherdess, she refused to drink water, even on the hottest day, and she wore a rope knotted tightly around her waist as a reminder of the suffering of others. Then she devoted herself to a long, cloistered life of devotion.

"Lastly, I want to say more about her courage to face obstacles. She and the other children were ridiculed and threatened and bullied, but they stood strong and insisted on the truthfulness of their visions. What a better world we would have if all of us showed such courage in the face of opposition."

Elisabetta didn't have the slightest appetite and had only tasted her dessert out of politeness. She put her spoon down and blurted out, "No one has shown more courage in the face of opposition than you, Holy Father."

He smiled gently. "I wasn't fishing for a compliment."

"I know, but I wanted to tell you how much I've admired your bravery and fortitude. You've done so many principled things and stood your ground against powerful critics. Your papacy—"

He wagged his finger at her to stop. "You sound like you're composing my memorial. Are you that worried about tomorrow?"

"Of course I'm worried," she exclaimed. "We have a specific and credible threat, and we haven't been successful getting to the bottom of it."

"Where is our intrepid scholar Professor Donovan?"

"The last we spoke, he was driving to the home of Charles Graves's brother."

"He really believes that this English priest is the key to the mystery."

"He seems convinced."

"Well, let's see how he gets on. There aren't so many grains of sand left in the hourglass. He has suffered a lot these past days. Evil is stalking him. Tell me, Sister, what kind of man puts his life on hold for the sake of another to endure these kinds of sacrifices?"

"A good man, I would say."

He bobbed his head in agreement. "And a good friend. I like that he's not intimidated by my office and that he isn't the least bit sycophantic, like so many of the people in my orbit. Yes, he respects the papacy, but he treats me like a fellow man and gives me his candid opinions, as friends do. Da Silva, who is even closer to him, says the same about their friendship.

"When you're the pope, friendship can be an elusive commodity. Old friends treat you differently. They can't help it. They can't see beyond the fisherman's ring. Those in the Curia have agendas that prevent them from becoming a true friend of the pope. I must tell you, in a different life, I would have been pleased to be your friend, Sister. You are a remarkable person—so bright and talented and well-informed. I've never for a moment regretted making you my private secretary. You saw how the wolves howled when a woman got the job. But I think, perhaps, this will be one of my most important legacies."

She felt herself blushing. All she could manage was, "Thank you, Holy Father."

He ate the rest of his ice cream and looked toward the serving counter, catching the eye of the night cook, who called over to ask if he wanted seconds.

The pope patted his belly and said he'd had enough.

He moved his chair a few inches back and allowed his legs to stretch under the table. "At my age, one can't help thinking about legacies. Well, maybe it's a bit more than my age. Since

278

receiving this warning, I keep seeing the mythical sword of Damocles hanging over my head by its gossamer thread."

Elisabetta rushed to say something reassuring. "My brother and Commander Studer will keep you safe tomorrow. I'm sure of it."

"Yes, I'm sure they will. Nevertheless—" He got distracted by the bowl in front of her. "Your ice cream has melted. You've hardly touched it."

"I wasn't hungry."

He stared philosophically at his empty bowl. "Nevertheless, I wonder how the pontificate of Celestine the Sixth will be remembered."

"It's premature to think about these things, Holy Father, but if I were asked, I would say that your pontificate shone a light on the teachings of Christ and brought the Church back to its true mission—to serve the spiritual needs of all the faithful, in particular the poor and disadvantaged, who are desperate for Christ's blessings. Yours is an open and welcoming Church. You always preach that we should see and act with mercy. Humility and mercy. In my opinion, these will be the twin pillars of your legacy. But not now, because, God willing, you will be pope for years to come."

"I pray you are correct, Sister. The alternative view is that I will be remembered as the pope who sold Michelangelo's *Pietà*." He pushed himself onto shaky legs and touched the tabletop for stability. "I must finish the homily now. Would you like to review it later?"

"With pleasure, Holy Father. I'll be up late, waiting for a call from the professor."

The three women watched the baggage carousel at Logan Airport going round and round. Carrie's bag arrived first, followed by Margo's, and when Jessica's failed to materialize, they went to the customer service desk to find out why. They were tired and talked-out, and all they could do was stare daggers at the baggage clerk as he worked the computer.

"Bad news," he finally said. "It looks like Miss Nelson's bag is still in Rome."

Carrie led the charge. "How the hell does something like this occur? We all checked in at the same time. Our bags are here."

"We have a saying at the airline," the clerk said. "Shit happens. It's already been routed onto the next flight. We'll have it delivered to your door tomorrow. Promise."

Carrie was on a hair trigger and started reacting like one of her surgical residents had accidentally cut an artery. "This is completely unacceptable, and—"

Jessica stopped her with a pat on the shoulder. She was physically and mentally as flat as roadkill and didn't seem the least interested in theatrics. "It's okay, Carrie. Let's just say this hasn't been my week."

They told the Uber to drop Jessica off first, and they ignored the driver's offer for one of them to ride up front. Instead, Margo and Carrie sandwiched Jessica between them in the small back seat to keep protecting her as best they could.

In the sickly, greenish light of the Sumner Tunnel, Margo asked her if she was going to be okay on her own. "I can stay with you a few days," she said. "No husband, no worries."

"I'll be fine. I need space. I can hardly breathe."

"We'll give you as much space as you need," Carrie said.

Jessica elbowed both of them in the ribs. "No, I need space right now. I can hardly breathe."

The three of them burst out laughing.

"Glad you haven't lost your sense of humor," Margo said.

When they surfaced from under the harbor, Jessica's building, the Millennium Tower, was looming. Her handbag was between her knees, and she fished for a tissue.

"You sure you're going to be all right?" Carrie asked. "Maybe you should take it slow and stay home for a couple of days."

"That's the last thing I want to do," Jessica said. "I need to get back to work and get ready for my FDA meeting. I refuse to spend a minute more thinking about what happened. I want to forget this week. I want to forget that Cal ever happened. I—"

She broke into sobs. Her friends each reached out to touch an arm. The Uber driver checked the dramatics in her rearview mirror.

"The only problem," Jessica said, "is that I'm still in love with the bastard."

They all knew that, whatever happened in the morning, this would be their last meeting, but there seemed to be an unspoken desire to avoid melodrama. As each man arrived, Hugo served them their usual beverages, and for the first time since they began gathering at his apartment, he put out plates of food. It wasn't a feast. There were potato chips and nuts, a block of cheese, a loaf of bread, some cold meats and condiments. He had purchased nothing for the occasion. Everything was from his kitchen. There was no sense leaving food behind to spoil.

Hugo let them eat and drink in silence. The only sound was the clatter of utensils on plates until finally he said, "Will you be at the Mass?"

They looked at one another. Martin took a sip from his beer and was the first to speak. "I'm not sure I can," he said, dropping his head in shame. "I support you, Hugo, you know that, but I'm afraid it will be too hard for me to be there."

"It doesn't matter," Hugo said. "As long as I know you're with me in spirit. That goes for all of you."

Martin got another beer from the fridge. "It was an abstraction until now. It suddenly feels very real."

Leone said, "How long will we have to wait? After it is done?"

"Give yourself to prayer," Hugo said. "It will happen when it happens."

Leone pressed him. "Are you sure it will come to pass?"

"If I weren't, do you think I'd go through with it?"

With his encouragement, plates were filled again. He didn't want leftovers.

"You haven't told us about Donovan's friend," Martin said. "I assume all went to plan in Sicily and that Donovan is back in America."

"There were problems," Hugo said, stunning the room back into silence. He studied their faces. The only one who didn't seem shocked was Christopher, who was calmly drinking his tea.

Martin recovered and asked, "What problems? Don't tell us the woman was hurt."

"She's fine. The police found her. She wasn't harmed. The same can't be said for the men Nino hired."

Angelo ran his hands through his hair. "More killings. What have we done?"

"You know what we've done," Hugo said. "You know the stakes."

"What of Donovan then?" Leone asked.

"He didn't return home. He's back on the hunt in the UK. He has reason to believe that Lúcia gave the Fourth Secret to an English priest, who is now dead. His brother may now possess it, knowingly or unknowingly."

"How do you know this?" Martin asked. "How do you know his every move?"

Hugo said, "I told you that Nino is resourceful."

"I know my cousin," Angelo said. "He isn't that clever. Where else are you getting your information from?"

"The less you know about what I know, the safer it will be for you," Hugo said.

"But surely Donovan's run out of time," Leone said.

"Not until tomorrow morning," Hugo said. "That's why we must stop him tonight."

"For God's sake, no!" Christopher said. "We cannot abide more killings."

"He's right," Angelo said. "No more killings. Please, Hugo."

Hugo softened his tone. "I'm not suggesting anything that drastic. I only want Nino to bundle him up, as it were, to either prevent him from finding it or, if he does find it, to prevent him from communicating with the Vatican. And I had this thought: If *we* could obtain the text of the Fourth Secret written in Lúcia's own hand, wouldn't that be an opportunity to justify after the fact what will happen tomorrow? Anger and outrage would turn to understanding and support. Better to be remembered as a martyr than a murderer. In any event, I have last preparations to make, so this is the time when we must say our farewells. You are all fine men and fine comrades. We have made something great together. We all have had a hand in the creation of the perfect world we've been promised. Please do not shed a tear for me. My joy knows no bounds."

He rose and limped to each man for a collegial embrace and a few personal words. Christopher was the last, and when they took hold of one another, he whispered in Hugo's ear, "We need to talk."

When the three others were gone, Hugo sat back down and looked at Christopher expectantly. "Talk about what?"

The skeletal priest remained standing. "I've done everything you've asked."

"I know you have."

"After Professor Donovan went to Paris, I dishonored myself and my position by eavesdropping on Sister Elisabetta's office line and reporting her conversations with Donovan and the Holy Father to you."

"You did what had to be done for the greater good. After tomorrow, your guilt will turn to rapture."

"I have doubts. They have become grave."

"Doubts are natural. Go home. Do something to relax. It will be over soon."

Cauchi shook his head defiantly. He was so slight that he gave the appearance of a child standing up to his father. "I want you to call off tomorrow. The pope is misguided, but I don't want him to die."

"Look, Christopher," Hugo said, "this is Stockholm syndrome. You've been working for the pope, and you've come to know him personally. Your access and proximity to the papacy made you appealing to me as a comrade in arms. I'm not surprised you like him as a man—he has some appealing personal qualities. But never lose sight of your repugnance at what he has done to the Church. He has trampled on every orthodox foundation of our faith. Don't you remember why you wanted to join with me?"

Cauchi looked bereft, as if his world were collapsing, and he began to shake uncontrollably. "I remember."

"Never forget. You didn't become a priest to be a pope killer, Christopher, and neither did I. As much as I disliked Celestine hailing back to the early days of his pontificate, it wasn't apparent that the Fourth Secret that Lúcia divulged to me at her deathbed confession had anything to do with him. Only later, by his actions, was the truth shouted to me."

Then he dropped to a near whisper and said, "And I knew, Christopher, that it was my calling to be the one to fulfill the prophecy. And it was this realization that led me to violate the sanctity of Lúcia's confession. But only to the four of you, all like-minded men, all brother priests."

Cauchi looked like a man who was hell-bent on unburdening himself. "It was me," he cried out. "It was me who warned the Holy Father about the Fourth Secret. As the time drew close, I decided I couldn't let him die. I offered him a way out. I did it anonymously. I said resign before the canonization or suffer a terrible consequence. If he wanted to know why, he had to find the Fourth Secret. That is when Professor Donovan was summoned. All I wanted was for Celestine to have cause to cancel the canonization."

"Did they leave any food?" Hugo said distractedly as he limped over to the spread.

Hugo's insouciance seemed to confuse the Maltese priest, who mumbled that he should go.

The cheese knife had never been used for meat, but it slid cleanly and without the least resistance between the ribs of that rail-thin torso, and although the blade was not long, there was enough steel to pierce the heart. Hugo thrust the knife not in anger, but in disappointment and betrayal. He liked the man, but he had seriously misjudged him.

He had never killed any creature higher than an insect, and for a moment, he was unsure of the result, as there was little blood to see. Everything about the violence and its aftermath had conspired to make the act easy on both perpetrator and victim. Father Cauchi had said nothing unpleasant, nor did he make disturbing noises. He simply slumped in gentle slow motion and lay on his side with a look of mild surprise. The bleeding was largely contained within the chest. There was no emptying of bladder or evacuation of bowels, so Hugo wasn't obligated to do anything more than cover the body with his spare blanket and get on with the rest of his evening. He imagined that the police would come to his flat in the hours following the Mass tomorrow and they would find the body before the residents of the building were subjected to unpleasant odors. He knew that tomorrow's violence wouldn't be as effortless, but he knew he wouldn't have to deal with the aftermath.

18

Nino drove his Transit van down a hedge-bound country lane in the mellowest of evening lights, one eye on the road, the other on the moving red triangle. Cal's BMW was to his north, no more than a few miles ahead. The signal from the tracker was good, and there was no need to speed. He smoked and hummed an Italian ditty. This was the part of his job he liked best—the unhurried pursuit with the outcome assured. Outsourcing carried risks—to wit, the deceased brothers from Palermo—whereas he had full faith in his own abilities. He had never failed to complete a job. He had never spent a day in jail. He was always paid.

His burner phone chirped to life, interrupting his reverie.

"Yes, what?"

Hugo said, "There has been a change of plans."

"What kind of change?"

"I want Donovan dead. Can that be done?"

"Anyone can be killed. That's not the problem."

"Then what is the problem?"

"You paid me to follow him, not kill him. Killing him would cost more."

"How much more?"

Nino decided to double his usual quote. His typical employers knew the market rate. This guy didn't.

"That's a great deal of money," Hugo said.

"Take it or leave it."

Hugo didn't hesitate. "All right, I'll pay."

"How? I'm in England. You're in Italy. I only take cash."

"I'll pay you when you're back in Rome."

"I never do a job unless I'm paid in advance."

Hugo stepped around Father Cauchi's blanketed body on his way to his whistling kettle. "I beg you to make an exception. You will be paid."

It was a lie. There was no more money. Lying used to be among his greatest sins, but now it was a triviality. Nino would have difficulty collecting his due from a dead man.

Nino watched the red triangle for a few seconds. He had nothing but contempt for the privileged American prick, and, truth be told, he probably would have done him for free. He said, "I know where you live. I know who you are."

Hugo replied, "I'm not surprised. You are an enterprising man. Your job is over tomorrow morning. When you're back in Rome, call me, and we can meet."

"Don't think about crossing me," Nino said. "You'd suffer a lot before you die."

"I understand. But there's something else I want."

"Now you're busting my balls."

"Hear what I have to say, tell me how much it will cost, then decide if I'm busting your balls, as you say."

"Go on."

"Donovan is on his way to see a man named John Graves, who inherited a book from his brother. That book is hiding something I need."

Nino grunted. "Didn't we do this already in Paris?"

"It's a different book."

"What book?"

"I don't know that. I need you to persuade this man, Graves, to show you all the books that belonged to his brother."

"Persuade? How?"

"However you do something like this."

"This would also be extra."

"Of course. Name your price."

He threw out another big number, and Hugo readily agreed.

"If you find an extra page hidden inside one of these books, take a photo and text it to your cousin."

"Why Angelo? Why not you?"

"Because Angelo knows what to do with it."

Nino ended the call and began to formulate a plan. The road was lightly traveled. He'd seen just one car in the last several miles. He could overtake Donovan and cut him off, finish him in the usual way, put the body in the van, and find a quiet place to dump it. As the plan got traction, his foot pushed down harder on the gas, and the gap between him and the red triangle began to close.

At this speed, it took only a few minutes for Cal's BMW to come into view. Nino kept his foot down, and soon he was within a car's length. He drew the last of the cigarette into his lungs, stubbed it out, and cursed at the road. It was too narrow to pass, and there were no shoulders, because the hedgerows were encroaching on both sides. Either the road was going to open up or he'd have to turn the van into a dozer.

When the van filled his rearview mirror, Cal checked his speedometer to see if he was being unreasonable. He wasn't, and it didn't take him any time to get annoyed. "Don't be a jackass," he murmured, looking for a place to pull to the side and let the jerk pass.

When the van got right on his bumper and tapped it, he let his window down, translated an American one-fingered salute into a British two-fingered one, and swore into the rushing wind. He checked the mirror again and got a good look at the driver. He was smiling.

The response to his hand-waving was a second harder jolt as the bumpers came together hard.

Cal leaned out and shouted, "Hey, asshole, what the fuck?" and then accelerated. The BMW was smaller and lighter, but the van, with its powerful diesel engine, kept up. Nino was enjoying the chase, and he had lit another cigarette, clamping his lips onto the filter, when he made contact with Cal's bumper again.

This hit got more than Cal's attention. It got him thinking that there was more to this than a local, high on testoster-one and whatnot, pissed at a BMW blocking his way. Was this the Paris killer? Was this the guy behind Jessica's kidnapping?

He put the gas pedal to the floor, and the BMW leapt into overdrive.

By keeping his foot down, Cal opened up a quarter-mile lead on the van, but Nino responded by pushing his larger beast to keep up. The next time he made contact, it wouldn't be a love tap. He'd ram the American into the hedges, climb out, and hammer him.

Cal sped past the junction of an even smaller lane, where a red car was signaling to turn. As soon as he cleared the junction, he saw the red car take a left and slip in between him and the van. He wordlessly thanked the driver and let up on the gas a little. He'd been white-knuckling the steering wheel, and he needed to give his hands a rest.

Beyond the junction, the hedges petered out, and the road opened to fields of barley. His GPS showed six miles to his destination. He'd pass through the village of Easton. There was probably a police station. He'd stop and report the van driver and have him held while he finished the job he had to do.

Nino unleashed a string of abuse at the red car blocking his way, and he accelerated onto that driver's bumper just as the road opened up and a strip of grassy shoulder materialized. He jerked the van to the right, bumped along the grass, and just barely managed to pass the piggy in the middle. That's when he heard the siren and glimpsed the flashing blue lights in his mirrors. A policeman on his way back to Easton had been behind the red car at the junction, waiting his turn to make a left. The speeding Transit van was a fat turkey to be plucked.

Cal also heard the siren and saw the reflected blue lights as he passed the sign for the village. Another glance confirmed the van driver's fate. He wouldn't have to find the police. They had found him. He breathed easier. Either his luck was turning or it was the providential hand of God. Either way, he'd take it.

Nino slowed and pulled onto the verge, allowing the gleeful driver in the red car to pass, waving contemptuously.

The policeman followed Nino onto the shoulder, parked, and entered the registration plate into his computer. Nino undid his seat belt, closed the tracking app on his phone, and calmly finished his cigarette.

The tap to the window came, and Nino rolled it down. The policeman was a fresh-faced ginger with a broad Norfolk accent that Nino struggled to understand.

"Do you know how fast you were going, sir?"

"How what?"

"How fast."

Nino offered an exaggerated shrug. "I don't know how fast. The gauge is in miles per hour. I don't know miles. I know kilometers."

"You're not from these parts, are you? Where's home?"

"Home? Italy."

"This is a rental?"

"Sì, I rented it."

"All right. Let me see your license, passport, and rental agreement."

Nino produced the documents. The rental contract was the only one that was real. The policeman went back to his car, and Nino lit up again and took a particularly deep drag.

When the policeman returned, he said, "Mr. Mario Tullo. Is that you?"

Nino said, "I am Mario Tullo."

"It seems your license and passport are not authentic, Mr. Tullo," he said with a sterner demeanor than before.

"What means, not authentic?"

"They're fake. You appear to have a problem beyond excessive speed and illegal passing."

"How can we fix?"

"I can't fix it. It's going to take a magistrate to fix it. I'm placing you under arrest."

Nino kept his composure. The officer didn't appear to have a firearm. If he was going to be arrested, this was a good country for it. "Please, sir, is there anything we can do? I have an appointment."

"What kind of appointment?"

Nino laid down some cover in case his bag was inspected. "I do construction. I have a job maybe."

"Where?"

"In Norwich, sir?"

"Going the wrong direction for Norwich."

"I think I'm lost. This job, it's important for me."

"Sorry, mate. You need to exit the vehicle. You're under arrest, and you'll have to come with me."

Nino got out. "What about my van?"

"We'll leave it here. The rental company will have to collect it. Can't have you driving on an illegal license, can we?"

"Where do we go?"

"The Easton police station's just ahead. We'll sort this out with my sarge."

"I need my bag. I won't leave it here. Could be stolen."

"Anything illegal in there? Any knives, guns?"

"Nothing, sir."

"All right, take it with you and get in the back."

"No handcuffs?"

"This is the UK, sir. Handcuffs are at the arresting officer's discretion. Unless I believe that you've committed a violent crime, or you're a risk for flight, or you pose a risk to my safety or the safety of the general public, then restraints are unnecessary."

"This is a very nice country," Nino said climbing into the car.

In the time it took the officer to shut the rear door and get behind the wheel, Nino had extracted his new blue hammer with its nonslip rubberized grip from his bag. With one blow, then two more, he ended his brush with the law.

The GPS announced that Cal had arrived at his destination. Passing through the ornate iron gates, going down a long drive of white gravel, and getting his first look at John Graves's vast country estate, Cal felt he had indeed arrived. The house appealed to his aesthetics. There was a grand symmetry to its three stories of iron-rich red limestone, and despite its air of formality, its twenty-six front-facing windows gave it a welcoming feel.

He left his car on the gravel forecourt and rang the bell on the massive oak door. He waited for a time but held off on a second ring. This was a very large house, and it might require a hike to answer the door.

The response came in the form of a small man in his seventies with a rubrous nose and silvery hair wearing a double-breasted pin-striped suit that covered a portly frame. Reading glasses hung from a cord around his neck. Incongruously, his loafers were scruffy, and one of them had a partially separated sole. As soon as he opened his mouth, fumes of alcohol escaped.

"You must be Donovan," he said. "John Graves here. Come in. Found us all right?"

"The GPS led me right to your door," Cal said. "Thank you for seeing me at, well, almost no notice."

"No problem whatsoever. Come in. Ann's somewhere about. What say you to some libations?"

The fellow was a period piece. Cal said, "I say, yes, please."

The entrance hall was all millwork, rose-colored marble, and bas-relief plaster. Cal's low whistle of appreciation delighted his host.

"Glad you like it," Graves said, bringing him through to one of the reception rooms. "It's a bit of a gem. Very few know about it. We don't do tours, we don't rent it out for films, and we've never done magazine spreads. We're blissfully private. I know some chaps with estates that are inferior to ours who are constantly flogging themselves on Instant Face, or whatever the hell the social media thing is. We don't go in for any of that."

The great reception room was oak-paneled, with a frescoed ceiling, a massive oriental rug, and enough sofas and chairs to entertain a crowd. The vault of the hearth was large enough to hold a breakout meeting.

"Ann!" Graves shouted. "Where art thou?"

A fairly young woman in an apron appeared, but it was the cook, not the wife.

"Mrs. Graves is dressing," she said.

"That's fine," Graves said. "Could you sort us out with bevvies? What about you, Professor?"

"Can you do a vodka martini, no vermouth?" Cal asked.

"I think we can manage that," the cook said with a smile. "Same again, Mr. Graves?"

"That would be lovely, yes. We have something in common already, Professor."

"Oh yes?" Cal said.

"I have my gin and tonics sans tonic water."

Drinks appeared quickly, and the two men sat on facing sofas for a getting-to-know-each-other chat.

"I must say, I was surprised to get your call," Graves said. "Truth be told, brother Charles doesn't often make it to front of mind. He's been gone for quite a long time. You said you were at Harvard."

"That's right. Here's my card."

Graves pulled on his readers and inspected it. "Divinity School! My word. You know I've got something of an oblique Harvard connection myself. Went to Emmanuel College, Cambridge. Your founder, John Harvard, was an Emmanuel man back in the day."

"What did you study there?"

"I read history. Wasn't much of a student, really. I went straight to the City and was rather better at making money. Did that for a while until the old man shuffled off the mortal coil, then came back to Graves Hall to manage the estate. We farm over five hundred acres, you know. You would have passed some of it on your way in."

Cal was conscious of the time and was desperate to get down to task, but his host clearly needed to be eased into it.

"How old is the house?"

"Built between 1736 and 1740. Sir Anthony Graves was a rare bird in his day, a prominent Catholic who was favored by the Protestant monarchy. He did something dodgy, no doubt, to ingratiate himself to King George the Second and was rewarded with this land. Tore down something crumbling and Tudor and built this rather good house. It's a bit much for the two of us—thirty-four rooms, twelve bedrooms—but where else would we go? In my father and grandfather's day, the place was crawling with help. We only have a cook, a gardener, and a couple of cleaners—none of them live-in. Times change."

"Did you and your brother grow up here?"

"Indeed we did. Happy enough childhood. Never needed a psychiatrist. I got on with life, quite independently. For some reason, Charles was a weaker sort. I think the real world terrified him. He gravitated to the life of a churchman because they told him what to do and what to think at every turn. If he'd been a different sort of chap, he would have been drawn to the military for the same reason. Sadly, he lived a very small life, teaching at a very small college until he died of a very large brain tumor."

Brotherly love, Cal thought, grateful to be an only child. "I take it you weren't all that close, then."

"We were not. Of course, thanks to his career choice, I inherited the lot of the estate, which suited me fine. In return, I felt a certain obligation of care. When he took ill and had to leave his college, I had him brought to a local place for his last years." Graves gestured vaguely toward the direction of the care home and said, "So, you spent the afternoon at Heather Grove. Is that unpleasant fellow RP Entwistle still associated with the place?"

"It's his son now."

"And how is it you learned I'd taken some of Charles's books?"

"The night he died, their assistant manager was on duty, a Mrs. O'Hara. She told me about your visit."

Graves brightened. "I remember her! Striking woman.

Excessively Irish. But why would brother Charles's books interest a professor from the Harvard Divinity School? I don't recall any interesting volumes. In fact, quite the contrary."

"It's not the books per se. It's what might be hidden inside one of them, a book that would have been given to him by a nun named Lúcia dos Santos."

Graves produced an unpleasant sort of eye roll. "Poor old Charles, the Fátima obsessive. Got into that swampland so deep he needed hip waders."

"I take it you're not a big believer in Marian visions?"

"I'm not a believer in any religious hocus-pocus. Charles and I were chalk and cheese on religion. I would describe myself as a grounded individual. Charles was off in outer space. In his later years, he claimed he communed regularly with the Virgin Mary and Jesus Christ. I know the doctors ascribed it to his tumor, but he was predisposed to it. If I got a brain tumor, I'd hallucinate about first editions and naked women."

Cal seized on the opening to segue into the business end of his visit and said, "I take it you're a book collector."

Graves sprouted an impish smile. "Take your drink and follow me. Let me show you my little library."

Nino got back into his van, opened the tracking app on his phone, and drove through the village of Easton, past the police station where he would have been held, and into the parish of Great Melton, where the triangle had come to rest.

The van had to be dumped. He was sure he'd find a car to steal to get back to London. He found some dense woods not far from Cal's location and drove through them as far as it would go before getting hung up on a fallen tree. He lit a cigarette and trudged along until the woods gave way to a field of sugar beets. In the distance was a large reddish house, and while he walked, he swung his travel bag at his side, with a claw hammer dripping bright-red blood onto his change of clothes.

19

Cal had spent much of his life as a denizen of libraries. He had seen his share of wonderful examples in private homes, but the one in Graves Hall took the cake. From the ground floor, they took a wide staircase, with chocolate-colored balusters and tan handrails, which undulated like a long python, and passed through a plastered arch in the upper hall to enter the enormous library vault that occupied the first and second floors at the center of the house. Graves told him, "The kitchens are the stomach of the house. My wife's rooms are the brains—she's the clever one who actually manages the estate. The library is its heart."

And what a heart it was. There were two decks of twelve-foot bookcases lining a room larger than most family homes. The upper gallery had gilded railings, each section centered with the family crest. The coffered ceiling, too, was gilded. Multiple seating areas of couches, armchairs, and standing lamps were arranged on a vast red-and-gold carpet. Natural light streamed through two pairs of tall front-facing windows.

"Incredible," Cal said.

"My obituary will begin with John Graves, noted bibliophile."

"Not a bad legacy. How many books do you have?"

"I can't give you a precise number," he said. "I obsess about the editions I purchase, not the tally. I imagine there are well in excess of fifteen thousand."

"How many did you personally collect?"

"Oh, goodness. Hundreds and hundreds. Perhaps a thousand or two. Each generation has added to the collection. We have some that date back to Anthony Graves's day. However, it was my grandfather, Bertram Graves, who was the first great bibliophile in the family. I would say that two-thirds of the books trace to him. He was the one who reconfigured the house to accommodate a galleried library. My father was no slouch either, but I think I've surpassed him, not in quantity but in quality. I'm the last of the Mohicans I'm afraid. No children."

He became distracted and began looking around the room. "I've got a copy of the first British edition of James Fenimore Cooper somewhere about, you know. In any event, no children means the whole kit and caboodle is going to wind up with the National Trust. Sweaty tourists, docents—I'm glad I'll be dead and gone. Would you like to see my Second Folio?"

He didn't wait for the answer, and Cal followed him over to one of the cases. "Here's where we keep the crown jewels, mostly firsts and incunabula," he said, removing the hefty book of plays. Among the jewels, Cal spotted copies of *Ulysses*, *Gulliver's Travels*, *Paradise Lost*, *The Canterbury Tales*, a complete set of Dickens. "I have many children, but the Shakespeare is my favorite. It's the Hawkins imprint, 1632. There are six others known to be extant. I won't tell you what I paid for it, but here's a clue: a lot."

In any other time, Cal would have loved to take a book such as this to a chair and spend quality time with it, but he heard the clock ticking in his mind. He paged through it long enough as not to insult his host and returned it to its place.

"Your brother's books. I wonder if you could you show them to me?"

Graves began to laugh, waving his hand over his head in circles. "Easier said than done. All I can tell you is that they're in this room. Where, I have no idea."

Graves's mirthfulness infuriated Cal. Yes, he didn't know the stakes, but surely the man could see the despair on his face. "I'm sorry. I don't understand. You don't know where they are?"

"Couldn't tell you if my life depended on it. Let me tell you how I operate. Other than the crown jewels—the really valuable ones—I treat my library like a wild garden. There's little order to it. Seeds get scattered by the wind. My great pleasure is wandering around with a tonic-free gin and tonic, discovering and rediscovering my books."

"The analogy is charming," Cal said, "but the wind doesn't put books onto shelves. Human hands do."

Graves wiggled his fingers. "Mine are intimately involved with the crown jewels. All the other acquisitions have been shelved by people in my employ. I'm known in these parts as an avid collector, and people come and drop off all sorts of tripe, imagining I'd be interested. Sometimes, they're looking for me to buy them—which I never do. Sometimes, they're just clearing out the home of a dearly departed. What I do is take the odd book of interest and use the rest for landfill. In the course of a year, I'll have accumulated a few dozen keepers in a closet, and I'll have a lad—usually a local sixth former—find space among the stacks and put them wherever they fancy. Charles's books would have spent time in closet limbo before getting elevated to the library for their heavenly rest." He chuckled at a memory. "I had one young chap who liked to group books by color, except that he was green-blue color-blind. I recall another who was very particular about matching heights."

"Who would have handled your brother's books?"

"No earthly idea. It was long ago. Mists of time."

"I assume there's no catalogue."

"What would be the fun in that?"

The hopelessness of the task settled in and fogged Cal's brain. "I need to start looking. Do you mind?"

"Looking for what? What title?"

"I don't know. Something about Fátima? A book of prayers? Something in Portuguese or Spanish?"

"Quite absurd. Nearly impossible absent an extended visit. You mentioned on the telephone this was time-sensitive. How much do you have?"

"Until tomorrow morning."

"Someone has set you a labor as challenging as Hercules cleaning the Augean stables in a single day."

"Hercules succeeded. I'd like to get started."

Graves rubbed his hands together like a greedy child. "As soon as we've had supper. Ann will make her appearance shortly. We've had Cook prepare a feast. It's not every day we get a professor from Harvard University to grace our table. Ann couldn't be more excited. She Googled you and thinks you're a looker."

Graves insisted that Cal accompany him to the cellars to pick out something special for their meal. There was nothing to do but respect his wishes. It was his house and his library, and if the only way to get to work was to break bread with him, then that's what Cal would have to do.

To get to the wine cellar, they took a stairway by the kitchen into a warren of dank rooms filled with old furniture, building materials, tools, and paint. The wine cellar had floor-to-ceiling racks of dusty bottles that were organized better than Graves's books—reds here, whites there, champagnes and ports. As Graves dusted off bottles and rattled off anecdotes about the vintages, Cal had a reckoning with a pang of guilt. Jessica would have been in heaven down here.

Mission accomplished and bottles in hand, they ascended to the ground-floor dining room, a baronial chamber with moody oils of Graves's ancestors staring from the walls. The lady of the house was waiting. Ann was at least a decade younger than her husband, taller and sleeker, a handsome woman who glided across the room like a laser-guided missile.

"Professor Donovan," she said in a posh London accent, "it's such a pleasure. I've been online since you called John, immersing myself in your glittering career."

Cal apologized for crashing into their lives with little warning, but she brushed him off and clucked. "My husband's manners," she said. "Your glass is empty. What are you having?"

Graves piped up, "He takes his vodka like I take my gin. I'll see to it."

"Here's you," she said, patting a chair at one end of a table that could seat twenty. "John was vague on the details of the reason for your visit, but he's vague about everything other than the books he's purchasing. He's rather like an idiot savant— good at one thing only."

Cal didn't know why he needed to defend the man, but he did so to a limited degree with a wincing smile. "That seems a little harsh."

"Does it? Perhaps you're right."

"I'm not sure if you knew your husband's brother."

"The mad priest? Yes, I knew Charles. Sad story, all around. What about him?"

"Your husband took some of his books after he died. One of them could be important, and I need to find it."

"Important how?"

"A Portuguese nun is being canonized at the Vatican in the morning. The book might contain some information Pope Celestine would like to know in advance."

"And he has an American professor at his bidding? Can you say more?"

"I don't think I can."

"How mysterious! I'm afraid I'm a boring old Protestant. We don't have these kinds of fascinating doings and intrigues. Martin Luther must have been dry as a bone, no fun at all. Does John think the book is in the library?"

"He does, but he doesn't know where. It's a big library."

"Yes, I've noticed."

"I'm sure you have. It looks like I may need to pull an all-nighter."

Graves returned with a tray of drinks. His wife took hers, a Pimm's cup, and said, "The professor was saying he needed to stay up all through the night looking for one of Charles's books." She inspected the bottles from the cellar. "I'd volunteer to help, but you know me after a few glasses of vino. I'd be utterly useless and might risk a topple from the gallery. Where's Cook? She's made a really nice bisque for our starters. I hope you like langoustines. Be a dear and tell her to bring it in, John."

The dinner that ensued was agonizing on many levels. Cal had precious little in common with the couple, and despite Ann Graves's professed interest in his career, she and her husband were more invested in talking about themselves. Over four courses—they followed the French tradition of serving a salad in between the mains and dessert—Cal was subjected to discourses on horse breeding, crop rotation, grain prices, British estate taxes, and the vagaries of the antiquarian book market. In ordinary circumstances, he would have knocked back enough drink to anesthetize himself, but he had business to do and needed a reasonably clear head.

More painful above all else was the passage of time. It was past nine when the coffee was served. Graves announced that the menfolk would take port in the gun room, where he'd show Cal his collection of heirloom shotguns.

"Finest collection in Norfolk, I've been told by those in the know. Worth half a million. Christie's has been banging on at me to sell, but why would I? Asset appreciation's the name of the game."

Cal had to draw the line. "This was a wonderful meal, and you've been gracious hosts, but I really need to get stuck into the library now."

Mrs. Graves said, "I'll show you to your room first."

He told her he didn't need a room, that he'd be working through the night and then heading back to London in the morning.

"Nonsense," she said. "You'll at least have a place to freshen up. It's on the first floor, east of the library. We are west of the library, so you'll have complete privacy."

"No shortage of bedrooms here," Graves said.

"Twelve, wasn't it?" Cal said.

"Good man," Graves said. "Paid attention. Meet you back in the library in a bit."

Cal dutifully inspected the bedroom that he wouldn't be using and then rendezvoused with Graves on the main level of the library.

"Need to show you the shortcut up to the gallery. I usually tell people, 'I'd show you, but I'd have to kill you,'" Graves said, chuckling at this original bit of humor. "See this case? Push this rosette on the corner here."

There was a click, and the section of bookcase turned on its central axis, revealing narrow stairs.

Cal thanked him for the reveal and said, "So, what's the standard method of execution at Graves Hall?"

"In the day, it was hanging. Think we'll give you a reprieve. We're early risers, but if you take your leave before we're up, kindly leave me a note on how you got on. Curious as hell. If you leave through the kitchen, you only need to pull the door closed to lock. We don't set an alarm. Nothing untoward happens in the parish. Well, good night and good luck."

Alone, Cal surveyed the expanse of shelves, puffed his cheeks, and let the air out noisily. Every bookcase had to be checked, with the exception of the crown-jewels cases, and given his host's seeds-scattered-by-wind analogy, Charles's books could have wound up anywhere. The only procedure that made sense was to be methodical and go case by case, shelf by shelf, book by book, and if the lower level was fruitless, head up to the gallery.

During Ann Graves's interminable discourse on stud fees, Cal had thought about the kind of book that Lúcia might have given Charles. Other than the religious studies she had made in pursuit of nunhood, she had no formal education, and as far as Cal knew, she spoke and read Portuguese only. Her personal books would have been in Portuguese.

However, she had spent some of her early years in the convent in Tuy, so it was within the realm of possibility that she could have acquired books in Spanish from that period in her life. Toward the end of her days, a simple, devout woman such as Lúcia might have possessed Bibles, prayer books, perhaps copies of her own memoirs, and books written by her hero, Pope John Paul II. He knew she had given the Portuguese missal *Visitas ao Santissimo Sacramento e a Maria Santissima* to Sister Ana, and this reinforced his belief that the gift Charles had received was also a book.

He also knew, from John Graves, that none of the inherited titles had any obvious value to a serious book collector, so the book given to Charles would have been, on the face of it, ordinary. Yet Charles's afterword referred to "a truly wonderful gift I will treasure for my remaining days." What kind of book would have struck him as wonderful? Cal's money was on a signed copy of her memoirs.

He chose a bookcase as a starting point with the intention of moving clockwise around the room. He began crouching at the lowest shelf, stood for the majority, and wheeled a library ladder over for the top two. He had eleven and a half hours until ten in the morning Rome time, when Celestine would begin Lúcia's Mass.

After an hour, he decided to reassess his strategy. He had covered all of three bookcases, and not counting the crown-jewels zone, there were over fifty left on the main level and the gallery. Despite his belief that the book would be in Portuguese or Spanish, he compulsively examined English titles too, and that meant pulling each one. There wasn't time to keep this up. He needed to motor.

Moving to the next bookcase, he scanned the spines and ignored anything unless it screamed Portuguese nun, and each book on every shelf was quiet. What had taken over twenty minutes per case now took five. He made his bargain, sacrificing accuracy for time, and moved clockwise through the night.

With time, the books became a blur. Given the antiquity of the library and John Graves's bona fides as a bibliophile, at least half of them, at least on the lower level, were leather-bound, predating the mid-nineteenth century. Most were works of nonfiction—history, philosophy, natural sciences. British publishers began abandoning leather for cloth in the 1820s, and among the cloth-bound books on the shelves, novels appeared. Of every hundred or so books he scanned, one was in a foreign language—Italian, French, or German. He didn't come across a single Portuguese or Spanish volume. It had gone midnight when he pushed the corner rosette on the secret bookcase and climbed to the gallery.

At the first case he inspected, he experienced a glimmer of recognition, followed by a tinge of excitement. There, at eye level, was a copy of Charles Graves's Fátima book. Perhaps one of the students John Graves had hired to shelve books had placed all of Charles's in the same bookcase. That possibility drove Cal to furiously examine the adjacent books and the nearby shelves, but there was nothing remotely evocative of a gift from Lúcia. He pulled out the Fátima book and saw it was a copy signed for his brother on the year of its publication.

He returned to his solitary clockwise search.

Nino waited patiently in the cooling, moonless night, keeping watch over the limestone mansion. He circled it at a distance and, hearing no dogs, moved closer.

Donovan's rental car was parked out front. The ground floor was dark, but lights glowed brightly from pairs of windows on the top two floors at the center of the house. There was a faint light from a first-floor window on the eastern side, and brighter lights and the flickering of a television coming from windows on the western side of the same floor, bedrooms, no doubt. When those lights extinguished just before two o'clock, he trod over a lawn of dewy grass heading to a rear door he had identified as a good entry point.

He peered through cupped hands into the dark kitchen and faced a moment of truth he had faced many times before. There was nothing he could do to change what would happen next. An alarm would either sound, or it would not. In his experience, city dwellers used alarms, country dwellers less often. If a siren cut the air, he would have to run. The house was too large to find his target and retreat before the arrival of the police, who would be on heightened alert because of the ginger officer.

He put on a pair of leather gloves and punched his knuckles through a pane. There was the sound of tinkling glass and nothing else. He reached in and unbolted the door.

He had a penlight that gave off a thin beam, the kind doctors use to look at throats, and he used it to maneuver through the kitchen and dining room and into the reception rooms in search of a staircase. In a room at the front of the house, he stopped and shone the light into a glass-fronted cabinet, and in Italian, he thanked God. He was nothing if not opportunistic, and it would have been foolish to pass up this opportunity. The case was not locked, and he had the pick of the litter. A dozen ornate shotguns stood shoulder to shoulder, like soldiers awaiting orders. He chose an over-under model with beautiful brass scrollwork and felt its heft. There were boxes of shells in the drawers. His bloody hammer would stay in his hooded sweatshirt tonight. This rich man's gun could be traced back only to its owner.

He found the wide staircase in the front hall and began to climb.

Cal was dead on his feet, struggling to stay awake. Ann Graves's fear of toppling over the railings of the gallery walkway wasn't that far-fetched, especially when up on the ladder. He had made it halfway around the upper level. The gallery books were generally second-class citizens relative to their main-level brethren, with a preponderance of twentieth-century material and many more novels and poetry books. He completed his inspection of one more bookcase, climbed down from the ladder, and moved one tick clockwise.

Squatting at the lowest shelf of the new case, he immediately saw three more copies of Charles's Fátima book. He pulled one out. Facing the title page was a bookplate: Ex Libris Fr. C. Graves. The two others had the identical plates. *This is good,* Cal thought. *This is very good.* These were Charles's personal copies. Where else could they have come from if not Heather Grove?

The rest of that shelf and the two above it were filled with novels by John Fowles, Graham Greene, Ian McEwan, and other fairly contemporary authors. None had Charles's bookplates. Then, at eye level, a dozen or so books caught Cal's interest. They were textbooks of a religious nature, on subjects such as interpreting the Gospels, a guide to the Second Vatican Council, and understanding the catechism. Each one had Charles's stamp of ownership. Whoever had placed the books had planted these seeds in one place.

His mental fogginess cleared, and his eyes darted from book to book, shelf to shelf. He found a Charles Graves book here, another one there. The highest two shelves required the library ladder, and he clambered up.

He spotted it right away. A tattered blue binding with gold lettering on the spine. In Portuguese.

A Cidade Mística de Deus— pela Venerável Maria de Ágreda

Mystical City of God by the Venerable Mary of Ágreda. The memo about Lúcia from the Vatican Archives. How many days had it been since Cal had seen it? It was only a week ago, but it seemed a distant event. Still, it came to him photographically: *Memo from Maglione to P XII, 2 May 1944, Inventory. Holy Father, The inventory at Pontevedra was as follows:...Ágreda's Mystical City of God in Portuguese.*

From his ladder perch, he reached for the thick book and opened the cover. It was a 1918 edition, and on the title page, it was signed in pencil, *L. dos Santos, Pontevedra, Espanha, 1932.*

It was no wonder she had obtained a copy of this book in her youth. The seventeenth-century nun Mary of Ágreda was much like her, a young woman visited by the Virgin Mary, who delivered a vision of the divine plan for the salvation of souls. It was no wonder she kept the book her entire cloistered life. And it was no wonder that Charles Graves, upon receiving it, would consider it a truly wonderful gift that he would treasure all his days.

Cal didn't want to waste a second. He remained on the ladder and feverishly paged through the book, looking for the prize but finding nothing. He cursed in frustration. *What am I missing?* He held the book by the cloth-covered cardboard cover, opened it like the spread wings of a bird, and gave the pages a shake. Still nothing, but when he turned the book on its side to close it, something gossamer fell from the cavity of the bowed binding, caught the air, and fluttered over the railing and settled onto the red-and-gold carpet below.

Boom!

Once you served in the army, you knew what gunfire sounded like.

He jumped from the ladder and glanced over the railing at a folded piece of onionskin.

There was another *boom!* that rumbled the old house. It came from a floor below, he thought, the west wing. The onionskin would have to wait. The army taught you to run toward gunfire, and that's what he did.

The secret staircase was narrow and twisty. He opted for the more maneuverable, wide staircase from the upper landing to the first floor and flew down it, looking for the corridor leading to the Graves's bedrooms. There was a dark hall that he entered cautiously.

"Hello?" he called out. "Is everything okay? I heard gunfire."

There was a room to his right, facing the front of the house, an office or a study. In the darkness, he made out prints of racing horses on the walls.

"Hello?"

There were partially open double doors at the end of the hall, and he crept forward on the balls of his feet.

"Mr. and Mrs. Graves, it's Cal Donovan. Are you all right?"

At the threshold, he picked up an acrid whiff of gunpowder. His hands felt pathetically empty. He wished he had something he could swing.

He took another step into the darkness and let out a weaker "Hello?"

He swept the wall with his hand, feeling for a light switch and found one, and then froze as an overhead fixture cast a harsh light.

A haze of gunpowder hung in the air, as if a fog had rolled in.

Two destroyed and bloody bodies were under a white duvet. John Graves's face was pulp.

A standing mirror caught a reflection, a movement from the closet, the barrel of a long gun.

Cal jerked toward the double doors as the hammer fell, blasting buckshot from one of the barrels. Plaster splattered, and he felt a stabbing pain in his left shoulder. In an instant, he entered survival mode and began hurtling down the hall, pumping his legs like pistons. He turned toward the landing as the other barrel let loose, and a spray of shot pocked the walls and ceiling.

On the landing, he had to make a swift choice: up or down. Instinct drove the decision, and he headed toward the ground floor. He figured the shooter had to make a decision too—to give chase immediately or to pause to reload what was probably a double-barreled weapon. Halfway down the stairs, Cal wished he'd taken Graves up on the offer to see his shotgun collection. He had no idea where it was kept.

He heard rapid footsteps coming from behind and then the sound of shells clattering to the floor, followed by the clunk of loaded barrels locking into place. The realization hit him as hard as the pellet that had pierced his shoulder—the shooter was a pro, who was reloading on the run.

At the bottom of the stairs, on the landing, a quick left would have taken him to the vast entrance hall and the huge oak door out to the forecourt. But he knew it would take several seconds to bound across the polished tiles and then more seconds to work out how to unbolt the door in the dark. An image flashed through his mind of being peppered with shot and dying in that hall.

There was another staircase heading down, and he made the snap decision to take it. He'd been in the basement and had a rudimentary sense of the space. It would be terra incognita for his pursuer.

He flung the basement door open and began running through the labyrinth of rooms, but his footsteps were echoing loudly off the vaulted ceiling, making it ridiculously easy to follow him. He ducked into a storeroom with a disused washer and dryer, kicked off his shoes, and took a second to probe his shoulder and feel the warm blood wetting his shirt. He clenched his jaw in pain but got himself moving again. He couldn't let himself be trapped in the dead-end space.

Now, the only audible footsteps came from the man with the shotgun. He was close, too close. To his right, Cal noticed the dark forms of wine racks. He stopped running and went inside the wine cellar only far enough to grab a bottle and hurl it with his good arm, sending it crashing against other bottles. Then he took off again.

A few seconds later, the trailing footsteps skidded at the opening of the wine cellar, and a deafening shotgun blast rang out, followed by the sound of shattered bottles raining down and a waterfall of good wine.

Cal kept moving, making his way in the dark as best he could, looking for another staircase and trying not to bump into anything that would give his position away. The basement brightened slightly, and from behind, he saw a glow coming from the wine cellar, where the shooter had found the lights — to look, no doubt, for his body.

The footsteps resumed just as Cal found a heavy door similar to the one at the bottom of other stairway. He turned the knob. The good news was that he had found the second set of stairs.

The awful news was that the hinges screamed, for lack of oil. He bolted the door behind him and started to climb.

His pursuer was fast and relentless, and the bolted door was little more impediment than rice paper. Another shotgun round obliterated the knob and the bolt, and Cal was left with a paltry lead. At the top of the stairs, he kept going. But he knew he wasn't going to outrun the shooter.

He needed a place to hide.

Reaching the first floor, he headed for the bright lights of the library, and entering through an unfamiliar side archway, he tried to get his bearings. A striped armchair across the room was the beacon he needed, and he ran toward it, hesitating for a fraction of a second at the sight of the folded piece of onion-skin on the carpet across the room. He desperately wanted it, but stopping to retrieve it could mean death. He chose life.

He felt for the carved rosette on the bookcase near the striped chair and pushed it. The latch popped, and the case swung open. He climbed through and swiveled the case back until the latch caught. Gasping for air, he collapsed onto the narrow treads and listened for his attacker.

Nino was attracted to the light flooding through the archway and ran into the library, where he became momentarily disoriented by the bright colors and the volume of the huge chamber. Then, across the room, he saw and heard something that another might have missed—a subtle motion at the corner of one of the bookcases and a faint click as the rosette latch reset itself.

He stopped to catch his breath and reload.

"Donovan! I'm here for you, Donovan! I'm tired of chasing you all over Europe! It's time we met face to face, man to man!"

Cal worried that light might be leaking from the secret staircase. He reached for the switch, and just then, he saw a manual bolt to secure the bookcase from the inside. He slid it into place and crept halfway up the staircase.

Nino went straight for the rosette and depressed it with his hand. Cal heard the latch pop and saw the bookcase shake with each of Nino's shoves. The bolt held.

There was an enormous ear-shattering blast, and the staircase filled with splintered wood and shreds of cardboard and paper from disintegrated books.

Cal ran up to the top of the stairs just as the bookcase swung open.

He had made it halfway around the gallery when he heard, "Stop!"

He slowly turned his head and saw Nino pointing a shotgun.

"You're bleeding," Nino said.

The back of his white shirt was soaked through. He felt dizzy from blood loss and exertion as he turned to face his attacker.

From his accent, Cal knew where the man was from. "Who are you?" he asked in Italian.

Nino smiled and responded in kind. "I'm a working man."

"Someone is paying you. Who?"

"Some guy. I don't ask questions. I do my job."

"Killing people for money. That's your job."

"Maybe the second-oldest job in the world. You're a history professor. You should know this. Before I kill you too, I have to ask—did you find it?"

"Find what?"

"The paper. In a book."

"Do you even know what it is?"

Nino kept sighting down the barrel. "I don't need to know why I'm killing a guy."

Five people who started the week alive are now dead, Cal thought. He would be the sixth. In a few hours, Pope Celestine might be the seventh. All for a piece of paper he'd never get to read, written by a woman on the precipice of sainthood. He stared at the man who was about to wipe away his existence and managed a smile.

"Why are you smiling?"

Cal gestured expansively with his good arm. "Do you see how beautiful this place is? I always said I'd like to die in a library."

Cal was watching the man's curled finger, and as it tightened against the trigger, he flung himself down and flattened his body against the gallery floor. He heard the thunderous discharge and felt pellets raking his scalp and his back.

Get up. You're not dead, he thought. *He's spent both barrels. Get up before he reloads.*

Nino swore at him, broke the barrels, and reached in his pocket for more shells.

Cal was charging, his nostrils flaring, screaming at the top of his lungs. They taught you in the army, in hand-to-hand combat, scare the other son of a bitch with a war cry.

Nino abandoned his reloading, snapped the shotgun closed, and flipped it around to use as a club. He hadn't counted on the hot barrel, and he didn't get a good enough purchase on it before Cal was on him. At first contact, the gun slipped from his hands. Nino hadn't been in a fight since the brawling days of his youth, but he had two good arms and he was strong. Cal was a boxer with a knockout right hand, but with his left arm hanging limp, it was his only weapon.

Cal caught him square on the face a few times with straight punches and uppercuts. Nino, squirting blood from his nostrils, bear-hugged him into a clinch and used his fist to bash his bleeding shoulder from behind. Cal howled in pain, and to get him off his back, went for an eye gouge with his right thumb.

Nino staggered, swearing his head off, and stooped for the shotgun. They both grappled for it, pressing up against the gallery railing, but Nino's two arms were better than Cal's one, and as the Italian was about to get control of the gun, Cal lunged forward, pushing Nino over the top of the railing.

Both men were falling.

Nino was no longer his enemy. Gravity was.

Cal experienced an exhilarating few moments of flying, followed by an explosion of catastrophic pain, and then, nothing.

20

Dawn came gently that morning. Heavily overcast skies gradually brightened, lumen by lumen, until westerly winds over the North Sea nudged the cloud cover inland. In one moment, the parish of Great Melton was drained of color, and in the next, the sun broke through, painting the countryside green and yellow. At Graves Hall, a shaft of golden light suddenly streamed through the library windows and fell upon Cal's upturned face.

His eyelids twitched open, and he groaned. There were too many sources of pain to process all at once. His eyes hurt from the light. His shoulder throbbed where he had been shot. His head ached from the concussive fall. His right leg felt like it was on fire. He explored the ground with his good hand. He was on a carpet, but which carpet and where? When his eyes adjusted to the light, the room came into focus, and he saw he was surrounded by books.

His mind opened. He remembered arriving at Graves Hall. He remembered his dinner with Ann and John Graves. He remembered finding *Mystical City of God* and hearing shotgun blasts. He remembered seeing their bodies. He remembered fleeing through the house and grappling with the killer. But he couldn't remember how he came to be lying on the floor.

And the killer, where was he?

In a panic, Cal tried to push himself up, but the combination of a bad left arm and a bad right leg was a formidable obstacle. He felt along his leg and found an excruciating deformity at the middle of his shin, a fracture, for sure. He was near a sofa and managed to use his two functioning limbs to prop himself in a sitting position against it, and that's when he saw legs. He crawled a few feet to get a better look. Nino was lying between the sofa and a shattered side table. A brass table lamp was embedded in his chest, the lampshade pancaked and bloody. It was then that he looked toward the gallery and retrieved the memory of the last seconds before the plunge. It could have been him run through with brass.

How long had he been lying there? He patted his trouser pocket and felt the edges of his phone. The screen was cracked, but it came to life. It was July 13, 9:34 a.m., and there were five missed calls from Elisabetta, three between two and three, two more between seven and eight.

The canonization Mass. It was scheduled for ten o'clock.

"There's still time," he said out loud. His mouth was a desert, and the words came out thickly.

Then his brain autocorrected. *Time zones, remember them?* It was 10:34 in Rome. The Mass had begun.

The folded onionskin was across the room, and he set off for it in a slow and painful crab-like crawl, pushing off with his left leg, pulling himself with his right arm. What would have taken seconds took minutes, but with one final exertion, he had it in his hand and managed to sit up.

He unfolded the gossamer paper and started to read the unmistakable scrawled penmanship of Sister Lúcia.

Our Lady of Fátima revealed her Fourth Secret on 13 July 1917 to me and my dear cousins. Jacinta and Francisco have gone to Heaven, and I am left alone to contemplate a secret I must never reveal, a secret that fills me with terror and awe, which I will take to my grave. No one is allowed to know it, but I must never forget it. I write it down so that I might always remember the words told to a young shepherd girl in the Cova da Iria, on a hot summer day many years ago.

This is what Our Lady told us.

An Italian pope will show himself to be a pretender to the throne of St. Peter when he sells the relics and treasures of the Church to those who care more for money than faith. This Italian pope will be consumed by fire on the day that the shepherd girl Lúcia becomes a saint. When this has come to pass, the sign of the Son of Man will appear in the heavens and Our Lord and Master Jesus Christ will come again to judge the living and the dead. He will return, and His Kingdom will have no end.

21

It is said that the happiest day in the life of the Catholic Church is the day a new saint is proclaimed.

The faithful who streamed into Saint Peter's Square and passed through the metal detectors were in a festive state of mind. They took their first-come, first-served places on plastic chairs arrayed before the basilica in neat rows. Near the start of the ceremony, there were tens of thousands of pilgrims taking pictures of the raised platform where Pope Celestine would conduct the Mass, waving Portuguese and Italian flags bought from vendors outside the gates.

The Hyundai popemobile was in position at the staging area near the basilica. Emilio Celestino and Eric Studer waited for the pontiff to appear, communicating with their command teams on their radios. Both hid their nerves behind stoic, clench-jawed expressions.

Elisabetta appeared from a side door of the basilica and said, "Five minutes."

"We're ready," Studer said.

"Anything from Donovan?" Emilio asked.

"Nothing," she said. "I've tried to reach him all morning. I'm extremely worried."

Studer scrunched his face. "What's going on? I thought he went home?"

Emilio was happy for Elisabetta to field the question. "There was a last-minute change of plans," she said. "He received a lead he wanted to follow."

"Where is he?" Studer asked.

"England."

"Why wasn't I told?"

She fell on her sword. "I'm sorry, Commander, it was my fault. It was an oversight."

"Well, it appears his time is up," Studer said icily. "I never thought this would be a productive exercise. And, no, you don't have to remind me that it was the Holy Father's idea."

Pope Celestine appeared, punctual to the minute, accompanied by his long-serving master of pontifical liturgical ceremonies, an Italian archbishop who would assist him at the Mass. The pontiff's white cassock flapped in the stiff breeze. He turned his tired face into the wind and pressed his lips into a thin, appreciative smile, as if remembering a gusty day from a time gone by.

Emilio said, "Your Holiness, we are ready for you. The pilgrims are in place—I would say eighty to ninety thousand. Nothing suspicious was found during our screening procedures. However, given the high threat level, we have installed the glass cage for the motorized processional."

"Whatever you think best," Celestine said. "I don't want to keep them waiting. I'm ready."

Celestine and his archbishop climbed the stairs to the platform of the popemobile, and Celestine gripped the railing. A videographer standing behind him began recording. Emilio and Studer took their positions by the front wheels, accompanied by a contingent of gendarmes and Swiss Guards. The vehicle began its slow roll.

As it turned into the square, the crowd erupted in joy. At least a third were from Portugal or members of Fátima organizations, and a sea of photos of Sister Lúcia appeared. Celestine lit up at the spectacle and waved vigorously at the crowd. In return, they cheered him like a hero.

Elisabetta walked around to the front of the basilica, taking a path behind the raised stage to the adjacent VIP stand, where members of the Curia, Portuguese dignitaries, and heads of Fátima lay groups were assembled. Seating was reserved, and she needed to find her spot.

"Sister!" Cardinal Da Silva called out from one end of the front row. "You're over here, next to me."

She stepped onto the riser, and as she made her way across the stand, her nose wrinkled. The smell was incongruous, and it puzzled her. She sniffed the air again, but the breezes were shifting and whatever it was, was gone.

A staff member of the Office for the Liturgical Celebrations waved at the dignitaries from the ground to get their attention.

"Ladies and gentlemen, the Mass will begin shortly. Please place your phones on mute."

At ten o'clock, the popemobile had completed its circuit of the square without incident and deposited Celestine at the foot of the stage. With his archbishop at his side, the pontiff ascended.

By tradition, the rite of canonization took place in the wider setting of a Papal Mass, as a way of demonstrating that the proclamation of a new saint fit, hand in glove, with the pinnacle of Christian life, the celebration of the Eucharist. Celestine stood at the altar, took a profound bow, and venerated the altar by the waving of incense censers.

Emilio and Studer took to the stage, one to the pontiff's right, one to his left, earpieces in place, rounds chambered in their holstered pistols, both ready to die for him.

Celestine leaned into the microphone, and the loudspeakers carried his voice into the square.

"In the name of the Father, and of the Son, and of the Holy Spirit."

The crowd replied in unison, "Amen."

Celestine extended his hands in a gesture of welcome and said, "The grace of Our Lord Jesus Christ, and the love of God, and the communion of the Holy Spirit be with you all."

After the Kyrie Eleison, the choir sang the hymn "Glory to God in the Highest," and Celestine proceeded to the chanting of the Litany of the Saints, the roll call of the Church's saints, and after each name, the crowd answered in refrain, "*Ora pro nobis*," pray for us.

Then Celestine yielded the altar to Cardinal Alonzo, the prefect of the Congregation for the Causes of Saints, who began making the obligatory three petitions.

"Most Holy Father, Holy Mother Church earnestly beseeches Your Holiness to enroll Blessed Lúcia dos Santos among the saints, that they may be invoked as such by all the Christian faithful."

When he was done, Celestine took the altar and responded,

"For the honor of the Blessed Trinity, the exaltation of the Catholic faith, and the increase of the Christian life, by the authority of Our Lord Jesus Christ, and of the holy apostles Peter and Paul, and our own, after due deliberation and frequent prayer for divine assistance, and having sought the counsel of many of our brother bishops, we declare and define Blessed Lúcia dos Santos to be a saint, and we enroll her among the saints, decreeing that she is to be venerated as such by the whole Church. In the name of the Holy Father, and of the Son, and of the Holy Spirit."

And with that, the assembled masses erupted in collective rejoicing.

The text of Celestine's homily was placed on the altar, and he began to praise the new saint and extoll her extraordinary life of piety and her absolute devotion to the Immaculate Heart of Mary.

The Mass was drawing to a close. Lúcia was a saint, and Celestine said his final benediction.

"May Almighty God bless you, the Father, and the Son, and the Holy Spirit. Go in peace, glorifying the Lord by your life."

The faithful replied, "Thanks be to God," and then took to flag-waving. The square burst into the Portuguese national anthem.

Emilio and Studer sandwiched the pontiff and accompanied him down the stairs to the popemobile.

"We should do another circuit," Celestine told them.

"Please, Your Holiness," Emilio said. "Let's get you into the palace for the reception."

Celestine was drained of energy and didn't require convincing. "Very well."

The guests with invitations to the papal reception filed into the Apostolic Palace through the ceremonial bronze door. There, they presented their tickets to the Swiss Guards, and then, in an unprecedented measure of security, they passed through another metal detector before they either climbed the marble staircase, the Scala Regia, or rode a lift to the second floor. The Clementine Hall of the old medieval Palace of Sixtus V, a cavernous, ornate chamber covered in Renaissance frescoes, was used for large celebratory receptions, but also on the somber occasions when the body of a pope lay for private visitation prior to his funeral rites.

Celestine took his place at the head of the reception line along with Cardinal Da Silva and Cardinal Alonzo. It was Elisabetta's job to whisper into Celestine's ear the name of the next person in the line and hand him a medal to bestow. A special papal medal had been cast for the occasion for each of the honored attendees. On the obverse was a portrait of Pope Celestine, on the reverse, a portrait of a mature Saint Lúcia.

The reception line snaked forward.

Cal read Lúcia's onionskin only once and dropped it to his lap. There would be time to process it later, but at this moment, the only thing that mattered was reaching Elisabetta and sounding the alarm. As he grabbed his phone, dread melted his pain.

Elisabetta was unaware her phone was repeatedly vibrating inside the deep pocket of her habit. So Cal dialed Emilio. But the crowd in the square and the chatter in his earpiece occupied his full attention, and he couldn't hear the ringtone from his breast pocket. In desperation, Cal tried Elisabetta's office line on the chance that someone—Monsignor Cauchi, perhaps—might answer, but it too went into voicemail.

"Come on, for Christ's sake!" he raged at the walls of books. "Someone pick up the goddamn phone!"

No one heard his pleas. The only sounds in the library were his own heavy breathing and a grandfather clock ticking near Nino's impaled body.

⊙══════⊙

"Holy Father," Elisabetta whispered, "Rosario Diaz of the World Apostolate of Fátima."

The Mexican woman came forward on the receiving line, genuflected, and kissed Celestine's ring. She accepted the medal with tears in her eyes and moved along.

"Holy Father," Elisabetta whispered, "Joaquim Garcia da Rosa, the Portuguese ambassador to Italy."

As the medal was being presented to the ambassador, Elisabetta's nose wrinkled again at the faint, incongruous odor, and she sneezed. She shrugged it off—her keen sense of smell was a distraction sometimes, and she looked down the receiving line to prepare for the next introduction. Satisfied that she knew the gentleman's name, she reached into her pocket for a tissue and felt the last vibrations of a missed call.

She pulled out the phone to see a screen of missed calls and voicemails from Cal. Just then, Celestine cleared his throat, a signal to her that the next in line was waiting.

"Apologies, Holy Father," she whispered, "Monsignor Bonifacio Hugo Jordão, from the Congregation for the Causes of Saints."

Cardinal Alonzo, who was the priest's superior, beamed at the monsignor. "Ah, Hugo! Come, come."

Hugo limped forward, lifting his left leg high and slapping his paralyzed foot onto the marbled floor.

Elisabetta mumbled another apology and took a few steps away from the line to place the call.

Cal had been staring at his phone, and when it lit up with Elisabetta's number, he answered with a torrent of words. "Is Celestine all right?"

"Yes, he's right here."

Cal shouted, "They're going to assassinate him! It's going to be by fire!"

Cardinal Alonzo was telling the pope, "Holy Father, Monsignor Jordão has been working tirelessly for many, many years on Sister Lúcia's cause."

Celestine held out the medal and smiled.

Hugo reached into his cassock through its cut-out pocket. The device was pure simplicity and undetectable to the magnetometers, an inflatable life vest filled with a few liters of petrol, with a rubber tube running from it into wads of cotton wool taped around his waist. Hugo opened a plastic pinch clamp, and the petrol began to soak into the wadding.

Elisabetta sniffed again, and this time, she understood the smell.

Celestine held out his hand and said, "Congratulations, Monsignor. Your work is done."

Hugo had a butane cigarette lighter in his hand as he bent to kiss the ring of the fisherman. "Holy Father," the priest said serenely, "your work, too, is done."

Elisabetta was on the move as Hugo's thumb dragged the wheel of the lighter, generating a spark.

She threw herself onto the priest as he erupted in an orb of flames.

Emilio looked to his sister and looked to the pope, and he did his duty. He and Studer dragged Celestine away to a corner of the hall.

Cal listened helplessly via Elisabetta's open phone as the terror and chaos played out.

He heard Studer shouting for fire extinguishers and medics.

He heard screaming and running and the explosive hissing of fire extinguishers.

He heard Elisabetta's anguished cries.

He heard Cardinal Da Silva shouting, "Oh my God!" as he ran to Celestine's side.

And he heard Emilio bellowing, "Holy Father!" as Celestine clutched his chest and collapsed onto the marble.

22

General anesthesia erases time.

Cal was put to sleep in the operating theater of the Norfolk and Norwich University Hospitals, and an instant later, he awoke in the recovery room. Upon regaining consciousness, he didn't experience a moment of disorientation. He knew exactly where he was and what had happened, and he was tempted to join other patients in other beds in their chorus of groans.

A nurse appeared and filled his view with a smiling face. "There you are. I expect you could do with a little pain medicine."

"Wouldn't say no."

She squirted the contents of a syringe into his IV.

"Any chance you could put a shot of vodka in the bag?"

"You're a cheeky one, aren't you?"

While Cal had waited for the police and ambulances to show up at Graves Hall, he tried over and over to reach Elisabetta and Emilio. With the arrival of emergency services, he was swamped by first-aid procedures and urgent questioning by the authorities, who soon realized they had a major incident on their hands. He and his phone were soon parted.

"I need my phone," Cal said. "Do you know where it is?"

The nurse said, "I've charged it for you, luv."

"God, I love the NHS."

"No calls allowed, but you can check your messages."

He saw the headlines right away.

THE POPE IS DEAD
HORROR IN THE VATICAN
ASSASSIN PRIEST DIES IN FIREBALL, POPE'S SECRETARY HOSPITALIZED

He said Elisabetta's name out loud.

"It's a lovely name, luv," the nurse said, "but it's not mine."

The surgeon stopped by a short time later and explained what she had done. A shotgun pellet had lodged up against his scapula and had cracked the bone but hadn't displaced it. There was some muscle trauma in the area, but everything would heal nicely, she assured him. The orthopedics people had pinned his fractured tibia and fibula, and he'd be in a walking cast for six weeks or so.

"You're a popular man, Mr. Donovan," she said.

"How do you mean?"

"There's a squad of police in the waiting room to speak with you. We'll keep them at bay for a while."

It wasn't until the middle of the afternoon that he was taken to a room where he was allowed to use his phone. He called Elisabetta, but a man answered.

"Cal, it's Emilio."

"I read she was hurt. How is she?"

During the split second until Emilio answered, Cal suspected the worst.

"She got burned. I haven't been able to see her yet. All they've told us so far is that she's going to live."

Cal had been holding his breath. "Thank God."

"She saved the Holy Father from the fire. She couldn't save him from his own heart."

"Will you call me as soon as you know more about her condition?"

"Of course," Emilio said. "How are you? Where are you?"

"I'm in a hospital. I'll be fine. I'm going to get out of here and come to Rome as soon as I can."

"It was a priest, Cal. He was in charge of Lúcia's cause for sainthood."

"I saw. I met him briefly. He made no impression."

"I should have—"

Cal knew what he was going to say. "There was no way you could have known, Emilio."

"Maybe. We'll find everything out. It wasn't just Monsignor Jordão. There was a plot. It goes as far as the pope's second secretary, Father Cauchi."

"How do you know?"

"He was found stabbed to death in Jordão's apartment. The assassins turned on each other. Cauchi must have been listening in on Eli's calls at work. He shared her phone extensions. That's how they knew every move you were making. It wasn't Studer."

"I'll have to apologize to him."

"No need. He doesn't know you suspected him. Listen, I've got to go."

"When you see her, please give her my—"

"I know, Cal. I'll give Eli your love."

Martin Gifflin answered his phone at the Congregation for the Evangelization of Peoples at the Piazza di Spagna in Rome, one of the Curial departments located outside of Vatican territory.

"This is Father Gifflin."

The voice on the line was low and urgent. "Martin, it's Leone."

Martin stretched the phone cord to close his door. "Why are you calling me? How did you know where I work?"

"I'm sure you know where I work."

It was true. Martin knew everything about him. He was Monsignor Leone Serafini, a functionary at the Congregation for the Doctrine of the Faith.

"I'm hanging up," Martin said. "Never contact me again."

"No, wait. I tried to reach Angelo. He's not answering."

"That's because he's using his head. You aren't."

"Christopher is dead."

"I know."

"Hugo killed him."

"I know that too."

"I'm going mad, Martin. I don't know what to do. I wish I'd never met him. Do you think they'll find us?"

Martin lowered the phone into its cradle, swiveled his chair, and stared out his window at the carefree tourists on the Spanish Steps, taking pictures in the softening afternoon light.

It was well past sunset, and Father Angelo Pettinato had been walking for hours. When he took off that afternoon, he left everything behind at the Secretariat for the Economy—his briefcase, his phone, his jacket. He had removed his clerical collar and placed it in a desk drawer, and when he was clear of the Vatican walls, he even shed his clerical shirt, stuffing it in a waste bin, and made do with his white T-shirt.

He had been reading news stories all afternoon. To his colleagues at the secretariat, his shock and grief seemed to be on par with theirs, but it was very much greater. The last story he read before taking his leave was from the BBC, about a serious incident with casualties in a country estate in Norfolk involving an Italian national named Nino Pettinato.

He wasn't entirely sure if the destination was conscious or happenstance, but when he found himself at the Barberini–Fontana di Trevi metro stop, he entered the station, bought a ticket, and waited for several minutes on the crowded platform before crossing himself and stepping into the path of the train to Battistini.

The oily smell of burned petrol still permeated the grand suite of rooms at the Secretariat of State, one floor above the Clementine Hall. When Cal hobbled in, Cardinal Da Silva rushed forward but couldn't figure out how to encircle him with the crutches in the way.

"Sit, my friend. Please sit," the cardinal said. "I'm sure you've left the hospital too soon. How can you manage these crutches with your shoulder wound?"

"One word, Rodrigo: narcotics."

"Be careful with those and the Grey Goose."

"Thank you. I won't."

Da Silva called for coffees and sat beside Cal on matching Renaissance chairs. "You should have gone back to Boston to recuperate. Why come here, to what must surely be the saddest place on Earth?"

"I wanted to see Sister Elisabetta."

"I visited with her last night. She's making progress."

Cal's chest heaved. "I couldn't save him," he said.

"No, my friend, you saved him from a terrible death by fire. His own heart took him, swiftly and without undue suffering. He is with the Lord now. He is at peace."

"Who else was involved besides Jordão and Cauchi?"

"There was one other that we know of, a priest who worked at the Secretariat for the Economy. His cousin was a criminal, a paid killer. I believe you met him."

"Oh."

"There were probably others. Emilio Celestino believes they will be found."

"What drove them?"

"We have Monsignor Jordão's diary. Partly it was his hatred for the Holy Father's liberalism, the sale of artwork—you know, the typical bailiwick of the right. Then there was the Fourth Secret. He fervently believed that it was prophetic, and that he would be the one to bring forth the Second Coming."

"How the hell did he know about it, Rodrigo?"

"We know from his diary that he was sent by the Congregation for the Causes of Saints to interview Lúcia in Coimbra shortly before her death. In her confusion, she blurted it out and revealed there was a hidden text of it, though she couldn't remember where she had put it.

"Jordão kept it to himself for years, and when, as he saw it, an Italian pope gave away the treasures of the Church, he believed it was his divine mission to be the one to satisfy the prophecy. To pay for the killer who stalked you, he embezzled funds from his accounts at the Congregation for the Causes of Saints. It was clumsy. He would have been discovered at the next audit, but he believed he would be gone by then."

Cal took the folded onionskin from his pocket. "Well, here it is. This is why all these people died."

Da Silva unfolded the Fourth Secret, read it carefully, and said, "My goodness, what are we going to do with this?"

"I suspect you'll suppress it," Cal said.

The cardinal folded it back up and slipped it into his cassock. "I suspect you're correct, but it will be up to a future pope to decide."

Sister Elisabetta saw Cal from her hospital bed and waved at him with heavily bandaged hands and arms.

"Look at you," she said as he clopped through the doorway on crutches.

"Yeah, and look at you."

He had been right about her hair. It was black and silky but longer than he had imagined. More bandages protruded from the top of her hospital gown, extending to her neck. He wondered how it was possible for an injured woman to look so beautiful.

He sat beside her and dropped his crutches.

"We make quite the pair," she said.

"Don't we? How long will you be here?"

"They're doing skin grafts on my arms tomorrow. They say I'll be going home by the end of the week."

"I'm so sorry, Eli."

"I'll be fine. I only wish—"

Cal had vowed that he wasn't going to get emotional, but he was anyway. He wiped away a few tears and said, "Me too. I'm going to miss him."

She pushed out her lower lip and said, "The good thing about these bandages is that when I cry, I can use them as tissues."

"Hey, watch it," he said. "It hurts when I laugh."

"I apologize. So, you found it."

He nodded. "Lúcia gave Charles Graves one heck of a gift."

"Do you think she knew it was in the book?"

"I don't think she did. Toward the end, she was forgetful."

"I want to see it."

"I gave it to Da Silva. I didn't keep a copy, but I memorized it."

"Go on."

As he recited it, they looked into each other's eyes, and when he was done, she crossed herself with a bandaged hand.

"I don't know what to think," she said. "Is the prophecy

wrong? The Holy Father was not consumed by fire. You and I—did our actions prevent the Second Coming of Christ? Should we be happy or sad? Whatever will the future bring?"

"I'm no good at predicting the future, Eli. All I know is that there's going to be a conclave."

They sat in silence for a while, gazing at each other. He knew what he was feeling was more than one of his attractions. This was love.

"I have feelings for you," he said.

She smiled. "I know you do. A woman always knows."

"What should we do?"

She said, "Isn't the question, what should I do?"

"I suppose it is. I'm sorry."

"Don't be. From time to time, God tests our commitment. This is my test. I'll do what I always do in a crisis. I'll pray."

He reached through the railings and gently touched her gauzed hands. They talked until visiting hours were over, and as he left her room, his radar was pinging.

For the first time in a long time, he felt hopeful.

Cal was recovering at his house in Cambridge when he got a news alert on his phone.

It was only the second ballot of the first day of the papal conclave, but the smoke over Saint Peter's Square was white. He quickly switched on the TV and listened to the talking heads speculating.

In time, the cardinal protodeacon appeared on the Benediction Loggia of Saint Peter's Basilica. Cal had met him once, a perfectly nice Italian gentleman. He was accompanied by two bishops holding a microphone and a written proclamation. The protodeacon leaned into the microphone. Cal didn't need to wait for the commentator to translate the Latin.

"I announce to you a great joy; we have a pope. The most eminent and reverend lord, Lord Rodrigo Cardinal of the Holy Roman Church Da Silva, who takes to himself the name John the Twenty-Fourth."

Cal sprang up and stomped his walking cast hard enough to hurt his leg. "How about that!" he yelled.

The last Portuguese pope was John XXI in the thirteenth century. The last American pope was never.

He would need to book a plane ticket to Rome.

He had a papal inauguration to attend and a woman he wanted to see.

ABOUT THE AUTHOR

GLENN COOPER is an internationally bestselling thriller writer. His previous books, including his bestselling Library of the Dead trilogy, have been translated into thirty-one languages and have sold over seven million copies. He graduated from Harvard University, magna cum laude, with a BA in archaeology. Cooper attended Tufts University School of Medicine and then practiced internal medicine and infectious diseases in hospitals, clinics, and refugee camps in conflict zones before joining the biotechnology industry, where he was the CEO of several publicly traded companies. Now he writes full-time and lives in Florida and Massachusetts.

Learn more at:

GlennCooperBooks.com
Facebook.com/GlennCooperUSA
Twitter: @GlennCooper
Instagram: Glenn_Cooper